THE BALLOON MAN

Other books by
Charlotte MacLeod

Exit the Milkman
The Odd Job
The Resurrection Man
An Owl Too Many
The Gladstone Bag
Vane Pursuit
The Silver Ghost
The Recycled Citizen
The Corpse in Oozak's Pond
Grab Bag
The Plain Old Man
The Curse of the Giant Hogweed
The Convivial Codfish
Something the Cat Dragged In
The Bilbao Looking Glass
Wrack and Rune
The Palace Guard
The Withdrawing Room
The Luck Runs Out
The Family Vault
Rest You Merry

CHARLOTTE MACLEOD

THE BALLOON MAN

THE MYSTERIOUS PRESS

Published by Warner Books

A Time Warner Company

This book is a work of fiction. Names, characters, places, and incidents are the product of the author's imagination or are used fictitiously. Any resemblance to actual events, locales, or persons, living or dead, is coincidental.

Mysterious Press books are published by Warner Books, Inc., 1271 Avenue of the Americas, New York, NY 10020.

Visit our Web site at http://warnerbooks.com

A Time Warner Company

Printed in the United States of America

ISBN 0-89296-657-2

For Alexandria
My dear sister and dear friend

1

"I had the damnedest dream last night."

Max Bittersohn, art expert par excellence and scourge of the international art underworld, felt around with his bare right foot for his right-foot slipper. Of course he got the wrong one.

"What the hell? Sarah, would you mind counting my toes for me?"

"Why, dear?"

"To see how many feet I've got."

Sarah Kelling Kelling Bittersohn had been married to Max long enough to know that early morning was not his best time. With a big family wedding only hours away, time was becoming of the essence, if it already wasn't, but there would be no earthly use in trying to prod him into action before he'd had his second cup of coffee. She fished the errant slipper out from under the conjugal bed, hung it on her husband's left big toe, and poured a cup of the life-giving beverage from the carafe she had brought up from the kitchen.

"What did you dream, darling?"

"As far as I can recall, it was something about a goon squad of purple cockatoos in green velvet combat boots, shooting dried peas at me through bright pink peashooters."

"Aha, the Freudian element rears its outmoded head. No doubt the wedding inspired that vulgar image. But why pink, and why peashooters?"

"Why not?" Max had finally grasped the logistics of matching toes to slippers; he stuck out his footwork for Sarah to admire. "My guess is that the cockatoos had run out of blowpipes and were having to improvise."

"But why were they shooting peas at you? Beans would be more effective, I should think. Did it sting when they hit?"

"Nah, they always missed. How come you've got so many clothes on?"

"Because I had to get out at the crack of dawn and show the tent raisers where to raise the tents."

That got Max moving. Summoning all his energy, he reached for the cup. "Why the hell didn't you wake me up? I'd have raised them for you."

"Not to put it too crudely, my love, I'll bet you any sum up to a Kennedy half-dollar that I know a lot more than you do about putting up tents. Aunt Emma had me fully trained in the art of tent raising by the time I was twelve years old."

Max put on his most truculent sneer. "Don't hand me that nonsense, kiddo. You've never raised a tent in your life."

"Of course I haven't," Sarah replied sweetly. "We Kellings do not raise tents; we merely stand around harassing the tent raisers into doing precisely what we want them to do, as opposed to letting them do what they foolishly imagine we're going to let them get away with."

"I could at least have helped you with the nagging and harassing," Max insisted.

"No, dear, you couldn't. Talents like Aunt Emma's and mine are either bred in the bone or they aren't. I'm sorry to tell you this, Max, but you just don't have what it takes to terrorize a tent raiser. You lack the steely stare in your eyes and the je ne sais quoi in the tightening of your lips, just so much and not a millimeter more. Or less, depending on the circumstances. I'd better warn you right now that many a professional tent raiser has arrived on the job in the prime of health and vigor, only to stagger and collapse once he's felt the laserlike glint of the Kelling eyeball."

Max studied his wife with sleepy satisfaction. Kellings came in two sizes, long and short; Sarah was a pleasing example of the latter variety, with baby fine brown hair and greenish hazel eyes set in her small, squarish face. Her naturally pale complexion was pink with exertion and excitement, and the jeans and shirt she had assumed in order to bully the tent makers set off a nicely shaped figure.

Quite a contrast to the white-faced little creature he'd first beheld on a television newscast, shivering in front of the Kelling family vault on Beacon Hill, where a particularly inappropriate set of remains had just been discovered. That same night Max had met her in person, swathed in something warm and fuzzy and blue, and made the dreadful mistake of assuming she was Alexander Kelling's daughter instead of his wife.

After that Max had somehow or other happened to run into the younger Mrs. Kelling every so often, trying to think of her as a nice woman who lived on the Hill with her autocratic blind and deaf mother-in-law and her handsome, elderly husband. The fact that Max had been born and brought up on the North Shore, where the Kelling family had a rambling old summer place, made these happenings look a little more plausible.

He'd been visiting his parents the day the Kellings' vintage Milburn, which had been for so long one of the North Shore's most picturesque sights, had gone over the cliffs with Alexander and his mother inside. Knowing Sarah would be alone and in a state of shock, he'd hung around his brother-in-law's garage, hoping she would stop for gas on her way back to Boston. She had. Max had offered her a ride back to Beacon Hill; she'd cried all the way and looked like hell by the time they got there. That was when Max Bittersohn realized he'd been in love with Sarah Kelling ever since that otherwise abominable night at the Lackridges'.

Gradually he'd promoted himself to acting knight errant, telling himself that he wasn't making a nuisance of himself, just trying to help a sorrowing widow over a rough time; knowing all the time that he was lying his head off and wishing to hell she'd walk into his arms, murmuring, "Take me, Max, I'm yours if you want me." It had taken longer than he would have liked, but now, by God, she was his and he was hers, and Davy, the world's most intelligent child, was three years old.

"Did it work?" he asked.

"How can you ask? Though I must admit," Sarah admitted, "I've never seen such a bunch of incompetents as this crew. They didn't seem to know a tent peg from a parasol. However, thanks to Aunt Emma's expert coaching, I had that whole tent-raising crew groveling at my feet in four minutes and thirteen seconds this morning. Aunt Emma could have had them all straightened out and flying right in half that time, but of course she's had all those extra years of practice. Speaking of Aunt Emma, you might give some thought to getting dressed. Some of the guests will probably arrive early, in typical Kelling fashion, and there's a great deal to be done."

"Do you have to remind me?" Max growled. "Where's Davy?"

"Right out there on the seaward deck, fishing for cardboard minnows. See him? He's planning to send the minnows home to their mothers when it gets to be nap time. And you, my love, are detailed to drive him over to Mrs.

Blufert's. She'll keep him with her until after the wedding service."

Max hadn't been overly pleased to hear that his son wasn't going to be in the wedding party. "Why can't he stay here with us?"

"Darling, you ought to know what a distraction even one small child can be at a big family gathering," Sarah argued. "Davy has better manners than most three-year-olds, I'm happy to say, but a girl likes her wedding day to go perfectly. Tracy is a darling, and deserves the best."

"She is that," Max agreed. "I don't know how my nephew managed to snare her."

"Mike is a darling, too," said Mike's aunt by marriage. "Miriam has everything arranged to a fare-thee-well, so we'd better leave it to her."

Miriam Rivkin, Max's only sibling, was a happy mother today. Here was her son with a brand-new degree in engineering, and there was a wisp of a girl named Tracy all ready to put on a wedding gown into which Miriam had sewn a blessing with every stitch. And here pretty soon would come Mother Bittersohn to watch her greatest dream come true.

Max's mother had wanted a second daughter ever since her Miriam had proved to be such a jewel. She'd got a boy instead. She'd accepted him with relatively good grace and planned for him to become a wealthy podiatrist with an office not far from his parents' home. Unfortunately, Max wasn't attracted to feet. Eventually she'd had to face the fact that there was no way her boy would ever quit racketing around the globe in pursuit of other people's stolen property. She'd hoped he'd marry a nice Jewish girl; he'd married a member of the Codfish Aristocracy and sired a son who was already showing ominous signs that he'd turn out to be the spit and image of his father. But what could you do! as Mother Bittersohn herself often said.

Mrs. Blufert, Sarah's part-time housekeeper and babysitter, had two grandchildren of her own visiting for the day; they knew and liked Davy. The three would play for a while, eat a simple lunch, take their naps, and play a little longer. Then Mrs. Blufert would dress Davy in a clean suit, if he still had one by then, and send him home fresh and rested so that Sarah and Max could show their guests what a clever son they'd managed to bring forth now they'd got the knack.

"What's on my agenda besides Davy and the minnows?" Max wanted to know.

"Shave, shower, get dressed, deliver Davy, come back, and be ready to leap into any last-minute breaches that may open up. There are sure to be some. Make sure you put on your light gray suit instead of the dark one and stand around looking elegant and suave when you have nothing else to do. Think you can handle all that?"

"I'll work on it. Any more coffee kicking around?"

"Need you ask?"

Sarah refilled Max's cup, peeked out the window to

make sure Davy hadn't fallen into the minnow bucket, and treated herself to a sip of her husband's coffee.

"We'd better not drink too much of this," she warned. "You're jittery enough already."

"Who, me?" said Max. "What do you think, kätzele? Is it going to work?"

"Oh, I expect so. Tracy's people have sent some lovely presents, but I don't suppose many of the senders will show up in person. Most of them seem to be wrapped up in their jobs and their divorces. Her wretched old father didn't even respond to the invitation. I gather he's hot on the trail of wife number five. At least Tracy's mother is here. Her name's Jeanne, in case you've forgotten; Miriam says she stayed up half the night making knishes for the buffet. I think that's rather sweet, don't you? Perhaps it made Jeanne feel like a member of the family, poor soul. She's gone all to pieces since Tracy's father filed for divorce. Though why any woman would want to stay married to a selfish woman-chasing pickle manufacturer is beyond my comprehension."

"His millions might have something to do with it," Max suggested.

"That's what they're fighting about, I believe," Sarah admitted. "He doesn't want to give her a cent, and she's holding out for lots of alimony. Goodness knows that family hasn't much in the way of family feeling. Tracy's stepbrother claims he has to stay in his laboratory and tend his fruit flies. I hope they bite him. Tracy's such a darling; does it strike you that she's almost as much in love with Miriam and Ira as she is with Mike?"

"So? Is that bad?" Max wandered over to the window.

"Of course not. It's wonderful," said Sarah. "But I must get back downstairs. Brooks and Theonia will be along pretty soon with four dozen chocolate tortes which need to be refrigerated until it's time to set the dessert tables. Uncle Jem's coming with them if Egbert can haul him out of bed and get him dressed in time."

"You do have the damnedest relatives," Max remarked.

"They've been damnably useful to you, you ungrateful brute," Sarah said spiritedly. "Where would your detective agency be without Cousin Brooks and his Theonia, not to mention my who knows how many times removed cousin Jesse?"

"The ex-delinquent," Max agreed with a grin. "All right, my love, I'll give you Cousin Brooks and the beauteous Theonia and even Jesse. But your uncle Jem is another kettle of chowder. What wild scheme has he got in mind this time?"

"He claims he's going to bartend in his fancy vest and red satin arm garters, but Egbert says he isn't, not in front of Mother Bittersohn."

"Let's hope the faithful factotum can control him, then. I sure as hell can't." Max yelped and ducked away from the window. "Here comes a carload of revelers already. What the hell time is it? Did our clocks stop and I'm late before I start?"

"Of course not, silly. It's Cousin Anne with the bouquets and buttonholes. She promised to bring the flowers over early. Oh, they're beautiful!" Sarah sighed as she watched Anne unload the flowers. The large and intricately intermarried Kelling clan could be a nuisance at times, but its members boasted a diversity of talents. Percy Kelling, Anne's husband, was the dullest of dull sticks, according to Uncle Jem, but even Jem admitted that dullness wasn't necessarily a handicap to a first-class CPA. Sarah had had very little to do with Percy's wife, Anne, until Anne had called her and Max in to recover a treasured family painting that featured an oversize parrot and its owner. Since then Anne had attached herself to Sarah like a clinging vine of the Convolvulaceae family and had applied her horticultural talents to the improvement of the Bittersohn acres. What Anne could do with a sack of manure and a few flats of annuals was little short of miraculous, and her flower arrangements were works of art.

By the time Max emerged properly dressed in the light-gray suit and the gray-and-white tie that Mike and Tracy had decided would be just the ticket for an outdoor wedding on a lovely September day, a sort of organized pandemonium had set in. Mindful of Sarah's list, Max ate a quick breakfast, collected Davy and a few changes of clothing, and drove to Mrs. Blufert's, where he gave each of the three children a wiggly wooden alligator with little green wheels for feet and a red mouth that opened and shut most fearsomely when a child hauled it around on a string.

Max stayed to show the children how to run an alligator race. After he came in a poor fourth, he went home to tell his father, who had made the alligators, what a great time the children were having with their new toys and reported back to his calm and collected wife.

How Sarah had contrived a perfect day for Mike's wedding was a puzzlement to everybody but Max. He'd known from the start that it wouldn't dare to rain with his wife bossing the show. The temperature was exactly seventy degrees Fahrenheit and would not go much higher or lower until sundown. Every now and then a puff of white cloud wafted across the bright blue sky like a giant blob of whipped cream on its way to frost a celestial wedding cake. Far overhead, the sun beamed down upon the enchanted place that Cousin Anne and Mr. Lomax, the gardener, had created out of an ugly, water-worn hillside, a few truckloads of fish offal, and heaven only knew how many chrysanthemums, each single plant carefully selected, color-coordinated, and set into the fishgut-enriched soil by Anne Kelling's expert hands.

Following his wife's instructions, Max went to the library, where the wedding gifts were on display. Early-arriving guests were trickling into the room, most of them just looking, a few trying to peek at the donors' names and addresses, which had been written on plain white cards and stuck facedown under the gifts. Miriam and Sarah had tried to keep a running list of who'd sent what; it hadn't been easy. Parcels were still coming through the mail, by UPS, by

Federal Express, by personal visits from friends, neighbors, relatives on the Rivkin side, on the Bittersohn side, from classmates of Mike's and Tracy's, from people whose names hardly anybody could recall having heard before, even from a few Kellings who had the good sense to appreciate Max and his family.

The best of the presents weren't on display. Ira had already presented his son and future daughter-in-law with a meticulously restored 1956 Ford Thunderbird. Miriam's gift to the bride was a complete set of the finest cookware, along with a file of her own tried and tested recipes and a promise of cooking lessons as soon as Tracy had mastered the art of turning on the stove. Best of all was a joint gift to the newlyweds, the one building on the old Kelling summer place that had been worth saving.

For months now, a crew headed by the elder Bittersohns and financed by Sarah and Max had been remodeling the former carriage house. The ground floor had been divided in two: half for the Thunderbird, the other half insulated, paneled, and heated as a studio for Tracy, who was already gaining some notice as a potter. Upstairs, a pleasant bedroom and sitting room would catch the sunrises and sunsets over the ocean. There were also a small but functional bathroom, an office for Mike, and a kitchen just about big enough to hold Miriam's cookware and the cook. What with the largesse already heaped upon them and the gifts not yet unwrapped, the newlyweds were starting to wonder whether they should build an ell on the carriage house or open a general store.

Max examined the display with a considering, expert's eye and decided to ignore his wife's suggestion that he check the list she and Miriam had begun as soon as the gifts began to arrive. She'd just said that to keep him out of mischief. Anyhow, he didn't know where she'd put the damned list. Besides, it was impossible to do the job under these conditions, with people coming and going and wanting to talk and getting in the way. The pace was picking up. More guests were coming, more food being delivered, more people wanting to see the presents. Where, he wondered, had all this stuff come from? The glittering array covered the desk, the library table, and the other tables that had been brought in from various rooms and draped decorously in white linen. Six coffeemakers, four blenders, several other gadgets whose functions he was afraid to speculate about, vessels of silver, crystal, china, pottery, plastic, feathers . . . Max did a double take. They were feathers, dry, molting, faded feathers, covering a bowl the size of a washbasin. Its original function was questionable, its present utility nil. That had to have come from the Kelling side. The Kellings never threw anything away. Maybe this was one of Aunt Appie's family treasures.

Tearing his incredulous eyes away from the object, Max was pleased to see Egbert, Uncle Jem's aged and invaluable valet de chambre, companion, and all-round good egg. They exchanged greetings that were, at least on Max's part, heartfelt. The room was too crowded. People were getting fingerprints on the silver, and jostling the tables, and picking up those handy white cards and probably not putting them back with the right gifts. Egbert was up to the job. Max watched admiringly as Egbert moved from one group to another, murmuring hints about coffee and pastries on the deck and suggesting guests might care to stroll down to the carriage house for a look at the Thunderbird, the studio, and the upstairs living quarters, giving special attention to the curtains and pillow tops, all embroidered by Mrs. Bittersohn Senior using motifs taken from Tracy's prize-winning pottery, which could already be seen in some of the more prestigious decorating shops.

Finally the place began to clear out, and Max, who had decided to concentrate on looking elegant and debonair, relaxed. People were drifting toward the big tent, where the bridal couple would stand to take their vows. Egbert tactfully urged the last of the viewers away, leaving Max alone in the library. Max glanced at his watch. He'd better get out there and make like a host until the ushers had got everybody seated. He cast a final glance over the wedding gifts, and froze.

2

"My God! Where did this come from?"

Max knew he ought to be out in the tent by now, but he remained stock still, staring in disbelief at the wealth of gold and rubies that nestled snugly on the worn velvet of a rubbed leather jewel case.

Max had authenticated many jewels in his career, but he had a particularly intimate acquaintance with this necklace. He'd seen it in Brussels, Amsterdam, Rio, Dallas, Rome, and Hong Kong—and in the portraits and photographs of three successive Kelling wives who had been privileged to flaunt their husbands' wealth and dignity by wearing the Kelling rubies. Sarah's former mother-in-law, Caroline Kelling, had been the last to wear the opulent parure, before she had ruthlessly and efficiently looted her only son of valuables that were rightfully his. She had handed over the Kelling jewels, including the rubies, to her lover, who had sold them and kept the money for himself.

Sarah had known about the Kelling parure even before she'd married Alexander, but she'd never seen it, although the pieces should all have been hers for her lifetime. Caroline Kelling had ruled her son with an iron hand and hadn't even bothered to swathe it in a velvet glove. Though blind and deaf, she'd run the old house on Tulip Street to suit herself and treated her young daughter-in-law like a servant. Max would never forget the day Sarah had opened the safe-deposit box that ought to have contained the Kelling jewels, part of her inheritance from her dead husband, and had found it filled with bricks. He hadn't been surprised, but poor Sarah had fainted dead away. Small wonder, after losing her husband and learning from him, before he died, that his mother had killed several people, including Sarah's father.

Max closed his eyes, rubbed them, and opened them again. He hadn't been hallucinating. The necklace was still there. Or was it one of the copies of the necklace Caroline Kelling's lover, Harry Lackridge, had pawned off onto unsuspecting buyers in Brussels, Rio, Dallas, Rome, and Hong Kong, before a suspicious-minded lady in Amsterdam had pulled a reverse swindle and kept not just the necklace, but the rest of the parure—bracelets, clips, chains, tiara, a lavaliere, even a matching opera glass?

The rest of the parure. It wasn't until that thought entered his dead brain that Max saw the other velvet cases, modestly concealed under the large open case that displayed the necklace. It took only a few moments to confirm his hunch. The other pieces were there, too, even the opera glass. Glancing uneasily over his shoulder, he closed the cases and refastened them, sliding each small hook into its corresponding socket with fingers that were not as steady as they might have been.

Could this be one of the copies Lackridge had had made in order to swindle purchasers? Somehow Max didn't think so. The astute lady in Amsterdam was dead; she had passed on earlier that year. Maybe her heirs had sold the rubies, and they had come into the hands of one of Tracy's friends or relations. Her father had enough money to buy all the rubies he wanted; he was CEO of Warty Pickles Inc., and his products could be found on the shelves of every grocery store in the country. Max turned over the white card on which the donor's name and address were supposed to be printed. Both sides were blank.

The violin, the cello, the oboe, and the flute burst forth in beautiful unison. The bridal procession must be almost ready to process. Max couldn't see his mother, but he could feel her sending some pretty vibrant thought waves. He himself was slated not to join in the procession down the improvised aisle, but to lurk at the back of the big tent and make sure that everything was moving along in strict accordance with Miriam's ironclad schedule.

What the hell was he going to do with the rubbed velvet cases and their unbelievable contents? They couldn't be left out on the table. In Max's opinion the parure was a particularly repellent example of Victorian tastelessness, but the gold was eighteen karat and the rubies were very large and of the finest color, and there were a lot of both rubies and gold. What about the safe in an upstairs wall of their bedroom? Max dismissed the idea. The bridesmaids had been using that room as a dressing room all day. It was fifty to one that some frantic young bridesmaid was in there now, pinning up a broken strap or doing whatever excitable females did to make themselves beautiful. He reached up and hid the boxes behind a Morocco-bound set of Thackeray on the top shelf of one of the bookcases, made sure the library windows were locked as tight as he could get them, and double-locked the only door to the room before he put the only key into his breast pocket. This was the best he could do on such short notice; it would have to be enough for now.

The music that had been no more than a pleasant background noise began to swell and soar, gathering families and friends together in one joyful mass. Ushers were finding seats for the laggards, clearing the center aisle once most of the well-wishers were in their places, and going back to escort those who merited special notice.

Max took up his position at the back of the tent, trying to look as if he'd been there for hours. He was in time to see the bride's mother led to her place. Jeanne brightened up as soon as she noticed what a handsome young fellow Mike's best friend and head usher happened to be.

Next came Mother and Father Bittersohn, she in light blue silk, wearing a lovely corsage created especially for her by Cousin Anne and the sort of hat that Queen Elizabeth II might have chosen if she'd had Miriam handy to make it for her. The patriarch entered correct on all counts in his light gray suit and tie, his boutonniere, his tallis, and a handsome new yarmulke embroidered by his gifted wife.

Miriam Rivkin's sewing machine had been busy ever since Mike and Tracy had finally made up their minds to a family wedding with at least some of the trimmings. She'd created Tracy's gown of ivory lace over taffeta, the maid of honor's in pale yellow, and the four bridesmaids' in shades from gold to russet. Just as she'd thought she was finished sewing the last dress, Miriam had happened to spy a wonderful silk print splashed with subtly defined chrysanthemums. She'd sat up all that night at the machine; now she swished down the aisle, looking absolutely gorgeous, as she could when she chose. And now entered the bridesmaids, all in taffeta with matching chrysanthemum bouquets that ranged from russet to amber to brighter gold to the maid of honor's sunshine yellow. Finally, here came the bride, a princess straight out of a fairy tale in creamy satin frothed with lace and veiled in tulle. Even in high-heeled satin pumps and a coronet of charming little button chrysanthemums interspersed with sprays of the traditional orange blossoms, Tracy barely came up to her prospective father-in-law's shoulder. She kept glancing up to make sure Ira was really and truly there. He glanced back, proud as any father could be to show off his beautiful daughter, even though

Tracy would still technically be on loan until she and Mike had pledged their vows.

The bride's bouquet was Anne's masterpiece, its creams and whites mingled as subtly as the highlights and shadows that Miriam had created out of the lace and tulle and creamy satin, emphasizing the tiny waist and sneaking a little extra padding into the bodice, as many a young bride had done before her.

The wedding ceremony was neither too short nor too long, but it seemed long to Max, stewing over the necklace, and to the guests who wondered how soon the bar would be open and the food served. As soon as the inevitable photographers began taking the inevitable scads of pictures on the side lawn overlooking the sea, Max looked guiltily around to make sure Miriam wasn't planning to grab him for some reason or other and made a dash for the house.

With all that joyful noise outside, the library felt almost too quiet when Max unlocked the door. He made sure that the Kelling jewels were still hiding behind Thackeray and stood pondering. The more he thought about it, the more peculiar the situation appeared. How had the rubies got there? Those velvet cases hadn't been there when he'd first entered the library. He couldn't have missed seeing the necklace; its baroque extravagance stood out among the sleek modern shapes of plastic and silver like an alligator in an aviary. One of the guests must have slipped the parure onto the table while he wasn't looking, shoving aside the surrounding appliances and bibelots to make room for it.

If another guest had seen the anonymous donor, he or she would have assumed a last-minute gift had been delivered in person. There didn't seem to be any point in asking whether anyone had observed such a thing. He couldn't even remember who had been in the room or when, and a good number of the visitors had been people he didn't know. Maybe Egbert would remember something. He'd have to have a long talk with Egbert, and with Sarah, but not until after the newlyweds had left and the guests departed. His wife would consider even the miraculous reappearance of a lost family treasure unimportant if it spoiled Tracy and Mike's big day. Especially this treasure, with its miserable memories.

He was about to return to his duties when he became aware of a faint but unpleasant odor. It hadn't been there when he'd locked the room. Had someone had the gall to leave a bag of garbage under a table or in a corner? Max took a flashlight from the rack in which Sarah kept a few extras in case of downed power lines or other mishaps that people who live close to the sea are used to, and began prowling. The increasing pungency of the smell led him to the desk. There was something there all right, tucked away underneath, between the pairs of supporting drawers. Max bent over to inspect it more closely. He wished he hadn't. Even through the double-thick, man-size plastic bag that covered it, who could mistake the shape and smell of a decaying human body?

Max felt along the outside of that gruesome heap, hoping to convince himself that it was not that of a human form or what was left of one. Then he did the only thing he could do under the circumstances and picked up the telephone.

"This is Max Bittersohn at Ireson's Landing, and I need an ambulance right away. . . . No, we're all fine; it's the corpse I've just found under my wife's desk that's giving the trouble. Do me a favor and keep the siren mute if you can. We've got about a hundred guests and relatives attending my nephew's wedding, and— What the hell!"

The corpse had moved. Max was more or less accustomed to bodies, but he had had a hard morning. He jumped back, dropping the phone, and watched open-mouthed as a man crawled out from under the desk, shedding the black plastic bag like a moth emerging from a cocoon. Moths don't look like much when they first emerge, and neither did this individual, who was extremely unlikely to spread gorgeous wings and waft off into the blue. He made Max think of a ferret. Brooks Kelling could probably come up with a more interesting ornithological comparison, but ferret was what came to Max's mind. Some kind of rodent, anyhow. The man was of medium height, skinny as a rail, with a long pointed nose. The hairs under the nose might have been meant to be a mustache, but there weren't many of them, and they twitched like a rat's whiskers when he talked.

"Sorry to cause all this trouble, Mr. Kelling—I mean, Mr. Bittersohn—but I'm not dead. It's, er, my brother who's dead, at least I think he is, but he's not here, so, er, we don't need an ambulance, though it was very kind of you to—"

"Shut up," Max said. He picked up the phone, which was squawking agitatedly. "Cancel the ambulance, Jofferty. . . . No, nothing's wrong. No more than usual. I'll get back to you."

The erstwhile corpse was now standing upright. It was clad in black trousers and white shirt and a black bow tie. The hired waiters wore clothes like those.

"Who the hell are you?" Max demanded. "And how the hell did you get in here?"

"I just came to borrow a shovel. You see, my brother, well, I don't have any money for a funeral, so I thought the only reasonable thing would be to dig a nice big hole somewhere out in the woods and, er, um, put him in. You wouldn't mind lending me a shovel, would you? And maybe somebody to do the digging? My doctor says I'm not in condition to do anything strenuous."

"Your name isn't Kelling, is it?" Max inquired, hoping the answer would be in the affirmative. A hitherto unknown and even loonier than average Kelling would explain a lot.

The man shook his head regretfully. "I'm Dewey Maltravers—no, that's my brother. I'm Louie, and I'm a stand-in."

"What do you mean, a stand-in?"

"Well, see, when my brother was alive, which was until a

while ago, whenever that was . . . See, I never had to know what time it was because all I did was stand there. When I wasn't sitting down, that is. Or playing dead. Playing dead is my true calling, but mostly I have to stand. I don't know what's going to become of me now, there are far too many stand-ins around Boston already. You wouldn't care to take on a middle-aged actor with a case of chronic hiccups, I don't suppose? Right now, I have to tell you, my career is practically up the spout. That's why I thought you might be needing a reliable stand-in."

"You're an actor?" Max was trying to get a grip on the conversation.

"Well, yes, in a way. My brother and I used to do a lot of advertising commercials with collie dogs in them and sometimes a Peke or an Irish wolfhound, but nowadays it's all just cats, cats, cats. I'm allergic to cats. They give me hiccups. But I'm a real whiz at holding up lampposts. You know, the nonchalant slouch, the hat brim pulled down over the forehead, and the hands in the pockets. You've got a real handsome old lamppost out there, so maybe—"

"And that's all you do? You've never tried anything else?"

"Well, I wouldn't like this to get around, but I do have what you might call an avocation. I, er, fix locks."

"Ah," Max said, enlightened. "You don't mean you do hairdressing on the side?"

"Not exactly. I do mostly padlocks and dead bolts and things of that nature. Most people, I mean the ones who actually talk to me, call me Louie the Locksmith. I know, it's a comedown. I can see you shrinking away from somebody who's not an artiste but merely a tradesman of a certain kind."

"No," said Max. "You're the one who's shrinking away, Louie. Or maybe sidling is a better word. You're a skillful sidler, but if you think I'm letting you leave here without a better explanation for your presence than that string of nonsense, you can think again. What is that awful stench? Are you sure you don't have Dewey, or part of him, inside the trash bag?"

He had sidled along with the locksmith and was still between him and the door. He wasn't worried about Louie getting away; the man was six inches shorter and twenty years older.

"Stench?" Louie sniffed. "Awful? Why, Mr. Kelling, I mean Mr. Bittersohn, that is a delectable odor. You don't care for Gorgonzola?"

"Cheese?" Max sniffed, too.

"I left my sandwich in the trash bag when I heard you asking for an ambulance," Louie explained. "I had to stop you, since I wouldn't want to put our hardworking police to unnecessary trouble. Thank you for reminding me. I'll just get it. There is a good half left."

He pulled the trash bag out from under the desk and reached into it.

The next thing Max knew he was flat on the floor with two broken legs. After a dazed interval he decided they weren't broken after all, but the club or stake, or maybe it had been a shovel, concealed by the black plastic wrappings had caught him an awful crack across the shins. Luckily it hadn't hit the healing fracture he had sustained the year before. By the time he got his wits back and his legs under him he knew there was no hope of catching up with Louie. He reached for the phone. This time he didn't call the police.

3

"Uncle Max?"

Jesse Kelling, ex-delinquent and Max's apprentice in the detective business, brought his car to a crashing halt and ran toward the big tent where Max had been lurking, trying to avoid the eyes of his sister and mother and cursing the fact that he hadn't set eyes on his wife for what seemed like hours. A hell of a wedding this was turning out to be.

He said as much to Jesse, after cautioning him to keep his voice down, and then gave him a quick summary of the situation.

"Louie, or whatever the hell his name may be, must have been after the rubies. He told me a string of wild stories, but he wasn't lying about his talents as a locksmith. The way he got that locked window open was as neat a job as I've ever seen. Sorry to interrupt your day off, Jesse, but Brooks and Theonia are mingling and I need some help."

"You sure do. What do you want me to tackle first, the necklace or the burglar?"

Jesse was quivering with eagerness and raring to go. Max eyed him with some misgivings. The boy was shaping up well, but he was only seventeen and a bit and still trying to shed the foolishness he'd picked up from his parents. Lionel Kelling and his wife, Vare, were among Sarah's less appealing relatives, which was saying a good deal. They had raised their four sons by modern methods—letting the little monsters do whatever they damn pleased, in other words. It probably hadn't helped to name them after a notorious family of bandits. Jesse was the oldest of the four. Woodson, James, and Frank were his younger siblings.

"He wasn't a burglar," Max corrected. "Nothing was taken."

"You sure?"

"Don't teach your uncle how to suck eggs, you young squirt," Max growled. His shin hurt. "Part of my job is making quick appraisals. There wasn't a porringer missing."

"Would-be burglar, then," said Jesse. "That's why he had the trash bag, he was going to fill it up with—"

"Espresso machines and wine bottle openers? He was almost certainly looking for the rubies, though I can't figure out how he knew they were there, when I hadn't known myself until just before the ceremony. Never mind the parure, it's safely stashed away now. I made sure of that. What I want you to do is look for Louie. He may have made his getaway, in which case you'll have to question the kids who were parking cars. One of them may have noticed a guy who was in a hurry to leave. There's a chance he's still hanging around waiting for a second opportunity to get whatever it was he was trying to get the first time. He could be a waiter or a guest. Keep an eye out for anyone looking suspicious. And don't look at me that way, damn it. I know the description is vague. Just do the best you can."

"Yessir." Jesse snapped to attention.

Max returned to his hosting. There went Sarah now, dashing from hither to yon, smiling and nodding, being gracious toward relatives, her own or her in-laws', and some people she probably didn't even know. That didn't matter; Sarah had had so much practice in on-the-spot grace that she seldom had any trouble sorting out who was which, and where. Max sent a kiss after her silver heels and wished he could deliver it in person.

By now, everybody except the terminally voracious had done more than justice to the buffet. The dessert table was still in evidence, with the bride's cake as the chef d'oeuvre. It would be cut soon, before people began to drift away to stroll around the grounds or get started for their homes. Max wished to hell they'd get on with it.

The cake was duly cut, the bride and groom smiled beautiful smiles at each other, the music started. The tiny girl who had seemed such an incongruous bride for big, redheaded Mike Rivkin handed her bouquet to the nearest bridesmaid and came floating across the dance floor, her arms outstretched to her husband. Everybody else stood aside and let them stay in their private wonderland until the first dance was over. Then Mike dutifully steered his grandmother onto the dance floor, and Tracy danced with her father-in-law. Ira tried not to keep picking her up off the floor, but it was hard when he was so much taller than she. They laughed their way through a swoony waltz. Everybody seemed to be having a wonderful time, Max thought. Everybody except him.

Jesse seemed to be dividing his time with scrupulous fairness between the bridesmaids and the remains of the buffet, but he managed to cover quite a distance in his seemingly aimless wanderings. He caught Max's eye, shook his head, and went on wandering.

Max knew he ought to be out on the dance floor doing his duty by various female relatives and maybe even getting a chance to trip the light fantastic with his wife, but he didn't want to go far from the house. He'd been watching the door, thus far to no avail.

Percy Kelling wasn't dancing, either. Max would have avoided him if he could, since Percy was not one of his favorite Kellings, but Anne's husband seemed to be in an unusually affable mood. He nodded regally at Max.

"Quite a little charmer," he remarked, indicating the radiant bride, who was now waltzing with Brooks Kelling while the latter's wife looked on with a smile. "Elfin, one might say. Who is she? Was she, rather."

"The name is, or was, Pilcher," Max said absently.

"Not one of the Warty Pickles Pilchers?"

"Yes. Her father is the CEO of the company. Do you know them?" Percy had Max's full attention now.

"The old man's not one of my clients," Percy said, his tone suggesting he wasn't sorry. "I know of him, of course. Everyone has heard of old Warty Pilcher. Not here, is he? I thought not. Probably off at some ungodly expensive Shangri-la with his fifth or sixth or seventh incipient disappointment in the matrimonial line."

He dismissed the Pilchers with an aristocratic Kelling sniff. "I must say, Max, you've done a good job here."

Max started. "What?"

"With the property, I mean. I and some of the others were distressed when you tore the old house down, but I must admit it was a monstrosity, with a total lack of creature comforts such as stoves that warmed, plumbing that worked, and roofing that didn't leak through in fifty different places."

"I'm glad you approve," Max said.

"Mmm, yes. In fact, the only thing going for the place was the view."

"That's still here." It was, and it was magnificent, miles of ocean beating off the cliff and chasing itself back to Portugal. The new house that Sarah and Max had planned between them was as different from the old wreck as was possible, modern and convenient and beautifully designed. Some of the Kellings, including Percy, had raised Cain when the old house was demolished, even though it was none of their business, but that was the Kellings for you.

Max hadn't regretted their decision, and he hoped Sarah hadn't. Not only was the old house inconvenient, it held memories he wanted his wife to forget. Memories of her unhappy marriage to her fond, handsome, elderly cousin, memories of the vicious old woman who had owned the ruby parure.

Max groaned. How had the damned rubies got there, and why, and by whom, and what the hell was it all about? How would Sarah take the news that they had reappeared? How much longer was this wonderful wedding going to go on?

4

Max Bittersohn could hardly believe what he was seeing. Jeremy Kelling, beau ideal of Beacon Hill and environs, had shown up around noontime, bright-eyed and bushy-tailed, complete in his role as a turn-of-the-century bartender, with a black leather bow tie, a waistcoat that could be heard all the way to Pride's Crossing, and red satin garters holding up his shirtsleeves to keep them free of the donnybrook that he claimed he was expecting to referee as the day waned and the pace picked up and the wedding guests got down to the serious business of imbibing. He'd even tried on a walrus mustache; it made him look like a genuine walrus, so he'd settled for being his own curmudgeonly self.

But where did the bartender belong? Certainly not stuck behind a makeshift bar over which he'd had to keep shoving abominations such as white wine and some kind of fruit punch that must be seething with vitamins and contained not one single drop of anything even mildly alcoholic. Whatever had happened to the youth of today? Didn't anybody get bombed anymore?

"Damn it all, Max," snarled the toast of the swan boats, continuing his plaint, "look at that crowd. About as inspirational as a dead codfish. Don't try to tell me the old order isn't changing; and not for the better, if you want my opinion."

Max didn't want Jem's opinion, but he could hardly say so. "Jeremy" Kelling, former Exalted Chowderhead of the Comrades of the Convivial Codfish, was one of Sarah's favorite relatives. Max was rather fond of him, too, and he wouldn't have hurt the old coot's feelings for worlds. Jem was complaining for the fun of it, and also because he was so used to his own coterie of eccentric old coots and grousing antagonists that he didn't know how to act in a situation as normal as this. The Kellings were for once in the minority; it was the Bittersohns and the Rivkins who were adding a strong dash of unforced gaiety to the scene. So far, nobody except a few of the old Kelling-related diehards had asked for anything decent and sustaining like double martinis or whiskey sours or even a good dry sherry. Tea and coffee, of all things, were in high favor.

Jem looked as if he wanted to sneak off somewhere and have a good cry. Was J. Lemuel Kelling about to go the way of bathtub gin and the Black Bottom? He was feeling glum as a Grinch and wondering how soon he could get out of here when the bride herself, responding to her uncle Max's gesture, dragged Jem out on the dance floor and taught him how to dance the Pussycat Prowl.

At least he thought she'd taught him. Tracy herself was not so sure. Anyway, she'd made Jem a happy man, and what were bruised toes and an occasional stumble between relatives?

With the chairs and tables pushed back against the tent walls, there was plenty of room for dancing. Noticing that Max was looking a bit frazzled, Sarah had slipped off by herself to collect Davy from Mrs. Blufert. She and her son were now out on the floor with Tracy and Mike, learning the Pussycat Prowl under Uncle Jem's unneeded and not very reliable tutelage. Max was still trying to be genial while feeling as though platoons of small furry animals were marching up and down his spine, all of them with cold, damp, smelly little pink feet. He couldn't see Jesse anywhere. The guests were scattering all over the place, joining in the dancing, watching from the sidelines, moving out to the decks to gaze at the view, chatting with friends, nibbling, and sipping. Max couldn't stand it any longer. He headed for the house.

The library door was still locked. As soon as he unlocked it he was surrounded by people who claimed they had missed seeing the wedding gifts before the service or wanted to make sure their own offerings had been delivered intact, on time, and ready to be displayed in suitably prominent settings. He couldn't think of a reasonable excuse for keeping them out, so he switched on a couple of overhead spotlights so that those present could all get a good look at the plethora of largesse that was heaped around them; then he stood there, trying not to look suspicious.

Had the necklace come from Tracy's father, a belated gesture of goodwill, a sudden resurgence of conscience? A man who had a nickname like Warty didn't sound as if he had a conscience. And if he did have one, why hadn't he taken credit for the munificent, if inconvenient, gift? If the necklace had been sent or delivered through one of the legitimate channels, old Warty's name would be on that white card. Max had seen enough of Tracy during the past months to realize that she was as sensible as she was talented. She'd been sandwiching handwritten thank-you notes between her potting wheel and her kiln, taking care to list each gift as it came and not getting a single name or address wrong, and when she wasn't able to keep up with the deluge, Sarah and Miriam had helped her. Tracy hadn't seemed to expect much from her family. She'd been mildly gratified when her mother had evinced an interest in attending the wedding, and not surprised when the ex–Mrs. Pilcher, after a brief interest in knishes, had switched her attention to the best man.

The poor kid was probably used to being a memorandum on some secretary's desk calendar, Max thought. Well, she had a family of her own now. Mike loved her, Miriam loved her, Ira loved her, the elder Bittersohns doted on her, Sarah and Max had welcomed her, and Davy had promised to let her play with the alligator that Grandfather Bittersohn had carved for him, if she was careful not to let it bite her. She'd taken the whole family to her heart just as they had taken her to theirs. How could two such selfish people as Warty and Mrs. Warty have produced a child like Tracy? The more he thought about it, the more unlikely it seemed that the CEO of Warty Pickles had come through with a suitable acknowledgment of his daughter's nuptial day.

Eventually he got the belated sight-seers out of the room, checked to make sure there were no occupied trash bags under the desk and the tables, and locked the door again. By this time, the morning wedding had burgeoned into a day-long festival, but Max was relieved to see that the guests were beginning to wear out. They had seen all they wanted to see, eaten all they cared to eat or dared to drink, danced and made merry until their feet gave out; now they were only waiting for the bride and groom, in traveling clothes, to come out of their carriage house and be pelted with kisses and flowers and handfuls of rice. This done, they collected their boxes of wedding cake, each with a chrysanthemum tucked in under its russet satin bow, and began to take their leave. Some had trains or planes to catch or long distances to drive or pets to feed or plants to water or a strong desire to go home and flop on the living room couch. Max wouldn't have minded doing a little flopping himself, but he had a feeling it would be a while before he could.

For one thing, there was Davy, fresh as a daisy after his nap, flushed with triumph after his performance on the dance floor, and demanding attention from the cruel parent who had callously abandoned him that morning. He'd had a wonderful time with his favorite baby-sitter and her kids and their alligators, but daddies had to be kept in their places. Tugging at Max's hand, he tried to pull him onto the makeshift dance floor.

Max smiled fondly but wanly at the little face looking up at him from around the level of his aching knee. If there was anything he didn't feel like doing just then, it was the Pussycat Prowl. Looking around in the hope of rescue, he caught sight of an object he prayed would provide a distraction.

"Look, Davy. There, up in the sky."

Davy gasped. "It's a flying saucer! Martians, Daddy!"

It did have an otherworldly look, gliding serenely across the sky, its swelling shape striped in colors that matched the sunset. Max hated to destroy his son's innocent fantasy, but the stern duty of a parent demanded he speak the truth.

"I'm afraid it's not a flying saucer. It's a hot-air balloon, with Earthlings instead of Martians."

Davy obviously didn't believe him. He began jumping up and down, waving his arms. "Martians! Martians!"

"Does he know what Martians are?" inquired Sarah, who had come to join her two best beloveds.

Max put his arm around her. "He can't know what they are, because they aren't. Haven't you explained the basic facts of astronomy to him? What kind of mother are you?"

"I was raised to believe that imparting basic facts is a father's responsibility. How do balloonists manage to fly those things, do you know?"

"Vaguely. I believe the air is heated by propane gas. They warm it up or let it cool off, depending on whether they're interested in going up or coming down. It's a bit late to be horsing around in a basket at this time of night, in my opinion."

"It's so pretty, though. Nice of the Martians to arrange this. A lovely finale to a perfect day. I wonder where they're planning to land."

Max didn't know where they had planned to land or whether hot-air balloons could be set down on a precise spot, but he was beginning to suspect he knew where the thing was going to land. It was almost directly overhead now, and so low he could see the faces of the people looking down from the basket. He caught his son in one arm and his wife in the other and headed south as fast as he could move. The remaining guests, who had been gawking appreciatively at the balloon, were a little slower to react, possibly because they were weighted down by wedding cake and Theonia's superb chocolate desserts, but they too dispersed, squawking and screaming as the big wicker basket dropped with a majestic thump smack on top of the wedding tent.

Clutching his hostages to fortune, Max turned to survey the damage and let out a breath of relief when he saw no arms, legs, or other human parts protruding from under the basket. Everyone had been outside, having a last fling at the dessert table or the bar or drifting toward the field where their cars were parked.

Davy was shouting with delight and trying to pull away from his father so he could be among the first to greet the visitors from outer space. Some of the younger guests had already converged on the balloon. Obeying the vigorous gestures of a person whose head was encased in a green plastic helmet, the volunteers grasped the ropes he tossed out and held the basket steady while two other people, male or female—there was no way to label either by the garments they wore—clambered down a rope ladder they'd hung over the side of the basket.

"It would be only civil to greet them and congratulate them on a safe landing, I suppose," Sarah murmured.

"If we're the first, we're entitled to the champagne."

"What champagne?"

"Isn't that what they do? I read it somewhere." Max rubbed his forehead with one hand while keeping the other firmly on his son. Even to a man who spends his time pursuing art thieves across five continents, the situation was a little confusing. "They present a bottle of champagne to the astonished farmer or house owner on whose property they end up."

"If they're handing out alcoholic beverages, I'd better get to them before Uncle Jem."

Sarah knew her uncle well. She reached the aeronauts only a few seconds before Jem trotted up, still resplendent in crimson arm garters. Max arrived on the scene in time to hear his wife's courteous welcoming speech interrupted by one of the newcomers.

"Mind telling us where we are?"

"Where you've no damned business being," Jem remarked with typical Kelling courtesy. "Gate crashing a private wedding, or maybe tent crashing is what I mean. Where's the champagne?"

Even close up, the two tent crashers would have been hard to distinguish one from the other. They were bundled up against the chill of the upper air, in identical orange down jackets and heavy dark slacks. Heavy plastic helmets, like the ones worn by sensible motorcyclists, concealed any hair they might have possessed.

"What champagne?" The interrupter pulled off his helmet. His graying hair was cropped short, and his voice was definitely baritone. Not that that meant anything. Max had known a number of women, several of them related to Sarah, who displayed both characteristics.

Instead of answering, Jem peered keenly at the speaker. "You're a Zickery!"

Max nudged his wife. "What's a Zickery?" he whispered. "Any connection with the Shriners or the Convivial Codfish?"

"They must be members of the family that owns that ramshackle old mansion across the road," Sarah whispered back. "No one was living there in my time, but Uncle Jem probably knew the family."

The Zickery stared back at Jem. "And you're a Kelling. Should have known. Asking for booze before he even says hello. Is this Ireson's Landing, then? What happened to the old yellow house?"

"It was torn down and completely rebuilt about eight years ago by my niece Sarah Kelling and her husband, Max Bittersohn. I'm Jeremy Kelling. If you're my age, you must have been Harvard class of 1940, and gone straight from ROTC into the army with your second lieutenant's bar all shined up."

"Well, we do keep hearing that it's a small world. I remember you, way back from when we were children, though you've changed a lot, and not for the better. You always had a peanut-butter sandwich in your hand; we assumed you must be starving over there; though you certainly never looked as though you were."

Jem was enjoying himself. This was more like it, someone with whom to exchange insults. "We used to feel sorry for you because you had to go all the way to the general store to get anything to eat while we had so much good food right around us. So which one of the Zickerys are you?"

"Alister. You must have been at Harvard in my brother Emmett's time, then. I came along two years later. We ought to have a drink on that sometime. Your place, of course."

"Whatever happened to Emmett?"

"Not a great deal. He's still collecting postage stamps.

And making quite a good thing of them, surprisingly enough. He married one of the Tippletons; they have a philately shop in Manhattan, a country place in Sewickley, and a pied-à-terre on Nob Hill in San Francisco. They travel a lot."

Max was used to the Kellings' habit of maundering on about old times with anyone and everyone, but this was a bit much for a man who'd seen his nephew married, been smacked on the shins by a lunatic burglar, and found a ruby necklace that had no business being where it was. He was about to intervene when the mute, unmoving figure at Alister's side broke its silence.

"Allie. You are forgetting your manners."

"I'm sorry, Callie. Folks, I neglected to introduce my fellow aeronaut. My twin sister, Calpurnia Zickery."

Callie, or Calpurnia, as the case might be, removed her own helmet.

Davy tugged at his father's hand. "I told you they were Martians," he hissed.

"Davy!" Sarah went pink with embarrassment, and Max tried to hide his smile. He knew where his intelligent son had gotten the idea, from a science-fiction television show about clones. Except for the fact that Calpurnia's hair was a little longer than Alister's, they might have been decanted from adjoining test tubes. Davy's mother restricted his television viewing to high-minded educational programs and any children's show that did not feature purple dinosaurs, but some of Davy's mother's relatives weren't so fussy.

Uncle Jem had a weakness for old *Star Trek* shows, particularly the ones in which the female crew members sashayed around the *Enterprise* in sleek black tights and skirts that barely covered the essentials. Jem had been thoroughly put out when the producers of the show had yielded to the complaints of those who pointed out that this smacked not only of sexism, but of a certain lack of military discipline.

"How do you do," Max said. "I don't want to seem inhospitable, but we've got a wedding going on here and your balloon has just flattened the main tent. Couldn't you have set down somewhere else?"

"Frightfully sorry," said Alister Zickery. "We were heading for our own property, but one can't always put the thing down where one wants to. Air currents and, er, that sort of thing." He waved rather vaguely at the balloon, which was now crumpling ponderously onto the ground. The third member of the crew, in a matching helmet and orange overalls, was directing the operation, enthusiastically assisted by some of the younger guests.

Calpurnia had been looking fixedly at Davy. "Charming," she murmured. "What a sweet little boy. We're going to be neighbors, sweet little boy. Will you come down and see me some time?"

"No, you don't, Callie," her brother exclaimed. "No children. I told you that. I won't have 'em around."

"That's enough of that, Allie," his sister said sharply. "We've kept these good people too long. It's time we were getting home. Good night, all."

As one they nodded, wheeled, locked arms, and marched away across the lawn.

"Where are they going?" Sarah asked.

"The old Zickery house, I guess," Jem said.

"But it's a wreck! They can't stay there. Maybe we ought to—"

"Oh, no, you don't." Max caught his wife's hand in a fond but firm grip. "It's been a long day, süssele, and I refuse to welcome that pair to our home and hearth. If they planned to end their balloon ride hereabouts, they must have made arrangements for accommodations. You don't know that the Zickery place is uninhabitable. Maybe they've been renovating it. I've seen a few trucks heading down that overgrown drive during the past week."

"So have I, come to think of it," Sarah admitted. "You're right, darling, it's been a long day, and we have other responsibilities, especially to this young man."

Davy knew what that meant. "Not sleepy," he said firmly.

5

Except for the catering crew, who were still packing up left-over food, and hoisting tables and chairs into their trucks, everybody had gone except Jem and Egbert. Not having lived anywhere that wasn't within walking distance of Louisburg Square, Jeremy Kelling had never learned to drive a car. Egbert could drive, but like that of most senior citizens, his night vision wasn't as good as it had once been, and he preferred not to buck the city traffic after dark. The two elders had come prepared to stay overnight. In the morning Jem's faithful though frequently exasperated henchman would drive him back to the souvenir-laden flat on Pinckney Street where they had lived since before Sarah was born.

Jem was depressed. Except for the brief, refreshingly rude interlude with an old acquaintance, and the triumph of his performance on the dance floor, he had not had a happy day. He'd found his vaunted skill as a bartender redundant among a gathering where Earl Grey tea and hazelnut coffee were favored by a long shot over the near lethal double martinis that he was used to mixing for his comrades of the Convivial Codfish.

He had finally turned over the bartending to Egbert, who could pour a glass of Orange Crush, root beer, or Camel Cola without wincing. As for himself, he'd skulked off to gaze wistfully seaward to the gull's way and the whale's way where the wind was like a whetted knife, or might have been if the wind had been blowing harder and the knife more keenly sharpened.

All he'd asked, after all, had been a merry yarn from a laughing fellow rover and a long martini and a strong martini when the long trick was over. And what had he got? Heartburn, that was what. Little had he wotted while he'd been pigging out on far too many of those beguiling little pastries that some of the guests had called piroshki, others had called knishes, and the rest called simply yummy that they would all give rise in due time to pretty much the same kind of burp.

Never let it be said, however, that Jem Kelling did not know his duty. After the multitudes had departed and the survivors had settled down in the living room, he graciously offered to mix a drink for Max. Max refused on the grounds that he had his wife, his son, and his liver to think of, but he knew how to take a hint, especially from Jem. Retiring to the kitchen where the remaining bottles and glasses had been taken, he stirred up a martini from the recipe that had been handed down from Great-Uncle Serapis Kelling, a founding father of the Comrades of the Convivial Codfish. Passing over such frivolities as a stuffed olive or a twist of lemon peel, Serapis's procedure had been and still was, even though Serapis no longer graced the mortal scene, to lift the cork from the well-chilled vermouth bottle, wave the cork back and forth three times, slowly but not too slowly, over the well-chilled gin in the well-chilled glass, then shove the cork back into the bottle, pick up the glass, and carry on from there in the accustomed manner. It was really quite simple, once one got the hang of it. And a good thing, too, Max thought. He wasn't up to complex recipes just then. He managed to concentrate long enough to pour a glass of orange juice for his son and a slug of Old Blatherskite for Egbert, who seldom imbibed but who probably felt the need tonight. After profound cogitation he added a slug of schnapps for himself. It had been quite a day, and the worst was yet to come.

With so many good things available all day and so many good people telling their host and hostess how good it all was, the said host and hostess had had hardly any time to get any food for themselves. Sarah insisted they must eat something, and she and Egbert put together enough of the leftovers to make a light meal. Ignoring Davy's demands for wedding cake and/or knishes, she made him a bowl of milk toast and managed to get a few bites into him before he showed signs of falling facedown into the bowl.

"Never mind, kätzele," Max said, scooping the sleepy cherub into his arms. "You can be sure he had a good healthy lunch at Mrs. Blufert's. He's too tired to eat."

"Let him sleep it off," Jem agreed. The food, or more likely the martini, had given him his second wind. "That's what I always do. Good night, Davy."

By the time Max had exchanged Davy's once neat shirt and shorts for a pair of pajamas printed with dinosaurs and tucked him into bed with his alligator, the phone had rung several times. He joined the others in the living room, and Sarah reported on the calls. Miriam and Ira, back home in Ireson Town, nonchalantly slapping together a sumptuous gourmet dinner for some out-of-state cousins, had telephoned to ask if they hadn't changed their mind about joining the group. They hadn't, though Sarah expressed her appreciation between yawns. The newlyweds had phoned from the airport to send Sarah and Max a special message of love and gratitude for their wonderful wedding; but they'd had to hang up quickly because their flight was being called. The head caterer had stopped by to apologize for not striking the tent, which was hardly his fault since the remains of the tent were still buried under the crumpled folds of the balloon.

"I told him it wasn't our balloon and that I hadn't the faintest idea what to do with it," Sarah said. "What does one do with an abandoned hot-air balloon?"

"One calls on the owners and threatens them with legal action if they don't get the damned thing off our property," Max said. "I think it has to be folded up or rolled up, and loaded onto a truck, along with the basket."

"How big a truck?" Sarah demanded. "If they mess up Cousin Anne's beautiful landscaping, I'll murder them."

"We'll make sure they don't," Max promised, hoping he was not speaking optimistically. "Don't worry, darling, if the Zickerys don't show up of their own accord, burbling apologies, I'll run over there and speak a kindly word."

"I'll go with you and speak a less than kindly word," Jem promised. The prospect obviously pleased him. "Imagine that pair turning up after all these years."

"What do you know about them?" Max asked, hoping the question sounded casual. It had occurred to him, as it would to any trained searcher out of other people's treasures, that the appearance of the long-lost Zickerys might not be entirely unconnected with the other odd occurrences of the day.

Jem settled back to enjoy his reminiscences. "There were a lot of them. They came and went all summer long, just as the Kellings did. I don't know whether they had some kind of rota or whether it was a case of first in with the most luggage. I have a dim recollection of iron cots with thin mattresses and chamber pots underneath. We had pretty much the same kind of setup on our side of the road, but we weren't quite as barbaric as the Zickerys. They were an insouciant lot, they didn't appear to worry over dirty dishes in the sink until they ran out of things to put food in."

"From what I've heard about Aunt Tiberia, she wouldn't have allowed that sort of thing here," Sarah put in.

Jem chuckled. "That's right, you never knew Aunt Tiberia Kelling; she'd been gone for quite a while before you started coming here. She drilled us all to wash whatever dishes we'd used as soon as they were empty, and not to expect anything special in the way of food. The menu was porridge in the morning and sandwiches for lunch, to be taken outdoors so that we wouldn't be scattering crumbs all over the floor if it was fine, and to be eaten in the carriage house if it rained."

"That must have been fun," said Sarah doubtfully.

"Up to a point. At suppertime we ate simple food like meat loaf and baked beans. For dessert we might get biscuits with molasses on them. They were pretty good," Jem said, his eyes misty with memory. "We also picked berries and apples, which Aunt Tiberia made into blueberry slump or apple cobbler, whichever was appropriate. They were good, too."

"Did the Zickerys go berry picking with you?" Max nudged gently.

"Oh, no. They had a car that they used to go into town for supplies. We Kellings walked, two miles there and two miles back. There wasn't much there, only a little country general store, but we could get cookies and licorice whips and bull's-eyes. I haven't tasted a bull's-eye since I was about ten years old."

Sarah patted his hand sympathetically. He gave her a

rakish grin and reached for the cocktail shaker. "Gin's better."

"So go on," Max said. "Did you have any special friends among the Zickerys?"

"We Kellings didn't mingle much. There were always plenty of us around, of all ages, shapes, and descriptions; pinching the pennies, not wasting food, taking our baths in warm tidal pools because the ocean water was too cold for our tender skins and the undertow could be dangerous. On Saturday nights, we got to use well water for our baths. If it rained, we stood outdoors in our bathing suits and enjoyed the impromptu showers at no cost to us or the elements. Sometimes a Zickery or two would join in. You should have seen Zenobia in her two-piece bathing suit."

Jem smacked his lips and finished his martini. Sarah smiled at him. A two-piece bathing suit had not been then what it was today, if indeed today's was anything at all. Zenobia's had probably been a sturdy all-wool chemise that hugged the body tightly and snapped between the legs with strong grippers. Over this went an all-wool skirt secured with an inchwide belt of strong white webbing and a businesslike clasp. But back then the older ladies who haunted the beach with their parasols and pairs of binoculars with which to keep their eagle eyes on the nubile females and dashing young males would have been scandalized by Zenobia's shocking display of uncovered flesh.

Max was unmoved by Jem's lascivious memories. An

ear-splipping yawn lengthened his ruggedly handsome face, and Sarah said tenderly, "Darling, hadn't you better get to bed?"

"I wish I could," Max said. "I wish you could, too. I was tempted to wait till morning before breaking the news, but it looks as if tomorrow will be another busy day. Don't look so scared, süssele, it isn't that kind of bad news, nobody's been hurt or threatened."

After tucking Davy into bed, he had removed the velvet cases from the safe in his and Sarah's room and brought them downstairs, covering the case with copies of *Brides' Bulletin* so he could keep a weather eye on them without the others noticing their presence until he was ready to introduce the subject. Might as well let Sarah relax and Jem get well oiled before he stirred things up again.

His forlorn hope that Sarah would be able to explain the presence of the parure faded as soon as he uncovered the cases. Her look of mild surprise made it obvious she didn't recognize them. No reason why she should; she had never seen the actual jewels, only the painted or photographed images. He opened the case that held the necklace. Rubies and gold caught the light in a blinding glitter, and Sarah gasped.

"Max! Is it . . . It can't be. But it is. Isn't it?"

"Damn right it is," said Jeremy Kelling, squinting myopically at the extravagant object. "Good work, Max. I take it these other boxes contain the rest of the parure.

How did you manage to track it down, and whom did you hire to steal it back?"

"I appreciate your commendation, Jem, but I don't deserve it. The damned thing turned up this afternoon, on a table in the library among the wedding gifts. It hadn't been there an hour earlier, and there was no name on the card under it. So it didn't arrive by the usual channels?"

Sarah had got her breath back. "Good heavens, no. Do you suppose I'd have calmly added it to the collection and not bothered to mention it to you? I don't believe it! Unless—unless this is one of the copies. Maybe it's someone's idea of a joke."

"Certain members of your family, my dearest, have peculiar notions of what is and is not humorous, but even a copy would cost more than a Kelling would be willing to lay out for a practical joke. And this is not a copy. It's the original."

Nobody asked if he was sure. Max didn't make mistakes about such things. He went on to explain anyhow. "The copies were so good, they'd have passed even a close inspection. The gems weren't glass, they were modern synthetics, indistinguishable from the real thing except under a fluoroscope; the gold was genuine eighteen karat, but it was only a thin layer, electroplated onto silver. I took the liberty of scraping away some gold from the inside of one of the links. It's solid all right."

Sarah lifted the necklace from its bed of velvet and held it up.

"You could fool me," Jem grunted. "Who made the copies?"

"I never tracked the guy down. Wish I had, he's probably pulled a few other elegant swindles since. But back then I didn't have the time or the manpower for the job. You remember how Mrs. Kelling's lover operated; he sold the original, had it appraised and authenticated, and then substituted a copy, not once but several times. Some of the victims found out they'd been taken and, being no better than they should be, staged a robbery and put in a claim for reimbursement with their insurance companies. That's how I got into the act."

"Some woman in Amsterdam managed to hang on to the original," Sarah murmured. "Isn't that what you told me? Then how did it get here?"

"Damned if I know. What's so embarrassing is that Max Bittersohn, great detective, must have been in the room when the unknown donor put it onto the table among the brussels sprouts forks and the snail holders."

"Who else was there?"

"Who wasn't? Everybody and his sisters and his cousins and his aunts wanted to check out the wedding gifts. Some of them I knew, most of them I'd never seen before. There were waiters and a couple of guys delivering parcels, and God knows who else. And Egbert, part of the time. Hey, Egbert, did you notice anything unusual?"

The only reply from the faithful retainer was a gentle

snore. Worn out by well-doing and Old Blatherskite, Egbert had dropped off some time back.

"Don't wake him," Sarah said sympathetically.

"I'll ask him in the morning," Max agreed. "Though I doubt if he saw the perp. The place was a madhouse. Our best bet is to start at the other end of the trail, in Amsterdam. Tomorrow." He was watching his wife. "Try it on, why don't you?"

Sarah dropped the necklace as if it had burned her. "I couldn't. It's not mine, I don't want it."

Max hadn't even got to the part of the story about Louie the Locksmith, but he decided he'd better save that. Sarah looked as if she'd had all she could take for one day.

"Would you care for some chamomile tea to help you sleep, Uncle Jem?" she asked.

"I do wish you wouldn't confront me with obscenities while I'm pondering, Sarah. Or was that a tactful hint? I guess I can ponder just as well in bed. Give Egbert a shake, will you? If he sleeps in that chair all night he won't be able to get out of it without a chiropodist."

Sarah obliged, and she and Egbert yawned in unison. "Would you mind locking up, Max? I'm awfully tired."

"Your wish is my command, angela mia. I'll be along as soon as I've made the rounds. Need any help wrestling Jem up the stairs, Egbert?"

"Thanks, Mr. Max, but I can manage him well enough. Those martial arts exercises I've been working on lately seem to be helping quite a lot. If you're sure there's nothing you want me for, then, I'll go on up. Good night, Mrs. Sarah."

"Good night, Egbert. Sleep well, and don't worry about breakfast. I thought we'd have scrambled eggs with some of those muffins and Danish pastries left over from the wedding. Maybe when you get back to town tomorrow you could stop by the Senior Citizens' Recycling Center and give them the rest of the leftovers. If you wouldn't mind, that is."

"I don't mind," said Jem, who hadn't been asked. "So long as I don't have to see Dolph. He and Mary are still in Denmark, aren't they?"

"Yes, they wanted to get some tips on running an up-to-date recycling center and on various schemes for senior citizens' activities. The Scandinavian countries excel at that sort of thing. I hope they're also having a restful holiday; they deserve it. They've done a wonderful job with the SCRC."

"Mary has, you mean," Jem grunted. "Marrying her was the only smart thing that great tub of lard did in his whole life."

"Take him away, Egbert," Max said wearily, and assisted in the operation. He then ordered his wife to bed. When he joined her, after double-checking the locks on doors and windows and returning the necklace to the safe, she was sound asleep. He was pretty tired himself, but he lay awake for some time.

He was remembering his and Sarah's wedding. It had

taken place on a lovely day in June when the rickety old Ireson's Landing house was still standing but slated for demolition as soon as they could get the wreckers in. Sarah's cousin Dolph Kelling had given the bride away because he'd have raised four kinds of hell if Sarah hadn't let him. Max's nephew, Mike, then a freshman at college, had elected himself Max's best man for much the same reason as Dolph's. Cousin Theonia, by then Mrs. Brooks Kelling, had baked the wedding cake. Miriam Rivkin had baked the knishes. Few of the Kellings had ever tasted a knish before, but they'd been quite ready to eat as many of the bite-size delicacies as they could get. Sarah's devoted henchpersons, Mariposa and Charles, had stage-managed the nuptials in their usual efficient style.

Nobody had got killed or hurt or drunk beyond reasonable limits. No Kelling had wantonly picked a fight with any other Kelling. The sun had set in a blaze of glory, and the moon had climbed up out of the ocean as he and Sarah watched from the headland. It was a hard fight, Mom, but I won, Max had thought, taking a firm grip on his wife.

Now he wondered if he would ever succeed in laying the ghosts of Sarah's past. Just when he thought they were gone they rose up from their graves to haunt her. It wasn't nice to hate a dead man, but this wasn't the first time he had cursed the memory of Sarah's handsome, spineless, elderly husband. Alexander had loved her devotedly and had tried his best to protect her from his murderous mother, but he hadn't had the guts to cut the apron strings and face the consequences, unpleasant though those consequences would have been. The train of disaster Caroline Kelling had set in motion was still on track.

6

"Where is that damned kid?" Max growled, slamming the phone down.

Sarah refilled his cup and pushed it toward him. "That's not a nice way to refer to your only son. He's outside with Egbert, watching the removal of the balloon and hoping the Martians will come back."

Max gave her a sheepish smile. "Sorry, kätzele. You know I wasn't talking about Davy."

"Are you apologizing? What a pity. I was hoping we could have a knock-down fight and then make up."

"I'd be willing to skip the first part."

Sarah slid away from his outstretched hand. "Stop that, you sex maniac. The scrambled eggs will burn, and if I don't get those muffins out of the oven within the next sixty seconds, they'll be leathery."

"You made muffins, after all that schlemozle yesterday? What a woman!"

She didn't look haunted this morning. Her soft brown hair was tied back with a pink ribbon that matched the rose-and-pink print of the caftan he had brought her from Cairo. "So what kid were you damning?" she asked, taking a pan of muffins out of the oven.

"Jesse. He was supposed to report to me yesterday."

Sarah popped the muffins into a napkin-lined basket, spooned eggs onto two plates, and joined Max at the table. "We'd better eat while things are relatively calm. As a matter of fact, Jesse telephoned last night."

"What? Why didn't you tell me?"

"Because you knocked me head over hocks with that tasteless bauble, that's why," his wife said spiritedly. "What's Jesse supposed to be doing, tracing the parure?"

"Not exactly." Max finished his first muffin and reached for a second. He wasn't strong enough to begin the unbelievable saga of Louie the Locksmith. "Anybody else call?"

"I told you about Miriam and the newlyweds. The only other call was from Theonia. It was rather odd, actually. She said she had to talk to you, and when I told her you were putting the alligator to bed she sort of mumbled at me and then Brooks said something I couldn't make out, and Theonia said it probably wasn't important, and that she'd see us soon."

Coming from Theonia, that was odd. She was now a Kelling by virtue of marriage to Sarah's cousin Brooks, but all she knew about her own family tree was that she'd been born under one. Her young, terribly frightened mother had given birth to a girl child half Gypsy and half a legacy from an equally frightened young anthropology student who'd got too involved with his homework. Where that had been, and where the young man had gone to, she'd never known and preferred not to guess.

Nowadays Theonia was the very model of an upper-crust Beacon Hill matron; but she could switch in a wink to a shuffling old woman wearing holey sneakers and carrying a worn-out shopping bag crammed with salvage out of the city's trash bins. Or she might be an ageless beauty wrapped in an aura of mystery and a gown that whispered knowingly of Paris but was in fact a negligee she'd garnished with sumptuous lace from a pair of the late Caroline Kelling's pure silk crepe de chine step-ins, circa 1928. She made her own clothes from outdated garments she picked up at sales, turned them into haute couture, and left professional designers sobbing in their Campari. Her most successful coup had been Brooks Kelling, who had worked his own special magic on his chosen lady with the mating call of the ruffed grouse and a plain gold wedding band.

Had Theonia seen something or heard something that had aroused her suspicions? Max tried to remember where she had been during the festivities and drew a complete blank. He had caught glimpses of her and Brooks from time to time, during the dancing, and among the people scampering out from under the descending balloon. The last time he'd seen her she'd been standing out in front of the house, waiting for Brooks to bring the old Cadillac around. Brooks and Theonia had picked up Anora Protheroe's stepson, George, and a couple of George's assistants from his atelier in the Back Bay and were heading out to Anora's cluttered ark at Chestnut Hill for one of her little teas.

If Theonia or Brooks had observed anything of importance, she would have said so. Or would she? It might have been impossible to find a chance to speak in private. He hoped this wasn't one of the occasions when Theonia's Gypsy half took over. She'd been reading tea leaves in a run-down café when she moved into the boardinghouse Sarah had started after her husband's death. Like most of the men who were privileged to behold her voluptuous contours, Brooks had fallen in love at first sight and wooed her with birdcalls and avian courting rituals. It had been a while since Theonia had had one of her visions. Max didn't believe in them. But she'd been uncannily accurate a couple of times.

He'd meant to get in touch with Brooks and Theonia anyhow, since he'd probably need their assistance. First things first, though.

"I'd better go out and make sure Davy doesn't get in the way of that truck," he said, hearing a heavy engine start up.

"Egbert has him leashed," Sarah said comfortably. "Or vice versa. He's being a camel—Egbert, that is—in the caravan of a dashing African explorer. Camels will run away if they aren't firmly tied to the explorer, you know."

"I didn't, but I'm relieved to hear it. Are the Zickerys there?"

"No, just the truck and a crew of husky young tent rollers, and an old geezer who seems to be in charge of the balloon. Davy was sadly disappointed. He still thinks the Zickery twins are Martians."

"So do I," Max said. "All right, darling, I'll leave you to keep the home fires burning while I make a few phone calls."

The office had three phones. The green was the one they used for family calls, the white was the business phone, and the red had a number known only to themselves and Cousin Brooks, Theonia's husband. Theonia probably knew it, too, since Brooks was putty in her exquisitely plump white hands. Max couldn't blame him.

Brooks was in charge of the Boston office, a little cubbyhole in a building on the corner of Boylston and Tremont. Since the nature of their business didn't lend itself to regular office hours, it was more than likely Brooks wouldn't be there so early, especially if he'd been whooping it up with Anora and company after the wedding. Jesse might or might not be home. Hoping he was, and that he was asleep, Max picked up the white phone and dialed the number.

Jesse might have been sleeping, but he snapped to attention when he heard the voice of his revered leader. "Morning, Uncle Max. I expected you'd call me back last night."

"Why should I? Obviously you didn't find out anything useful. What were you doing, chasing bridesmaids?"

"Not just chasing. Remember the pale yellow one?" Jesse added hastily, "Don't get mad, Uncle Max. I'd already covered the place like a blanket and hit one dead end after another."

"You're mixing your metaphors. No luck finding Louie?"

"No, sir. So I got to talking to Jennifer—that's her name, Jennifer—and we, well, we decided we'd split, and some of the others decided they'd come, too, and we went to the Bucket of Clams, and what with one thing and another . . . You aren't mad, are you, sir?"

In fact Max was marveling over the repeated "sirs." Before he and Sarah had taken Jesse in hand, that word would never have passed the childish lips of any of Lionel's offspring. A string of obscenities would have been more likely. It was necessary to maintain discipline, however, which he did by keeping a stony silence.

"Aw, come on, Uncle Max. I'd have told you right away if I'd found any trace of the old geezer. Don't tell me you never got distracted by a pretty girl starving for clams?"

"Never," Max said stoutly, crossing all the fingers he could spare. A lie of that magnitude demanded more fingers, and probably his toes as well, but the latter were inside his slippers and inaccessible.

"What do you want me to do now?" Jesse asked humbly.

"Nothing. I'll let you know. Stay cool," he added, hoping that attempt at modern lingo didn't date him too badly.

Brooks wasn't at the office, so Max tried the Tulip Street house. Sarah had inherited the place from her husband and had run it as a boardinghouse while the lawyers were trying to straighten out the complex train of illegal second mortgages and general chicanery instigated by Caroline Kelling and her lover. It was during that period of her life that Sarah had formed close friendships with Mariposa and her significant other, Charles, who now ran the house for Brooks and Theonia and any other members of the family who happened to be in Boston.

Brooks answered on the second ring. His first question made Max's hackles rise.

"Is everything all right?"

"Why shouldn't it be?"

"Didn't you read Theonia's note?"

"What note? Damn it," Max sputtered, "can't we stop conversing in questions?"

"If you prefer," Brooks said agreeably. "She said she'd slipped a note into your pocket yesterday, before we left for Anora's."

"It must still be there, then. What did it say?" Realizing he had slipped back into the interrogatory mode, Max answered his question with the one Brooks would logically have asked. "Why don't I read it? Yeah, right, I will. That's not the reason I called. Something odd has happened. Remember that ruby parure that was stolen from the safe-deposit box?"

"The Kelling parure? How could I forget? Don't tell me . . ."

Max told him. Brooks let out a long musical whistle, probably the call of some exotic bird or other, had Max been able to identify it.

"Well, well, fancy that. I won't waste your time in idle theorizing, Max, since I'm sure the various possibilities have already occurred to you. Yes indeed, a business conference is definitely in order. Will you come here, or shall we come to you?"

Max had already worked it out. "We'll come there. I want to get Uncle Jem and Egbert back to Pinckney Street; they stayed overnight, you know, since Egbert doesn't like to drive after dark. I'm not happy about the old boy driving before dark, either, especially in city traffic, and I'd been trying to think of a way of playing chauffeur without hurting Egbert's feelings. I'll head on over to Tulip Street after I deliver them, and you and Theonia, or Jesse, or somebody, depending on how the investigation develops, can drive me home tomorrow."

"Excellent," Brooks said crisply. "Is there something you want me to do right away? I had planned to spend the morning cleaning up the matter of those missing Utrillos, but—"

"No, that's fine. At the moment I don't know what the hell is going on, much less what to do about it."

When he returned to the kitchen to tell Sarah what he'd arranged, he found her less than enthusiastic. "There's an awful lot to do here, Max. Much as I'd love to see Brooks and Theonia, I really ought to get the presents packed up and recorded and taken to the carriage house. I haven't been able to use my desk for weeks. Then there are the tent people to deal with. They said they'd remove the remains as soon as the balloon was out of the way. I telephoned earlier, and they said they'd come right away."

"How'd you accomplish that?" Max asked respectfully. "More intimidation, à la Aunt Emma?"

"Not exactly. I just refused to pay them until they'd finished the job. And what would we do about Davy?"

"Take him along," said Davy's doting father.

Sarah looked doubtful. "I'd like to get him back on a regular schedule. He's had a lot of excitement the past few days. Speaking of which, why don't you go out and relieve Egbert? He's been a camel for over an hour, and Davy is apparently refusing to let him off the lead."

Max glanced out the window. He could see the small figure of his son running circles around the crumpled yellow-and-white folds of the tent. The camel was unquestionably staggering.

"Poor old Egbert. All right, süssele, I'll assert my parental authority. Why don't you roust your uncle out of bed so we can get ourselves organized?"

"I'd rather be chewed by scorpions. Do scorpions have teeth?"

"I doubt it, but I get the idea. I'll send Egbert in."

Davy didn't want to go in. "Even camels need to be watered, fed, and rested," Max pointed out. "An experienced explorer takes good care of his livestock."

"What do camels eat?" Davy asked curiously.

"Muffins," Max said. "They prefer blueberry."

Davy remembered that explorers also liked blueberry muffins and led his puffing steed away. Egbert gave Max a grateful look.

Max watched them with a fond smile. Davy was walking slowly and administering encouraging pats to the camel. He was a good-hearted kid, once he was reminded of the frailties of animals less energetic than a three-year-old human.

He didn't blame Davy for lingering. It was a beautiful morning, with blue skies and a gentle breeze just cool enough to be refreshing. He'd have liked nothing better than to spend the day playing with his son, helping his wife with the wedding gifts, and even listening to Jem Kelling's lies about the good old days. If it hadn't been for that damned parure . . .

Hands in his pockets, he wandered down the drive toward the road. Should he go to Boston with Jem and Egbert and leave Sarah to deal with the tent people? He didn't doubt she could, but he hated to leave her alone. Max had the check all written, but he was planning to let Sarah be the one to hand it over. He'd missed watching her intimidate the tent crew; he could only imagine what a genuine, dyed-in-the-wool fifth-generation Kelling might look like when in the process of having to part with a rental fee. Maybe he should call Brooks back and ask him to come to Ireson's Landing instead. There wasn't much point in going to Boston. He'd left a message for his man in Paris, Pepe Ginsberg (pronounced "Geens-bair"). Pepe hadn't been in the office; he seldom was, since he had to cover a large territory—France, the Low Countries, and Scandinavia. He'd been instructed to check his answering machine daily, though, and would return Max's call as soon as he could.

It would take even Pepe a while to get results, Max knew. The last known address of the astute buyer of the necklace had been in Amsterdam, but that had been seven years ago. She might have moved, or been on vacation, when she died. She might not have left a will. People often didn't.

Max realized that, absorbed in thought, he had reached the end of the drive. He turned to retrace his steps and found himself blinded by a sudden eclipse.

7

Max Bittersohn was not a man to panic. After the first flabbergasted second he realized the vast, choking cloud of total blackness was only some misguided half-wit's notion of a joke. He had recognized the acrid stench of a smoke bomb—not the baby-size kind he had once, in his distant, misspent youth, set off under the kitchen window when his mother was making latkes, but a much larger variety, like the simulation hand grenades used by the military in training recruits and by the motion picture industry in lending an air of authenticity to vampire flicks and burning buildings.

His mother hadn't been amused, either.

One good thing about smoke was that it could not be corraled. The air was still dark as the underneath portion of a witch's lingerie, but Max could feel the breeze against his face. The cloud would disperse in due course; all he had to do was stay right where he was, near the bottom of the long, steep driveway. The real danger from a situation such as this was in growing impatient. One or two false steps might put him out in the road, directly in front of a car with a disoriented or understandably frantic driver behind the wheel. Any sensible driver would stop or pull off the road when he found himself unable to see past the windshield, but even a sensible driver might panic under those hellish conditions.

Even as the thought entered his mind he saw a pair of headlights on high beam pierce the blackness. The vehicle zigzagged across the road, missing him by about four feet, and bounced off a telephone pole or a tree trunk.

Max started forward, then forced himself to stop. The smoke was beginning to show signs of thinning out and moving on, but he still couldn't see across the road, and if another car hit him while he was trying to go to the assistance of the driver, it wouldn't do him or the victim much good. He called out, "Anybody hurt?"

The answer was a burst of sound from the engine and a squeal of tires as the maniac in the vehicle reversed, turned, and roared off into the artificial night. Max waited, wincing, for another crunch, but heard nothing.

He headed back up the drive as fast as safety dictated. The house was at the top of the hill; it might have escaped the worst of the smoke. Sarah was bound to be worrying about him, though, and the police had to be notified as soon as possible. Too bad he hadn't thought to bring a flashlight, but how could he have known that sudden night would descend?

He ought to have known something would go wrong, Max thought sourly. He'd been a cockeyed optimist to assume that the reappearance of the rubies was a harmless, isolated incident, to be investigated at his leisure. He'd had enough experience with art treasures to know that objects so valuable carried a trail of danger and crime. The smoke bomb had to be related to the rubies; it was too much of a coincidence that some nitwit would pick that morning to play a sick joke. There had to be a reason for someone wanting to shroud the place in darkness.

One reason leaped to mind. Max broke into a run and immediately regretted the decision when he tripped over something and fell heavily onto his hands and knees. He fumbled around and found the offending object. It was Davy's alligator.

The next thing he ran into was Sarah with a battery lantern in her hand and no doubt a steely glint in her eye, though it was still too dark to make out such details.

"You idiot!"

Max heard the catch in his wife's voice as she dropped the lantern and threw her arms around him. "What do you think you're doing? You could have fallen and broken your leg again. Where did this black cloud come from?"

"It wasn't me," Max protested.

"I didn't suppose it was. Max, you are limping. What

happened? Did I hear a crash? What were you doing down there?"

Max explained what had happened as they made their way toward the house. "Though I'm damned if I can explain why it happened. Was there any trouble at the house?"

"Not unless you consider a sudden volcanic eruption trouble. We dashed around closing doors and windows, so the awful stuff didn't get into the house, but we couldn't see a thing outside." Sarah managed a feeble laugh. "Davy adored it."

"Martians?"

"Of course. It's thinning a little, isn't it?"

"Seems to be. I'd better go back down and see if there's any sign of that fool driver. How about you calling the police?"

Sarah wasn't falling for any of that he-man stuff. "How about you sitting right here on the steps and resting your leg? You said the car had gone."

"Okay, if you say so." Max was quite willing to bask in wifely concern. With all of them running around checking doors and windows, a would-be intruder would have been spotted immediately. "You might bring me one of the portable phones."

In addition to the official instruments in the office there were telephones, corded and cordless, all over the house. Max ran up ferocious bills keeping in touch with his personal secret service connections at strategic points at home and abroad. Sarah opted for a cordless one, those being of the sort that the neighbors could tap into should they desire to do so, as they frequently did. It was neighborly gestures like this that kept the Bittersohns' popularity rating high. They seldom had time for socializing, so the least they could do, Sarah argued, was stay in touch via this modern version of the old party line. She carried the phone out onto the step, pushed the 911 button, passed the handset over to Max, and asked him to give Sergeant Jofferty her regards.

Max knew everybody on the local police force. He was a third-generation immigrant from Saugus, and everybody knew his brother-in-law, Ira, the only honest garage owner in the area, and his uncle Jake, one of the few honest lawyers in the area. Max had a more intimate acquaintance with the local constabulary as a result of his involvement in several local crimes, most of them involving Sarah. She and Sergeant Jofferty had formed the foundation of a warm friendship on that fateful day when her elderly first husband and his autocratic mother had hurtled over a cliff into the sea in their 1920 Milburn Electric.

Jofferty sent his regards to Sarah, and then listened in only mild surprise as Max told him what had happened. He'd got used to peculiar goings-on at the Kelling place.

"Smoke bomb? You mean one of those things we used to set off on Halloween?"

Max admitted he'd set them off, too, and explained the difference between those examples of boyish joie de vivre and the industrial-size variety that had been used. He could give no accurate information as to how long a smoke bomb took to disperse and was not inclined to acquire such data the hard way, but he didn't think it would take very long unless the wind backed around and blew the cloud inshore again, which it probably wouldn't. In fact, it was dispersing rapidly. However, he advised Jofferty to take it easy when he approached the Kelling place, since there had already been one accident, though it obviously hadn't been serious.

What with one thing and another, Sarah was kept on the doorstep longer than she'd expected to be. A mitigating circumstance was that Max was holding her within easy kissing range while getting on with his telephoned report. The circumstances proved to be so distracting that they were still sitting there when the police car drove up and Jofferty got out.

"All clear now," he reported unnecessarily, since they could see for themselves that the worst was over. "You folks okay?"

"Yes, except for Max's leg," Sarah said. "Let me have a look, darling."

"What happened to it?"

"I fell over Davy's alligator," Max said. Knowing Sarah would do it herself if he didn't, he rolled up his pant leg. Sarah let out a cry of distress.

"Darling, that's a terrible bruise. You couldn't have done it tripping over Davy's toy."

"It's a long story," Max said. "Why don't you come in and have a cup of coffee, Jofferty?"

"Thanks, but my wife's decided I'm drinking too much coffee and I've got to cut down. The heck of it is, she's right."

"Tea, then, or milk or mead, or anything that suits your fancy. This may take a while. By the way, was there any sign of that idiot who crashed his car?"

"Nope. To tell you the truth, Max, I didn't bother making out a report on that. The car couldn't have been damaged much or the guy wouldn't have been able to drive it, and nobody else was involved."

The steps were getting cold. Sarah was about to suggest they go indoors before Max got a chill in his fractures when she saw a truck approaching. "Finally, there are the tent people. They said they'd be right over."

"Maybe they were held up by the smoke bomb," Max said.

Jofferty looked out across the lawn toward the sprawl of crumpled fabric. "How come they didn't pack the tent up yesterday? When my niece got married the caterers were in such a hurry to finish up they practically grabbed plates and glasses out of people's hands. My sister-in-law had a fit about it."

"They would have done it yesterday if the balloon hadn't landed on the tent," Sarah explained.

"Balloon? Gosh, Mrs. Bittersohn, you people sure lead confusing lives."

"This is going to take even longer than I thought," Max said. "Mind if we get the tent business over and done with first, Jofferty? I'm getting a little confused myself. You've got the check, haven't you, Sarah?"

"Yes, dear. I'll go and get it while you find out how good you are at terrorizing tent makers."

Accompanied by Jofferty, Max started off across the lawn toward the tent makers' truck. It was a sorry-looking affair, rusty around the fenders and sagging around the edges. One of the back tires was almost bald. The man in charge, or so Max supposed him to be, came to meet them. Like the others, he was wearing a pair of grubby white coveralls with yellow trim. The words "Omar Inc." had been applied, also in yellow, across the chest.

"Sorry, Mr. Kelling," he began.

"Bittersohn," Max said.

"Oh? Sorry again, Mr. Bittersohn. We would of been here before this, but I'm short-handed, one of my guys walked out on me yesterday, and then we ran into this weird black cloud, if you can believe it—"

"I believe it."

"—and José and Willoughby were late anyhow, they don't own cars, and the bus they usually take was full up and wouldn't stop, and the next one—"

"That's all right," Max said loudly. "So long as you're here. How long will this take?"

He shouldn't have asked. The foreman was an embittered man, with a lot on his mind. His explanation ended in a tirade. "How do they expect me to get good people when they pay peanuts and only hire part-time? Look at that bunch of bumbling jackasses. Half of 'em are senile and the other half are illegal. I swear, I don't know what the world is coming to. The time is out of joint."

"Oh, cursed spite," Max agreed politely. Maybe it did take a steely-eyed Kelling to get this bunch moving. What was taking Sarah so long? He decided it would be unmanly to wait for his wife to do the job for him. Squaring his shoulders, he suggested that the bunch of bumbling jackasses might get on better with some expert leadership and led the way toward the heap of fabric. The men weren't even bumbling. They stood in a huddle, muttering among themselves.

"Well, get on with it," the foreman said irritably. "What are you standing there for?"

"Uh—we don't know what to do with it, Mr. Mortlake."

The speaker, a gaunt, grizzled man of advanced years, gestured toward the nearest fold of fabric.

"Don't know what to do with it? Damn it, Willoughby, I spent a good ten minutes yesterday showing you how to roll up a tent."

"Yessir. It ain't the tent, Mr. Mortlake. It's the body. We don't know what to do with it. You never told us what we was supposed to do with bodies."

Sarah could have sworn she'd put the check in her purse. It wasn't there. She went through the drawers of the dresser and nightstand, her search considerably hindered by Davy, who trotted at her heels, demanding that she admire the drawing he had made of a flying saucer, complete with Martians. Finally she located the check in the pocket of the shirt she had worn on the day in question and was able to turn her full attention to her son.

"It's a beautiful drawing, darling," she said warmly. "Now I have to give Daddy this check. I'll be right back."

"I come, too."

Sarah couldn't think of any reason why he shouldn't.

Somehow she wasn't surprised to see that nothing had been done. The men, including her wonderful husband and the able Sergeant Jofferty, were standing perfectly still, staring blankly at the folds of fabric. Bless their hearts, men did have a way of engaging in endless discussions about how things ought to be done instead of getting on with the job.

Max turned, started, and came hurrying toward them. "Go back to the house, Sarah. Don't let— Here, you young rascal, where do you think you're going?"

He caught Davy by the collar and held on to him, despite his protests.

"What's the matter?" Sarah asked faintly. She had known when she saw the look on Max's face that something was wrong.

He hesitated, trying to think how to tell her without informing Davy. His intellectual son knew as much Yiddish as he did English, which was quite a lot for a three-year-old, and he was equally accomplished at pig Latin. "Our initial assessment of the aeronautical occurrence was erroneous. The evacuation of the premises was not complete."

"My God! Do you mean . . ." She got hold of herself. Davy had stopped squirming and was looking at her in alarm. She forced a smile. "What Daddy means, darling, is that the men are very busy and we'll just be in the way. Let's go and—and make more blueberry muffins, shall we? Your faithful camel ate them all, and Uncle Jem will want some for breakfast."

"What about muffins for me?" Max demanded with false heartiness.

The performance convinced Davy, though. He gave his father a measuring look. "Will you be a camel?"

"You strike a hard bargain, kid. All right, a camel it is," Max promised. "Hurry up, now, because I'm getting very hungry. Sarah, you might ring Brooks and tell him we won't make it this evening."

Sarah nodded. "Here's the check. You won't be long, will you?"

"No longer than I can help, süssele. Have I mentioned lately that I love you?"

Sarah stood on tiptoe and gave him a quick kiss. "Me too, as Davy says."

"Me too," Davy echoed.

Max waited until they were well on their way before he went back to the awestruck audience. Jofferty had his notebook out, but he wasn't getting much information out of the witnesses. The foreman kept shaking his head and muttering.

"Poor old Mac. What a way to go."

"How do you know it's him?" Jofferty asked patiently. It was the third time he'd asked the question, but he knew he had to wait till the witness had recovered from the initial shock. This was a nasty one. The damned balloon must have landed on the face of the corpse.

This time he got through. "Well, sure it's him. He's wearing one of our uniforms, and Mac was the only one who didn't show up this morning." He swallowed and averted his eyes from the battered remains of the face. "He's the same height and build, and there's that finger he mashed yesterday when he dropped his end of the pole, the pinkie on the left hand. Poor old Mac, he was a lousy tent maker, but he tried."

And what a lousy epitaph, Max thought, staring at the pathetic remains. The defunct tent maker hadn't been a young man. The hair that wasn't stained ugly brown was pure white. He knelt and ran his hand over one of the twisted legs.

"Don't touch anything," Jofferty said automatically. "Sorry, Max, I wasn't thinking. That's what I'm supposed to say at a crime scene. Not that this is one."

"Are you sure?" Max didn't look up.

"Well, it sure isn't murder. I mean, trying to mash a guy by dropping a balloon on him is a damned unreliable way of killing him. I rode in one at the country fair once—once was enough for me, I can't stand heights—and the balloonist, if that's what you call him, said only an expert could guide the thing, and even an expert couldn't bring it down on a precise spot unless . . ." Jofferty pulled out his handkerchief and wiped his perspiring brow. He'd seen plenty of mangled bodies in his time, including that of Alexander Kelling, but he never would get used to them.

"Right." Max stood up and brushed off his pants. "All the same, I think you'd better play this one by the book, Jofferty. You can use the radio in the cruiser to call in, can't you? Ask them not to use the siren, I don't want my family to know what's going on."

"If you say so, Max. Just let me get a little more information on the corpse. What was his name?" He nudged the foreman, who was still staring at the body. "He did have a name, didn't he?"

Mortlake shook his head. "Poor old Mac," he intoned. "He was a man, take him for all and all."

"His full name," Jofferty insisted. "Mac what?"

"Macbeth."

"Come off it."

"Macbeth, I said. Joe Macbeth. He said we should call him Mac. I have a hard enough time keeping track of the names of the crew, they come and go so fast, but I couldn't forget his. I happen to be a Bacon buff."

"Yeah? Me too. All those health nuts keep saying it's not good for you, but I say what the hell, something's gonna get you sooner or later."

"Just a minute," Max said, trying to keep a straight face. Laughter wasn't suitable for the occasion, but at that moment he was grateful for a little comic relief. "I don't think he means that kind of bacon, Jofferty."

"Certainly not. It wasn't Shakespeare wrote those plays, you know. It was a guy named Bacon. *Macbeth* is one of his masterpieces. Personally I thought Orson Welles's performance was the best, even though the critics tore him to pieces."

8

Max returned to the bosom of his family just in time to prevent the two most immature members of it from rushing out to find out what was happening and why. He managed to distract Davy by offering to play camel, but Jem Kelling rejected the invitation to be another member of the herd. He'd heard about the body from Sarah and was determined to offer his advice and assistance. He'd also polished off the last of the second batch of muffins, which was okay by Max, since it was almost lunchtime anyhow. By the time Max had been led across the Sahara and helped to discover a new pyramid (built by Martians), he was ready for a nap even if Davy wasn't. However, the elder Bittersohn was rescued from the younger by the devoted wife of the former and handed over to Mrs. Blufert, who took him off to his room for a picnic lunch. Jem had returned, accompanied by Sergeant Jofferty, and they settled down at the kitchen table for food and conversation.

Sarah refused Egbert's offer to play chef. "There are enough leftovers to last for a week. We'd better finish some of the perishable items before they go bad. Sergeant, would you prefer caviar or smoked salmon?"

"Only if he can't get bacon," Max said. "Don't bother looking for it, süssele, that was a joke. Not a very good one, I admit."

Nobody laughed when he explained. "It was murder all right," Jofferty said heavily. "How'd you know, Max?"

"Not enough blood," Jeremy Kelling said with obvious relish. "I'll have some of those pickled beets, Sarah."

"That was one indication." Max indicated he did not care for pickled beets. "The blows on the face were inflicted after he was already dead. He'd been killed elsewhere and the body placed under the tent after the blood had dried and rigor was well advanced. I don't know why the murderer went to all that trouble. Nobody would believe death was caused by the balloon."

"An insult to the force," Jofferty agreed, helping himself to pasta salad. "We may be hicks, but we're not stupid."

"What did kill him?" Sarah asked.

"We'll have to wait for the results of the autopsy, but even a hick cop like me couldn't help noticing that the back of the skull was a peculiar shape."

"Don't take it personally," Max advised. "A more important question is that of motive. The poor devil appears to have been an elderly itinerant, trying to eke out his Social Security check with whatever part-time work he could pick up. Mortlake said he'd been with Omar Inc. for less than a month. He'd moved here from Chicago. Said it was too damned hot in the Midwest in July."

"The classic innocent bystander?" Sarah asked. "Maybe he was killed because he saw something he shouldn't have seen yesterday."

"Like what?" Jofferty asked. He pushed his plate away and cast a hopeful eye at the remains of a chocolate decadence cake. "You said it was a long story, Max, but make it as short as you can, will you? I've got to report back to the station sometime today."

Max tried. He began with the discovery of the necklace and then described his brief encounter with Louie and his Gorgonzola sandwich. He tried to gloss over this part of the story, since he hated admitting a wizened old maniac had knocked him flat, but Sarah wouldn't let him get away with it.

"So that's how you got that awful bruise on your shin! Why didn't you tell me?"

"Because you were chin deep in relatives all day and dead beat last night. So far today we've had a smoke bomb and a corpse to distract us."

"You think all these things are connected?" Jofferty asked, polishing off the remainder of the slice of cake Sarah had cut for him.

Jem snorted. "Dash it, man, they must be."

"How?" Max inquired politely.

"Well, uh, I haven't had a chance to ponder them yet. Egbert, what do you think?"

"I try not to, Mr. Jem. However, it seems to me that we ought to consider our next move. We brought only enough clothes for an overnight stay. Your wardrobe will need to be replenished if we remain longer. With your permission, I will return to the apartment and pack a suitcase."

"I thought you were going home today," Max began.

"Abandon you and Miss Sarah and the child with a murderer running around loose? You can hardly suppose we would be so craven."

"Damn right," Jem agreed. "I don't need any more clothes, though. Max can lend me something."

Max was about to expostulate when Egbert took the matter out of his hands. "Not under any circumstances, sir. I have enough trouble keeping you from committing sartorial excesses with your own wardrobe."

"What does he mean by sartorial excesses, Max?" Jofferty asked curiously.

"Don't ask me, ask Jem. He's been to Harvard. I think it's like wearing white cotton sweat socks with your white tie and tails, assuming that you have any. It's the sort of thing you just don't do unless you happen to be the serf who scrubs the floor so that the women's ball gowns won't get too grungy around the bottoms."

Sarah's taut face relaxed. "Don't say 'bottoms,' for goodness' sake, Max. 'Hems' is easier to say and less likely to give offense. We do have to be on guard these days or we're likely to get swatted by a belligerent pronoun or hit with a preposition we didn't see coming. These are perilous times for the English language, in case you hadn't noticed."

Max smiled at her. Having Jem hanging around wasn't his idea of fun, but for Sarah it might work like the decompression process that deep-sea divers had to go through before they could come up to the surface and shed the load of weights that had felt all right in the water. She looked as if she could do with a little decompressing, after the frantic preparations for the wedding and the subsequent discoveries.

"Okay, Jem, if that's how you want it. But I'll be damned if I'll let you wear my clothes. I had meant to run you two back to Boston today, and stay overnight at Tulip Street with my assorted henchmen, but it's getting late and Sarah said she didn't want to disturb Davy's routine. I'm sure as hell not leaving her and the kid here alone. Sarah, why don't you and Davy come along, and stay with Brooks and Theonia until we figure out what's going on?"

Sarah wasn't having any of that. "And leave *you* alone? Maybe we're getting all het up about nothing, Max. It's been such pandemonium here for the past month or so that I can't think straight. I wish I could just do nothing except get the house in order, then sit down with Davy and read him a silly picture book. I'll read you one, too, if you want, but that's about as far as I'm equipped to go right now."

Jofferty took the hint, though it wasn't meant for him. "Thanks for lunch, Miz Sarah. I'll be on my way. There's just one more thing, if you don't mind. I wouldn't mind a peek at those jewels, if you happen to have them handy."

"They're not handy, but you're entitled to a peek." Max got the rubies out of the safe and brought them downstairs. Jofferty shook his head in wonder.

"My gosh! What do you suppose it's worth?"

"I couldn't give you a figure without doing some checking. I know what the last buyer paid for it, but that was over seven years ago and prices fluctuate according to the market."

"It's yours, isn't it, Sarah?"

"Yes—no—oh, I don't know, Sergeant. Legally it belonged to my first—to Alexander. The wife of the owner was entitled to wear it, but she couldn't sell it or lend it or even wear it unless she was entertaining royalty or a reasonable facsimile thereof. Only my mother-in-law did sell it, or rather she handed it over to someone else who sold it. She wasn't supposed to, but she did."

Jofferty nodded sympathetically. Sarah assumed he knew the story, or some of it, but he was gentleman enough not to say so. He had known Caroline Kelling. "The point is that the buyer acted in good faith and socked out a considerable sum for the horrid thing. I never got the money, but that wasn't her problem. As Max can tell you, the laws about stolen property, especially art objects, are subject to varying interpretations in different countries and at different times. We'd have had to go to court to get it back, and that would have cost a lot of money, which I didn't have, even supposing we had won the case. To be honest, I didn't want the thing. I still don't want it."

Her voice was unsteady. Jofferty removed himself as gracefully as possible, and Max put his arm around his wife's quivering shoulders. "I'm sorry about this, süssele."

"I don't know why you're sorry, it isn't your fault." Sarah wiped her eyes with her fingers. "Max, maybe it was meant for Tracy after all. It was with the rest of the wedding presents, wasn't it? I know it sounds a little crazy, but some of my relatives *are* a little crazy. We ought to have warned her what she might be getting into before she decided to marry Mike."

"Oh, I expect she'll bear up under the blow," said Max. "Her father's a pickle baron, and they're neither of them Kellings. That ought to help some. I'm afraid you're grasping at straws, darling, but it's a possibility that has to be investigated. Would you want Tracy to have the rubies?"

"If I had my way, I'd pitch every single one of them over the cliff," Sarah said with sudden violence. "I wouldn't wish the cursed thing on my worst enemy, much less that sweet innocent."

"The curse of the Kellings, is it?" Jem sniffed. "Get a grip on yourself, girl. A true Kelling wouldn't throw away money if it came with a dozen curses attached to it. Fix her a drink, Max, she's not herself. And you can get one for me while you're at it."

Sarah declined the suggestion, insofar as it pertained to her, and they left Jem happily ensconced with a pitcher of martinis at his elbow and Egbert lecturing him about socks. Max had returned the jewels to the safe and then joined Sarah in Davy's room. Against all the odds Mrs. Blufert had managed to get the scion of the Bittersohns into bed for a nap. They bestowed sentimental kisses on the oblivious cherub's brow and tiptoed out.

"I can't thank you enough, Mrs. Blufert," Sarah said gratefully. "I didn't mean to leave him with you so long, but we ran into a few problems."

"Why, it's no trouble at all, you know that. You want to start work clearing the wedding presents out of the library now? I can get that worthless nephew of mine and his friend over here in ten minutes to lug the boxes over to the carriage house."

"I don't think I have the energy to start the job now," Sarah admitted. "There's a lot of fragile china and crystal that needs to be repacked very carefully and put down where it won't get squashed, and someone will have to check the gift list to make sure everything is properly labeled with the name of the sender."

"You do look kind of worn out," Mrs. Blufert agreed. "Takes a while to rest up after the big job you did. I'll just do my usual cleaning, then, and get along home unless you're planning to go out this evening and want me to stay with Davy."

"We're not going anywhere tonight," Max assured her. "You did reach Brooks, didn't you, Sarah?"

"Yes. They'll be here around six-thirty, with Charles and Mariposa."

"Company for supper?" Mrs. Blufert shook her head disapprovingly. "You shouldn't take on so much, Miz Sarah. Suppose I just whip up a batch of potato salad and run home to get that ham I baked yesterday?"

Sarah gave her a quick hug. "Bless your heart. That's sweet of you, but there's still the biggest part of a ham left from the buffet, not to mention a dozen other things, and if I know Cousin Theonia, she'll bring her usual goodies. Max, what are you going to do about Egbert? He's bound and determined to drive into town, and it's getting late. He couldn't be back before dark."

"Should I offer to rinse out Jem's socks and underwear?"

"There's a grand new invention called a washing machine, darling, in case you hadn't heard. Let's see if Egbert will settle for that as a last desperate expedient."

Jem was in the living room, whence, as he indignantly explained, he had been chivied by Mrs. Blufert.

"Chivied?" Max repeated blankly.

"Harrassed, driven, annoyed with petty vexations, often for a specific purpose," said his intellectual wife. "I expect Mrs. Blufert's specific purpose was to clean the kitchen without you leering at her and making suggestive remarks, Uncle Jem. Did she chivy Egbert, too?"

"You'll have to ask him." Jem finished the last of his last martini, settled back in the chair, and closed his eyes.

"I will if you'll tell me where to find him," Max said.

"The garage, I expect, unless he's already left."

"Damn," said Max. "Maybe I can catch him."

He ran, but he needn't have bothered. When he got to the garage Egbert was still there, standing in the open doorway. Max began, "There's no need for you to drive to town tonight—"

"I beg your pardon, Mr. Max. Need is no longer a relevant consideration. The fact of the matter is that I cannot drive to town unless you would care to lend me one of your vehicles."

Max stared at the assorted vehicles. There were three of them, Sarah's little compact, his own elderly but elegant Mercedes, and the gleaming restored Thunderbird that had been Ira's gift to the newlyweds. There should have been a fourth.

"What happened to Jem's car?"

"I am not in a position to answer that question," Egbert said calmly. "Nor, to judge from your question, are you. Two possibilities come to mind. An inebriated or confused wedding guest borrowed it by mistake, or it has been stolen. In either case it would seem sensible to notify the police."

9

Max let Egbert make the call. This was becoming embarrassing. Smoke bombs, bodies, stolen vehicles, all happening under the very nose of the great detective Max Bittersohn, who hadn't the faintest clue as to what was going on. Anyhow, Egbert could supply the necessary information, including the license number and description. Let him explain why the keys had been left in the car. It had seemed like the logical thing to do at the time. Most of the guests had done the same, handing over car and keys to the stalwart local youths who were supposed to park the cars neatly and efficiently in the area roped off for that purpose. Since Jem and Egbert were staying overnight, Max had suggested they put the lovingly tended antique in the garage with the other family vehicles.

The culprit couldn't have been an ordinary car thief or a compulsive and impecunious collector of vintage vehicles. Most of the Kelling vehicles fell into the latter category. Once a Kelling got his or her hands on a car, only the death of the Kelling or the total destruction of the car parted the twain. Sometimes both, Max thought, remembering the antique Milburn Electric in which Sarah's first husband and his mother had plummeted to their deaths. The Kellings had had the Milburn ever since its debut in 1920; Alexander had been planning to bequeath it to the Larz Anderson Auto Museum when the time came. He'd checked it over carefully, as he always did before they'd started out for their usual ride around the cliffs. It was only by the mercy of God, and Caroline Kelling's dislike of her daughter-in-law, that Sarah hadn't been with them. She had stayed home to make clam chowder for their supper. She'd never served that meal; numbed by shock and horror, she had been on her way back to Boston when she happened to run into a guy named Bittersohn who'd been hanging around his brother-in-law's gas station.

Max didn't want to think about Alexander Kelling or his homicidal maternal parent, but he had to. He remembered something else he had to do. Leaving Sarah to calm her infuriated uncle, he sneaked upstairs.

His natty gray wedding suit wasn't where he had left it, draped over the back of a chair. He hadn't bothered to hang it up, since it would have to be sent to the cleaners anyhow, but Mrs. Blufert didn't put up with that kind of thinking. After some profane searching, Max found the garment in the closet and fumbled in the pocket of the jacket.

The note was there all right. If he hadn't been so tired

and distracted, he'd have emptied his pockets when he'd undressed. Or maybe he wouldn't have. His mother had tried to raise him right; she'd lectured him frequently about loading the pockets of his good jackets with heavy objects. That made the pockets sag or something, as if anybody cared except mothers.

Max's pockets often did contain heavy objects, especially when he was working on a case or when he was in the company of his son. Davy was a picker-up of unconsidered trifles, including rocks and feathers, shells and snails, and an occasional irritated caterpillar, all of which he wanted to take home, not in his own small pockets, but in those of his father. Max hadn't changed into his wedding suit until after he'd left Davy at Mrs. Blufert's, so the pockets were empty except for a crumpled paper napkin.

It was one of the ones supplied by the caterers, with the initials of the bride and groom inside a tasteful heart-shaped scroll. He was about to discard it when he realized there was writing on it.

Theonia's elegant flowing penmanship was distorted by haste and, he deduced, strong emotion. The pencil had dug holes in the thin paper.

"Max, be careful. Something's on the boil. I don't know exactly what, but it's out of the past and connected with Caroline Kelling. Do be careful, Max; very, very careful. It's you who've become the target, not Sarah; but keep her away from it if you can. You and I must talk, when I have something to give you."

She'd already given him more than he wanted. He remembered the night, not too many years ago, when Theonia had examined the dregs of her tea and, without a word, hurled one of Sarah's precious blue-and-white China export cups into the fireplace. She'd had one of her flashes, evil directed against their circle, and had taken that means of turning it back on the ill-wisher.

If you believed in that sort of thing, you could say her trick had worked. The ill-wishers had lost, the Bittersohn Agency had chalked up another success. You could also say that quick thinking, fast action, and good luck had solved the case and brought the perpetrators to a well-deserved end.

Max didn't believe in that sort of thing. He'd never have hurt Theonia's feelings by scoffing at her, but it didn't require extrasensory perception to sense danger when the agency was working on a case. People who steal expensive art objects resent being asked to return them, and they are inclined to think ill of the inconsiderate individuals who want to put them in jail.

That was the logical way to look at it, and Max Bittersohn was a logical man. Theonia's flashes were few and far between, though. Most of the time she was as cynical and skeptical as any woman he'd ever known. And how by all the blue-bottomed apes in hell had she come up with the name of Caroline Kelling, just before that demonic old woman's ruby parure had appeared out of thin air?

Could she have seen the necklace during the brief span

of time when it was in the library? That was possible, he supposed, but even if she had, would she have recognized it as part of the Kelling parure? Like all the other members of the group, she had heard of it, but she would have no reason to study the painted and photographed images intensively enough to identify it. There had to be some logical explanation, but he was damned if he could think of one.

He didn't wonder how she had slipped the note into his pocket without his noticing. Theonia's white-gloved hands had been fluttering like the doves to which her enamored husband often compared them; she'd been laughing and hugging people and cheek kissing as many cousins as time allowed. She could have dipped into the pockets of every member of the infatuated audience without being caught.

A thump and a whoop from the next room informed him that Davy was awake and ready to be up and doing. He shoved the note into his pocket and went to intercept his son. A single-minded child, Davy demanded the services of his faithful camel. Max didn't think his knees could stand much more crawling, so he swung Davy onto his shoulder and went downstairs and joined the others.

A conference of some sort had been in progress, but even Jem left off grumbling out of deference to youthful ears and subjects that shouldn't be mentioned in front of children. Davy was in a rambunctious mood, so they adjourned to the lawn, where he could run around in circles that would, his elders could only hope, tire him out enough to sleep soundly that night.

The disappearance of the tent was a bitter blow. Max had to explain in detail that it hadn't belonged to them and that they'd had to give it back. It was a mercy there hadn't been any bloodstains, since Davy refused to believe the tent was all gone until after he had inspected the area foot by foot. Deprived of the tent, he then demanded another balloon and/or a visit to the Martian lady who had been in it. What with one thing and another, Max could have cheered with relief when a car zoomed up the drive and came to a sudden stop. Nobody but a teenager drove like that. He welcomed his apprentice with a fervor that made Jesse blush and beam.

"The others won't be along till later," he explained. "Theonia said don't worry about food, she'd bring it. I didn't have anything to do, so I figured I might as well come on over. Hi, Dave. How are you doing, tiger?"

"He's running poor old daddy tiger ragged," said Sarah, joining them. "Jesse, you're a sight for sore eyes and a blessing to sore shins. Can you entertain the baby tiger for a while?"

"Keep him moving," Max advised. "But don't let him out of arm's reach."

"Sure. Has something happened?"

"Well, yes. We'll talk about it later." Sarah took her sagging spouse by the arm. "Come and rest, darling. What about a cup of tea?"

Tea was the last beverage he wanted just then, with Theonia's warning fresh in his mind. "I don't want you running around waiting on me, schätzele. Can I do anything for you? Cook, dust, rub your feet?"

He dropped gratefully into one of the pretty old wicker lawn chairs he and Sarah had picked up at a local auction. Mr. Lomax had applied a coat of fresh white paint, and Miriam had made chintz-covered cushions for the seats and back.

"There's more than enough food, especially if Theonia is bringing her usual bounty," Sarah answered. "Mrs. Blufert made potato salad, bless her heart."

"Who gives a damn about potato salad?" Jem demanded. "How's the gin holding out?"

"There's plenty, but you can't have any more until the sun is over the yardarm," his niece said severely.

"It's already over the yardarm in California."

"No, it isn't. You've got it backward."

"The Canary Islands?"

"You aren't in the Canary Islands."

The Kellings could keep this up for hours. Max turned to Egbert. "No word about the car?"

"One could not reasonably expect results so soon, Mr. Max. They said they'd do the usual thing. I don't know exactly what that means, but your Sergeant Jofferty seems a most competent individual. He did ask me to pass on a message. To quote him exactly, it was 'What the hell next?' "

"I wish I knew." Max stretched his aching legs and

forced himself to loosen up. Davy and Jesse were playing catch. Since Davy's catching and throwing skills were about on a par with each other, both parties spent most of the time running after the ball.

"I've been wondering about that smoke bomb," Egbert said. "Could it have been set off in order to facilitate the theft of the vehicle?"

"Driving an unfamiliar vehicle through a cloud of blinding black smoke wouldn't be my idea of fun. He certainly didn't come down the driveway. I followed it back to the house, and I think I'd have noticed if a car the size of Jem's had passed by or over me."

Egbert was not to be moved by sarcasm. "What about that track down the hill and through the pasture?"

"Even harder to negotiate in total darkness. I suppose I could have a look, though it's unlikely he'd have left tracks. It hasn't rained all week."

He made no move to do so, though. Sarah and Jem had finished thrashing out the ramifications of time zones and their effect on the consumption of martinis. She looked tired. Small wonder, Max thought. Conversations with Jem had that effect on him, too. Sarah was used to her relatives, but she'd had altogether too many people around for too long. He took her hand.

"Want to go down and walk on the beach for a few minutes? The rest of the gang won't be here for almost an hour."

Sarah's feeble objections were overruled by Jem, who

wasn't such a bad old goat after all, Max thought. He'd seen that Sarah needed a respite. "The food is ready, you said so yourself. If anything else needs to be done, Egbert will do it."

"With pleasure," said the gentleman's gentleman.

Down under the cliff the wind was brisk, blowing straight across the Atlantic. It blew fresh color into Sarah's cheeks. She let out a little sigh. "I'm so glad you thought of this, darling. It's so lovely and peaceful here. Nobody but us. Even the tide's gone out. That was one of Alexander's little jokes. Oh, Max, really I hadn't . . ."

"Hadn't what?"

"Hadn't thought much about him since Davy was born. I feel guilty about that. Alexander was such a good man, at least he tried to be. But it was awfully hard, with Aunt Caroline demanding his full attention every minute of the day and often half the night. He didn't have time to pay much attention to me after we were married."

Max had his own opinions about that and a lot of other things about Alexander Kelling, but he wouldn't dream of expressing them.

"You were very young," he said gently.

"I was only eighteen when Alexander and I got married. Alexander was forty-one. We were fifth cousins once removed, or something along that line. Nobody found the discrepancy in our ages anything special; it was just a matter of keeping the money in the family. Alexander and I stood up in front of the fireplace in what had been my parents' front parlor. The minister showed up, and half a dozen or so of the relatives. The minister said what he had to say and left. I made a pot of tea and set out a plate of cookies. The relatives ate the cookies, and then they left. Nobody kissed the bride, not even Alexander. That was not the Kelling way."

Sarah hadn't meant to sound sarcastic. She didn't know why she was dragging up that old stuff after such a wonderful day. Perhaps Max knew better than she. He encouraged her to keep talking.

"What happened to your parents' house?"

"It was sold furnished without my being asked what I might like to keep. That would have meant next to nothing because the house to which I was going must not be cluttered up with objects that poor brave blind Aunt Caroline wasn't familiar with and might stumble over. So I moved in with her and Alexander and started wearing my mother's clothes."

"Why, in God's name?"

"Because Aunt Bodie, I believe it was, took it upon herself to gather up the clothes I'd worn before the wedding and send all but the underwear to the Goodwill. I was a married woman now and mustn't dress like a child anymore. Unfortunately, she didn't offer to buy me anything more appropriate. Neither did Alexander; I didn't know why and thought it would be rude to ask. I did know that Father had left me some money in his will. He'd never mentioned how much, but I wasn't supposed to get any of it until I was twenty-seven. I wasn't trained for anything except what my governesses had taught me about art, poetry, and local history and what the cook we used to have showed me about cooking and housekeeping. So I did the best I could with what I'd learned at my father's house, tried to make over Mother's hand-me-downs so they wouldn't look quite so frumpy, and hoped for something good to happen."

Sarah heaved another, deeper sigh. "Max, dear, I'm sorry I've been boring you like this. I've probably told you most of it before, though I've tried not to."

"So what if you did? How many times have you listened to my uncle Jake's courtroom yarns? Sit down and rest your feet. This looks like a fairly comfortable rock."

"How did you know? This is my old wishing rock. Alexander and I used to sit on it for hours, looking out to sea while he told me stories about the mermaids who rode the waves on their thoroughbred dolphins. I made believe I could see them with their golden hair streaming out behind them and their silvery fishtails slapping the water."

Sarah's voice was shaky now. Max put his arm around her and felt her quivering; he didn't think it was from the chill that was coming up with the night mist.

"What's the matter, fischele? Can't find your dolphin?"

She turned into his arms and hid her face against his shoulder. "I did find it. I don't want to lose it."

Being compared to a dolphin wasn't one of the most graceful accolades Max Bittersohn had ever received, but he wouldn't have traded this one for the Nobel Prize, the Congressional Medal of Honor, or the plaudits of all the crowned heads of Europe.

"Fat chance," he said tenderly, holding her close.

Sarah raised a flushed, tearstained face. "Aren't we ever going to be rid of them? I want to lay Alexander to rest, as a gentle memory, but she won't let me! That sounds demented, doesn't it?"

"If you're referring to your ex-mother-in-law, I'm not sure it does."

"I'm being silly. I don't really believe in evil spirits or curses, but if anybody could make a deal with the devil, it was Aunt Caroline. She murdered her husband and my father, robbed me of Alexander's love and most of the money I should have inherited—not that I cared about that!—and she'd have disposed of me just as coolly if it had suited her purposes. Now that—that damned necklace has turned up. It's as if she won't let go, as if I have to go on fighting her. Well, she's not going to win this time!"

"That's my girl. Want to go back now? It's getting cold out here."

"And our valiant allies will be arriving soon." Sarah was herself again. "Thanks, darling."

"What for?"

"For letting me get it out of my system. I hadn't realized how badly those memories rankled. But if it hadn't been for Aunt Caroline, I'd never have met you, or Mariposa and Charles and Theonia."

"Quite the little optimist, aren't you?"

"Just call me Candide." She gave him a watery smile. "Among other things. There's something I have to tell you, süssele."

10

Theonia was resplendent in a black velvet gown she'd found in Filene's Basement, shortened to tea length, and trimmed with yards of jet-beaded lace looted from an otherwise moth-eaten robe de chambre she and Sarah had discovered during one of their forays into Emma Kelling's attic. Kellings never threw anything away, and Emma's attic was one of her sources for costuming her light opera group, but she had good-naturedly agreed that the garment in question was too far gone to serve even the duchess of Plaza Toro. With a black lace mantilla draped over her raven hair, Theonia was the spitting image of a Venetian noblewoman, and her husband, Brooks, could have stood in for the duke.

Like the great Savoyards who had played the part, Brooks was a trim, sprightly man only five and a half feet tall, with the bright eyes of a chipmunk and the inquiring mind of an investigative reporter. A man of many talents, he was particularly authoritative on the subject of the crested grebe. His birding interests had thus far been of limited use in his new profession of right-hand man to a pursuer of art thieves, but his other talents had made him invaluable to Max.

In deference to Theonia and because she too understood the effect of clothes on female spirits, Sarah had found time to change into a caftan Max had brought back on one of his foraging trips from a souk in Cairo or Damascus, or it might have been Beirut. She'd got accustomed to the comfort and elegance of caftans while she was pregnant with Davy, and although her wardrobe might have seemed rather outré for a Boston-born and -bred lady, in fact it was nothing of the sort. Some of Sarah's Boston-born ancestresses had probably been wearing caftans and djellabas and perhaps even saris in the privacy of their boudoirs ever since the days of the clipper ships. The long, loose robes would have been just the ticket to wrap a lady's feet in while she was relishing the latest of Ralph Waldo Emerson's delightful essays or teaching herself Hebrew so that, when the time came for her to do so, she could meet and talk with her Maker in his native tongue.

After wrapping the rainbow folds around her own feet, Sarah curled up on the sofa and waited for Max to begin the meeting. They were there, her valiant allies and dear friends. Brooks sat next to his wife, holding her hand as was his constant habit. Uncle Jem had his feet up and a jug of his special martinis at his elbow and Egbert hovering beside him. Jesse was looking a little frazzled. No wonder, Sarah thought. She'd read somewhere about a professional football player who had followed his three-year-old son around to see which of them would collapse first. The three-year-old had won by half a day. Jesse's sacrifice had not been in vain. Davy had succumbed shortly after dinner and was now tucked in his bed with his alligator.

The only missing members of the firm were Charles C. Charles, Sarah's erstwhile butler, and his whatever-they-were-calling-it-these-days Mariposa, who were in Miami making tactful inquiries into the present ownership of a sixteenth-century Madonna and Child that had once graced a church in Mexico City. Sarah wasn't about to suggest that they be recalled. The agency that provided all of them with income had to continue its normal routine. She missed them, though. She even missed her cousin Dolph, who was in Denmark or possibly Sweden with his wife, Mary, the former bag lady.

"Do you suppose Dolph would know something about the parure?" she asked. "I wouldn't want him and Mary to cut their trip short, but we could telephone them."

"I've been piously thanking God the old goat isn't here," her uncle Jem said. "What could he do except bellow and snort and paw the ground?"

Brooks shook his head disapprovingly. "You're confusing your zoological references, Jem."

"No, I'm not. Bull in a china shop, that's Dolph. Anyhow, he doesn't know any more than I do about the Kelling family treasures, such as they are. The long past history of the rubies isn't as relevant as what happened to them after they were sold. Right, Max?"

"I'm working on that," Max informed them. "Pepe hasn't called back, has he? I told him to try the office and the house if he couldn't reach me here."

"He hadn't called by the time we left," Brooks answered. "There must be something we can do from this end. You've no idea how the jewels got into the library?"

"Somebody put them there," Max said. "It wasn't one of us. Nobody was unwrapping parcels the day of the wedding, there wasn't time. I would swear the necklace wasn't on the table when I entered the library. It was there when I got ready to leave."

"You didn't see the person who left it?" Brooks asked Egbert.

Jem's henchman shook his head regretfully. "No well-bred individual would deliver a last-minute wedding present in such a surreptitious manner. I would certainly have noticed an action so out of the ordinary and drawn it to Mr. Max's attention."

"There's one obvious suspect," Jesse said. "The old geezer that laid Uncle Max flat."

"That doesn't make sense," Sarah objected. "If he was dressed like a waiter, he could have been in the library without being noticed, but why would he hang around after he'd done the job?"

"Especially in a trash bag," Max said sourly. "Forget it, Jesse. He sure as hell wasn't hiding under the desk when I locked up the room. I couldn't have missed the smell of Gorgonzola."

"Maybe he changed his mind," Jesse insisted. "And came back later. You said one of the windows had been jimmied."

"Not jimmied, unlocked. It was a neat job," Max admitted. "But any trained locksmith could have done it. I could have myself."

"Of course you could, darling," Sarah said soothingly. Max was still smarting over his defeat. A change of subject was called for.

"That seems to be another dead end," she said. "What about the body under the tent?"

"Joe Macbeth."

"An alias?" Brooks asked.

"Why should it be? There must be other people named Macbeth besides Shakespeare's character. According to his boss Joe was a harmless guy whose only irritating characteristic was a tendency to quote Scripture rather too frequently. He didn't drink, smoke, or swear, at least not on the job."

"What was the cause of death?" Theonia asked quietly.

"A sensible question, for once. To put it in nontechnical terms, the back of his head was bashed in. That proves it wasn't an accident. The basket of the balloon couldn't have hit him fore and aft. Anyhow, he'd been dead for hours before he was put under the tent."

"The smoke bomb," Sarah exclaimed.

Max smiled at her. "I think you've got it, darling. A

bunch of outraged orangutans could have been cruising around without being seen in that black fog. The tent crew was actually on its way here when the bomb was set off. If the murderer hoped to blame Macbeth's demise on the balloon, he'd have to stow the body away before the tent was removed."

"He'd have to be awfully stupid to think he could get away with that," Sarah objected.

"Unlike the inventions of ingenious writers of mystery fiction, most murderers are stupid, schätzele."

"It would behoove us, I believe," Brooks said in his precise Andover-Harvard accents, "to find out more about Mr. Macbeth. Presumably he took his departure with the rest of the crew, after the tent had been erected. Did he return later, in a less distinctive ensemble? And if so, why? If you like, I will begin investigations along that line first thing in the morning."

"The police may be doing the same thing," Max said. "Or they may not. Go ahead, Brooks, but check with Jofferty so you won't be duplicating your efforts."

"Certainly." Brooks made a neat notation in his little black book.

"How about me?" Jesse asked, stifling a yawn.

"Go home and go to bed," his employer said. "Modern youth is a degenerate breed. Look at you, completely wiped out by a three-year-old."

"You'd better have some coffee first," Sarah said. "Or

maybe you should stay here tonight, Jesse. I don't want you falling asleep behind the wheel."

"I haven't got any pajamas or a change of clothes," Jesse objected.

"Let's not start that again," Max said.

"He'll be all right," Brooks assured Sarah. "You underestimate the energy level of his age group. If you don't need Jesse, Max, he can do some of the legwork for me."

Max nodded. "You'll be in the office most of the day? . . . Good. I'll probably drop by around noon. Egbert will expire of embarrassment if Jem has to wear the same outfit any longer, so I'll drive them to Pinckney Street tomorrow morning. They can pick up what they need or think they need, and then I'll bring them back here, if they want to come."

Jem had dropped off into one of his little naps, but he heard that. "Damned right we're coming back," he said indignantly. "You think we'd leave you unprotected? Now then, what were we talking about?"

"I think we've covered most of it," Sarah said, smiling affectionately at him. "Would anyone like coffee? Or a cup of tea?"

She looked at Theonia. The queenly matron adjusted her mantilla. "Max told you?"

"Shouldn't I have? Damn it, we're conversing in questions again," Max exclaimed.

"He didn't tell me," Jem remarked. "What's all this, then?"

"I'll get the coffee," Sarah said, and fled to the kitchen. She'd started the machine and put the kettle on, in case someone preferred tea, when Brooks joined her.

"Can I help?"

"You can put the cups and saucers on that tray, and get the cream out of the fridge, if you will, please. And do we want the teapot?"

Brooks nodded gravely. "She'll try again if you want her to. I'm sorry if this has upset you, Sarah. Perhaps Max shouldn't have told you."

Sarah's hands were steady as she removed the teapot from the shelf and began spooning tea into it. "Of course he should have. I'm a big girl now, Brooks."

When the tea had steeped and the coffee had been poured into the Royal Prussian pot that had been in the family since Sarah's grandmother's time, she and Brooks carried the trays in. Max had told the others about Theonia's warning, and they were discussing it with varying degrees of skepticism.

"It's a pity your sources aren't more definite," Jem said. "Is that all you got?"

Theonia inclined her queenly head. "That's how it works, when it does work, which isn't often," she said calmly. "When I was doing my readings at that grubby little café, I got to be quite good at the standard gimmick. It's a combination of simple psychology and observation. The way people dress is indicative of the kinds of lives they lead and the social class to which they belong. There are other obvious clues such as a wedding ring, or even the indentation left by a ring, supposing the client is canny enough to remove it beforehand. You start talking more or less at random, throwing out tentative suggestions, and you watch the client's reactions. If you're good enough at muscle reading, a slight twitch of the lips or widening of the eyes can tell you whether you're on the right track. It's like that game children play, when they direct a searcher by telling him he's warmer or colder."

Jem said admiringly, "So that's how it's done. You mean when that psychic told me I'd had a hundred mistresses—"

"She was lying in her teeth," Max muttered.

"She was telling you what you wanted to hear," Theonia corrected. "I'll wager she started with ten and worked her way up till you stopped shaking your head."

"I didn't . . . Well," Jem admitted sheepishly, "maybe I did. I got kind of emotionally involved, you see. No, thanks, Sarah, I don't want any damned coffee, don't you know caffeine is unhealthy?"

"Unlike gin," said Max.

"My flashes, as I call them, are completely different," Theonia went on. "You remember the night I smashed one of your best teacups, Sarah dear. On that occasion it was Max who asked me to read the tea leaves; I knew he wasn't really serious, and I certainly didn't anticipate what happened. I didn't expect it this time, either. After the wedding I decided I'd had enough champagne and went to the caterer's tent for a cup of tea. I just happened to glance into my cup, and—well, there it was. Not since that other evening have I had such a strong sense of impending evil."

She took the cup Sarah handed her and let out a musical, genteel peal of laughter. "Oh, dear, Sarah, not your Haviland! Are you sure you want to risk it?"

"You can smash the entire set if you think it will do any good," Sarah said. "The last time you sensed danger directed against our circle. This time there was more, wasn't there? It's Max who's in danger."

"I'm afraid so." Theonia finished her tea more quickly than she would have done under normal circumstances and stared down at the dregs.

Under normal circumstances Max would have scoffed, at least to himself. But there was no getting around the fact that Theonia had seen danger coming from the past, specifically from the long-dead Caroline Kelling. She had written the note before he had told anyone, even Sarah, about the necklace. He hadn't bothered to ask Theonia whether she had happened to see it in the library. Self-deception wasn't one of Theonia's failings, and anyhow, he'd have seen her if she had dropped in to view the wedding gifts. Theonia stood out in any crowd.

Somehow he wasn't surprised when Theonia handed the empty teacup to Sarah. "Do you want to smash it, or shall I?"

11

Everything seemed unlikely this morning, Sarah thought. Could it be that the tumult and the shouting had really died; that on dune and headland had sunk the fire; and that all the pomps of yesterday were now one with Nineveh and Tyre?

They probably weren't, Rudyard Kipling notwithstanding. A smoke bomb, a balloon, a ruby parure, and a corpse couldn't be dismissed with poetry. Thank goodness those inappropriate distractions had waited until after the ceremony had been fittingly concluded and the bride and groom had left on their honeymoon. Weddings were a strain on everyone, especially the bride; Tracy and Mike deserved their time alone. They wouldn't have to find out what had happened until they returned, braced and ready for the hazards of matrimony. Being related, even distantly, to the Kellings was a hazard Tracy probably hadn't counted on, but it couldn't be helped. Maybe, Sarah thought hopefully, they could clear up the whole business before the newlyweds got back.

First, though, there was breakfast to be considered. Sarah decided she'd make popovers and take out some of the applesauce she and Mrs. Blufert had made from the fruit of their own trees. Mrs. Blufert would be along soon, with her crew, to help trundle the wedding gifts over to the carriage house. Mr. Lomax, their tried-and-true handyman, who had been at Ireson's Landing since before Sarah was born, would also be on hand. He'd have a fit when he saw what trucks and tents and feet had done to his beautifully tended lawn, but that couldn't be helped, either.

She had mixed the popovers and put the pans in the oven before anyone else appeared. It was the faithful Egbert, as she might have expected.

"Mr. Max is still in bed, and Davy is with him," he reported. "From the sounds they are making I deduce that a game of some strenuous nature is in progress."

"I hope poor Max isn't having to be a camel again. He really did get a nasty crack on the shins."

"The game appears to have something to do with alligators. What can I do to assist you, Mrs. Sarah?"

"Not a thing. You're a guest, remember? When do you suppose Uncle Jem will be down?"

"Pretty soon now, I should think," Egbert replied. "Would you like me to go and see?"

"That might be helpful. If you're still planning to drive

into town, you ought to make an early start. Early for Uncle Jem, that is."

The popovers were out of the oven and smelling wonderful. Sarah made a pot of tea, sat down at the kitchen table, and ate one of the popovers. She ate another and was debating the pros and cons of a third, wondering why she was still hungry, until it dawned on her that she'd had very little to eat for the past two days. Not because there hadn't been food enough to go around, heaven forfend, but because she'd been too busy making sure everybody else got plenty to remember that she had a stomach, too. She'd just about decided to eat a third popover when Max came down, impeccably attired in London-tailored suit and Italian silk tie.

"Hi, süssele. Want some help here?"

"No thanks. I can feed myself now that I'm a grown-up lady. My, aren't you handsome this morning. Why the fancy duds? Egbert is a bit of snob about attire, but he doesn't expect you to get all dressed up just to drive him to town."

"I thought I'd pay a call on a pickle baron while I'm in Boston. Since I don't know what pickle barons wear, it seemed safer to err on the side of propriety. Are those popovers to eat or to look at?"

"Whichever you prefer, my lord. Here they are, still warm from the oven. You'd better take some before Uncle Jem comes along and eats them all up. Is it Tracy's father you mean to visit?"

"How many pickle barons do we number among our acquaintances?" Max finished his popover and reached for a second. "It's unlikely that he sent the necklace to Tracy, but we ought to make sure before we go running off in all directions."

"Unlikely to the point of impossible," Sarah said with a sniff. "From what I've heard about him, he's a horrible man. I suppose you're right about checking, but why waste time going to see him instead of telephoning?"

"I can't give him the third degree over the phone." Max's evil leer would have been more impressive if there hadn't been a smudge of applesauce on his chin.

"You tough private eyes know your business best, I suppose. More applesauce?"

"By all means. Our own apples, right?"

"Right. What have you done with our son?"

"He's out on the deck, pulling his alligator around. He's crazy about that thing. When I went in last night, he had it in bed with him, tied to the bedpost so that it wouldn't bite anybody. Ah, here comes the man of the hour. Sit down, Uncle Jem. Would you care for a popover?"

"Oh, you know me, I'm easy to please. Just poke the dish this way and pass me the butter, not forgetting the apricot jam and the guava jelly. Are those going to be enough popovers?"

"If not, I can bake some more," Sarah assured him. "Did you sleep well last night?"

"Of course I did. I always do. My snores are as the snores of ten because my heart is pure. Or somebody else's heart. Ah, yes. Whatever became of Natalie? Dear old Natalie. I wonder who's kissing her now."

Sarah decided not to ask who Natalie was; or had been. "I don't want to rush you, Uncle Jem, but Max wants to leave sometime today. Could you possibly bring yourself to get dressed, or are you planning to travel in your bunny suit?"

The one-piece flannel garment, in a touching shade of pink, set off Jem's rosy face and white hair, but he did not appreciate the comparison. "What a vulgar thing to say! I'll have you know this is an exact copy of the siren suit Winston Churchill wore during World War Two. The word 'siren' referred not to bewitching nymphs partially covered with scales, but to the sirens that warned of an air raid. The garments, as you see, were warm, easily assumed, and modest."

"Churchill's was pink?" Max inquired.

"I don't believe so, sir," Egbert replied seriously. "But the pink fabric was on sale, you see, and Mr. Jem's tailor made up several of them at a quite reasonable price."

"This is a ridiculous conversation," Jem said. "Naturally I have no intention of appearing in public in my nightclothes. I'll get dressed as soon as I've had another popover. Are you coming with us, Sarah?"

"No, there's too much to do here. I have to keep tally of the wedding gifts as they get taken out to the carriage house."

"Now?" Jem snarled. "Didn't anybody have sense

enough to start a tally just as soon as the first wedding present reared its ugly head? That's how it's done. You just take them in order and make sure the names and addresses are firmly attached to the gift list. Otherwise you might as well go stick your head in a revolving door and brave the consequences."

"I know how it's done, and I did start a tally," Sarah informed him. "But toward the end so many things came in all at once, and there were three of us working on the list, Tracy and Miriam and me, so it's possible a few gifts were overlooked. I want to double-check and tell Mrs. Blufert where to put the boxes."

Jem reached for the last popover. Max looked ostentatiously at his watch.

"It's not necessary for you to come along, Mr. Jem," Egbert said. "I can pack for you."

"Nonsense," Jem mumbled. "Won't take me ten minutes. Any more applesauce?"

Max pushed his chair back. Hurrying Jem was an exercise in futility; the more you tried to hurry him, the slower he got. "I hear Lomax's truck. I want to have a word with him before we go. Take your time, Jem."

Jed Lomax stood by the drive, looking disconsolately out across the once pristine sweep of lawn. He didn't remove his dirty old swordfisherman's cap when Max joined him; he'd known Isaac Bittersohn's boy since he was no bigger than a mackerel and had watched his career with interest. A sad disappointment to his maw, young Max had been, chasing crooks instead of studying to be a rich foot doctor. He'd turned out pretty good, though, and he'd sure done wonders for poor young Mrs. Alex that was, Mrs. Bittersohn that she was now. Lomax had been tickled pink when they got married and decided to stay on at the old Kelling place, with him to look after it like he'd done for years.

"Sure made a mess, didn't they?" the handyman said morosely.

"Weddings are like that," Max agreed. They exchanged man-to-man nods. "I appreciate you coming today."

"Ayup, I figured you'd be needin' me to get the place redded up some, so I just come along in the truck, bein' careful not to drive into them chrysanthemum beds. Looks like they're the only thing that wasn't tore up. Damn shame; get a place lookin' just so an' see what happens."

"It wasn't so much the wedding as the balloon," Max said.

"Balloon?" Lomax gave him a questioning look.

"Some rather strange things have been happening here the last couple of days. Have you heard anything about them?"

He felt pretty sure Lomax had, but his native reticence wouldn't let him admit it. "Can't say as I have. What kind o' things?"

"Well, I guess the burglar was the first. I found him in the library under the desk, wrapped up in a plastic trash bag. Thought for a minute he was dead, but when I started to drag the bag out he came alive, and when I asked him what the hell he was doing there he caught me a wallop across the shins with a plank or something and made his getaway while I was rolling around on the floor."

"Caught you on that bad leg?"

Max appreciated the excuse. "He didn't do any real damage, but it hurt like the devil. By the time I got around to looking for him he'd disappeared."

"The library was where you had all those fancy wedding presents. Anything missing?"

"No. Maybe I showed up before he had a chance to steal anything." Max decided not to mention the jewels. Not that he didn't trust the old boy, but it was unlikely he could contribute anything useful.

"So then what?" Lomax demanded.

"Well, then we had a smoke bomb, one of those things that are set off when directors are making a war movie or the army's training rookie troops for the real thing, God help us. I'd gone for a stroll, down to the end of the drive, when all of a sudden everything went black, coal black, like the inside of a mine. It was the damnedest feeling. I didn't dare move for fear I might walk in front of a car or run into a tree trunk."

"I did hear somethin' about that," Lomax conceded. "Damn fool stunt, somebody could've been hurt. Any idea who did it?"

"No."

Lomax scratched his head. "Pure meanness an' deviltry. Sounds like the kind o' thing a Zickery might do."

"You knew the Zickerys?" He must have, Max realized. He was almost as old as Jem, and he'd lived in Ireson's Landing all his life.

"Used to see 'em at the store. They didn't have much to say to the likes of us. Crazy as bedbugs, all of 'em. One female used to walk around town in a one-piece bathing suit." Lomax permitted himself a slight smile. "She didn't show much, I guess, compared to what you see on the beaches these days, but back then it was a pretty startling sight. I hear a couple of 'em's turned up again."

"In the balloon," Max agreed. "One of those big hot-air balloons, like the ones they have at carnivals. Luckily it didn't come crashing down on the caterer's tent until after most of the guests had left."

"Sounds like the sort of damn fool thing they'd do. Been nobody over there for years, but I did hear as how somebody's fixing the old house up."

It hadn't occurred to Max to suspect the Zickerys of setting off a smoke bomb. There was no proof that they had, except for Lomax's memories of a bunch of bad hats who ought by now to be past childish pranks. The more he heard about the Zickerys, the less keen he was on having them as neighbors.

"I don't suppose we can suspect them of hiding a corpse under the wedding tent," Max admitted. "That happened yesterday—finding the body, I mean. The poor devil was apparently one of the crew that put up the tents, but that's all anybody knows about him. That's all, except for Mr. Jem Kelling's car being stolen."

"All?" Lomax permitted himself a tight-lipped grimace that was his version of a smile. "Sounds like a cartload of trouble to me."

"Nothing's happened today," Max said optimistically. "Not so far. I promised to drive Sarah's uncle Jem and his man, Egbert, to Boston so they can get into their apartment and bring back enough clothes to last the week. They claim they want to stay here and help out."

"That ought to be int'restin'."

"I expect they'll manage well enough. Sarah needs somebody around to watch Davy and tell him wild stories about the Wild West. Jem means West Roxbury, of course. He doesn't know the difference between a cowboy and a cowbird, but Egbert has sense enough for the pair of them. Whether any of them will last out the week remains to be seen. There's Jem, I'd better get him in the car before he thinks of something else he wants to do first. Keep an eye on things for me, will you, Jed?"

With Jed Lomax and Mrs. Blufert and her crew on hand, Max wasn't too worried about leaving Sarah and Davy. Anyhow, hadn't Theonia insisted the danger was directed at him?

Jem was pleased as punch to be chauffeured by somebody who wasn't afraid to drive over thirty miles per hour. Since Max had better sense than to waste time making obscene gestures at drivers who cut him off, tailgated, and committed other sins against common sense and safety on the road, Jem did it for him. In between shouting complicated invective out the window, he remarked, "This is a pleasant change. There's nothing like a whiff of carbon monoxide every so often. You haven't visited our little pied-à-terre for some time, Max; you'll be surprised at the changes Egbert and I have been making."

Max smiled and forbore to comment. The changes would consist mainly in finding a handier place to stash the extra gin bottles in an already overstuffed apartment. Jem had staked out his little claim on a half mile or so of Beacon Hill pavement many years ago; he was not likely to make any significant changes now. Whether he'd have the fortitude to last out a whole week of absence from dear old Pinckney Street didn't really matter; he thought he was helping, and if push came to shove, Sarah could find a way to cope with him. Max only hoped she wouldn't have to. She'd had to do too much coping already in her relatively short life. Max intended to make sure that her life became a long one, because what would be the use of living if Sarah wasn't with him all the way?

Getting into Boston was, as usual, a gamble with fate, but Max knew all the tricks. He even found a parking place not more than a healthful walk to the worn granite steps up which Jem had toiled so many times. He followed a tactful step behind, just in case, as Egbert and Jem puffed up the stairs and into the elevator that took them to the second floor.

The apartment was a shambles.

Worse than that, the apartment was occupied. Sprawled face-down across Jem's good sofa was a body. It was attired in a paisley dressing gown and a pair of backless leather slippers that were too big for it. One of them had fallen off the dangling foot.

"Good heavens," Egbert exclaimed. "He's dead!"

"Damned impertinence!" Jem growled. "He's wearing my dressing gown and slippers! I don't know what the world's coming to, people dying in one's clothes. What are we supposed to do now? Rent a wheelbarrow and dump him out on the Common?"

"That won't be necessary," Max said, wrinkling his nose. The odor was unmistakable. "Why did you do it, Louie?"

The corpse sat up, Gorgonzola sandwich in hand.

"Do what?"

"Steal Mr. Kelling's car."

"I didn't."

"Then who did?"

"He did."

"He who?"

"Him."

"Can't you talk straight for a change?"

"No."

Max shook his head. "Ask a stupid question and you get a stupid answer."

"Maybe he's still in shock, Mr. Max." Egbert was relieved to find they didn't have a dead body on their hands. "How did you get in here, Louis? We left this place locked up tighter than a drum; I've told you that Mr. Jem does not want you here when he's not around. We can't be changing the locks every twenty minutes."

Max stared at Egbert. "You know this guy?"

Egbert looked embarrassed. "Not to say know, Mr. Max. You see, what happened was that the Comrades of the Convivial Codfish decided the society ought to form its own musical group, so at Mr. Jem's insistence I advertised for people who could play a musical saw, an old-fashioned policeman's rattle, and a penny whistle. Louis here showed up a couple of weeks ago with a penny whistle—"

"Which he probably pinched from someone," Max interrupted.

"He doesn't play it very well," Jem remarked critically. "However, I remembered him from the old days, when he was a callow youth who used to hang around Danny Rate's Pub, near the Old Howard, picking pockets and stealing tips off the tables. He assured me he'd led a respectable life since, and he's quite well informed on English music hall ballads, especially the vulgar variety written and sung sometime around the turn of the century. I refer to the century that's now just about kaput, as opposed to the one that's waiting to clobber us with new horrors that I for one shall be happy to escape. Louie, do you know that little gem whose chorus ends 'And the body's downstairs'?"

"Let me think a minute."

"Damned if I will," Max snarled. "Hey, Jem, where the hell are you going?"

"For a brief nap, I expect," Egbert replied as his employer vanished into the bedroom and slammed the door. "He's developed napping to a fine art, you know, just flops down on his bed and sleeps for an hour or so, then he'll be fresh as a daisy for the next couple of hours. I think having Louis around tires him."

"He would tire me," Max agreed.

"I know, Mr. Max. But you see, Mr. Jem's used to having a lot of people around, and his old friends are starting to die off, and when he found out Louis knows more of those old music hall ballads than anybody else Mr. Jem has ever run into, he got in the habit of inviting him over for a friendly little sing-along, as you might say. You know how Mr. Jem loves to sing about the Fall River line and the old overnight boats. I must admit that Louis's habit of slipping Mr. Jem's gold watch and cuff links into his pocket can be annoying, but he always returns them when I ask."

Max was halfway to the boiling point by this time. "I don't believe this! No, I take it back. Knowing Jem, I do believe it. Did he give good old Louie permission to steal his car?"

"Did you do that, Louis?" Egbert looked disapprovingly at the stand-in, who had risen to his feet. "Shame on you!"

"I didn't steal it, I just borrowed it. It's parked just around the corner. I even adjusted the meter so it stays on two hours all the time, so you wouldn't get a ticket," Louie added virtuously.

Max sighed. "Dial 911 for me, would you, Egbert, and hand me the phone when you get hold of whoever's in charge of impertinent corpses and car thieves."

"It was only a bit of fun, for goodness' sake. Some people are so picky. Can't even take a joke. I can't sit around here all day twiddling my thumbs. I've got things to do."

"Such as what, for instance?"

"Oh, I don't know. Whatever happens, happens. At least I'm fairly sure it does. It always has, so far. Well, so long, folks. It's been great."

"Cut it out, Louie," said Max. "Your oblique conversational style may suffice to distract people like, uh, these kindly gentlemen, but I've had about enough. You aren't leaving until the police show up. And put Mr. Kelling's walking stick back in the umbrella stand. I'm not stupid enough to fall for that trick again."

"Dear me," exclaimed the former corpse, examining the heavy gold-headed stick in pretended surprise. "Did I pick this up? I do suffer from a harmless spot of kleptomania, you know; my analyst tells me my parents are to blame, or would be if they were still around, which they aren't, Mum having flown the coop some years ago with a traveling plumber, and dear old Dad—"

"I said, that's enough." Max took the phone from Egbert. "Who's this? . . . Oh, Kilkallen. This is Max Bittersohn. Remember me?" The telephone squawked at him.

Max grinned. "Yes, I remember the incident fondly, too. . . . Yes, I know you don't do car thefts or breaking and entering. We found a dead body at our place at Ireson's Landing yesterday. . . . Yes, I know that's not in your jurisdiction, but the suspect is. He stole Jem Kelling's car and fled to Jem's apartment in Boston, where I just found him. You know where it is. Send somebody over to pick him up, will you?"

"Hey, wait a minute," Louie exclaimed. "You can't pin that one on me. I never killed nobody in my life!"

Having received a profane acknowledgment of his request from Kilkallen, Max hung up the phone and studied his suspect with satisfaction. He'd pegged Louis the Locksmith as nothing more vicious than a petty crook, an inveterate scrounger, and a grabber up of anything potentially useful to Louie himself. The threat of a murder charge had sobered him.

"So you've decided to stop playing games, have you? We've got plenty to hold you on, Louie. Two counts of breaking and entering, one count of assault, one of auto theft. And I'll bet I can think up a few more if I put my mind to it, including accessory before, after, and maybe during a murder."

"I didn't have nothing to do with that!"

"You're protesting too much, as my recent acquaintance Mr. Mortlake would say. If you didn't kill the guy, Louie, you know who did. Don't you think it would be a good idea to come clean?"

"Oh, Mr. Bittersohn, you wound me! That would be a serious breach of etiquette. I may be a crook, but I'm never gauche. Surely you wouldn't want me to rat on a friend." He gave Max a calculating look. "However, I've no objection to spending a few days in police custody. It's the least I can do, I suppose, to make up for my inadvertent social lapses. Do you want to put the cuffs on me now?"

12

"It's beginning to look as though we might not make it back in time for lunch," Egbert said. "Shall I give Mrs. Sarah a ring and let her know we've been held up?"

The police had come and gone with their prisoner. Louie hadn't put up a fight or even an argument, but he hadn't admitted anything, either. His final comment had been "Don't bother putting up bail for me, Mr. Kelling."

"She wasn't expecting us for lunch," Max said. "Let's get this show on the road. Got everything you need, Jem?"

"No, blast it, I still haven't been able to locate that ballad about the body downstairs. Egbert, are you planning to spend the rest of the day folding my pajamas?"

"They're all folded and packed, Mr. Jem, along with your spare dentures and your nightcap. I was thinking that we might better save the ballads until we take that trip to England you've been talking about for the past thirty years or so. The Brits love that kind of stuff, or used to; they're bound to have scads of ballads over there."

Max put an end to the conversation by picking up the largest and heaviest bags before Egbert could get at them. Egbert took the smaller and lighter ones. Jem Kelling made heavy work of carrying a shaving kit that must have weighed almost a quarter of a pound. Max stowed the luggage away in the boot, as Jem insisted on calling it, and stowed his passengers in the tonneau, got in behind the wheel, glanced at his watch, swore, and switched on the engine.

"Excuse me, Mr. Max," Egbert said politely, "but would you mind seeing if we can find where Louis parked Mr. Jem's car? I've no doubt he can bollix a parking meter as efficiently as he can pick a lock, but I have been informed the police have other methods of ascertaining whether a vehicle has been left too long in a specific location and we ought perhaps make arrangements for moving it."

"Good point," Max admitted. "I should have told Kilkallen about Louie's ingenuous admission, but there was so much else going on that I forgot. Louie didn't happen to mention which corner he'd parked it around, did he?"

"I don't believe he did. Perhaps we could cast about, so to speak."

"The trouble is, I've got an appointment out in Sturbridge at two o'clock. I had planned to leave you two at a likely watering hole nearby and maybe even join you in a bite, but this business with Louie has taken longer than I expected. I'll have to drop you off and come back for you, and I don't have time to fight my way through this unholy maze of one-way streets. Suppose you telephone Kilkallen from the restaurant and let the cops look for the car? Ten to one it's been towed by now anyhow."

"What's this appointment?" Jem demanded.

Egbert coughed genteelly. " 'With whom is this appointment' would be better grammar, sir."

"Tracy's father."

"Aha!" Jem crowed. "Good thinking, Max. But you don't really believe that self-centered old satyr sprung for a gift of that value, do you? Not that the necklace isn't vulgar enough to appeal to him, but he'd be far more likely to bestow it on one of his floozies. I remember a diamond bracelet with which I won the lavish favors of the luscious Lucy Lazonga—"

"Tell me about it another time," Max interrupted. He didn't believe for a moment that any Kelling, even a self-proclaimed satyr like Jem, would have shelled out for diamonds. Paste or glass, possibly, if the Kelling in question were desperately enamored, but never genuine stones.

"I unquestionably will," Jem said. "And I can give the narrative the panache it deserves once I've got a couple of martinis under my belt. You're not leaving me and Egbert, though. I insist on being present to assist in the third degree."

"But you just said the old boy probably doesn't know

anything about the necklace," Max objected, sliding neatly past a taxi that had stopped to let off a fare.

"We won't know for certain until we've subjected him to intensive questioning," Jem said with relish. "Egbert, did you pack the rubber hose?"

Max had had about much cockamamie Kelling conversation as he could stand for one morning, so he concentrated on getting through the grisly city traffic as expeditiously as possible without jarring his elderly passengers. In fact, he mused, it might not be a bad idea to take Jem with him. Maybe they could play bad cop, good cop. Jem would love that, and he'd be good at it, too. Nobody could be ruder than a Kelling.

He wondered whether Egbert had packed a rubber hose. And of course the penny whistle.

"What about lunch?" he asked. "I doubt we'll have time to stop anywhere, and you must already be peckish, as Egbert would say."

"Oh, that's quite all right, sir." Egbert's genteel tones were accompanied by a rattle of paper. "I took the liberty of packing us a little picnic. One never knows what will eventuate, and it is best to be prepared for the worst. Would you care for chicken salad or pastrami?"

"Need you ask?" Max stretched an arm back and accepted a neatly wrapped sandwich and a cylindrical object encased even more securely in foil. "I might have known you wouldn't forget the pickle, Egbert. This wouldn't happen to be one of Warty's best, would it?"

"It certainly would not, Mr. Max. Only desperation would force me to add a product of Warty Pickles to our larder."

"That bad? Come to think of it, I've never seen a jar of Warty's on the pantry shelf at my mother's or Miriam's."

"Nor would you, sir. They are ladies of taste and discernment. Would you care for another chicken salad sandwich, Mr. Jem?"

"Pastrami," Jem said through the last mouthful of his first sandwich. "And a martini to go with it. Max, there's a place half a mile up the road on the right—McGillicuddy's. You'll spot it by the neon sign." Jem cleared his throat, hemmed a time or two, and burst, or rather slid, into song. "The shamrock, thistle, rose entwine the maple leaf forever."

And they did. Though the sign was not lighted by day, it was large enough to dominate the landscape for some distance. Max was too fascinated by this touching display of loyalty to a vanished past to object when Jem directed him to pull off the highway. McGillicuddy must be a displaced and homesick Canadian, he decided as Egbert got out of the car and went into the bar. Jem regaled his chauffeur with the first two verses of the ditty in question—"In days of yore, from Britain's shore, Wolfe the gallant hero came"—until Egbert emerged with a large plastic cup.

It was the first time Max had come across martinis to go. He had no objection. Drinking them kept Jem from singing. There were, he suspected, quite a number of verses to "The Maple Leaf Forever."

The Warty Pickles factory was not a pretty sight. In Max's critical opinion few factories were, but most of the newer establishments had paid lip service to the idea of landscaping, at least in front of the main office. There were no flower beds or swatches of close-cropped grass here, no pole flying a representation of the company logo, not even a pink flamingo. The building itself was faced with aged aluminum siding. The vehicles in the adjoining parking lot weren't antique or vintage, they were just old—except for the glistening stretch limousine in front of the main door. It was a particularly grisly shade of green. Pickle green.

Max pulled up behind it and helped his passengers out. He persuaded Jem to leave the plastic cup in the car. The lobby was as grimy and dispiriting as the outside of the building. There was an armed security guard and a much mascaraed blond receptionist. Both were chewing gum, or possibly tobacco. No wonder old Warty spent as little time as possible here, Max thought. As he'd explained to Jem and Egbert between McGillicuddy's and their destination, he had had the dickens of a time tracking the man down and bullying him into making an appointment.

He had to show the guard his driver's license before the receptionist would announce him.

"Tell him Mr. Kelling and his assistant are with me," Max said. He didn't like the look in the security guard's squinty eyes or the way he fondled the worn leather holster at his hip. If he'd been told to admit only the Mr. Bittersohn who had made the appointment, he might try to stop Jem, and then all hell would break loose.

After a mumbled discussion the receptionist jerked her thumb toward a door behind the desk without interrupting the even cadence of her chewing. Before they reached it the door was thrown open and there was the pickle king in person.

Max had never seen a man who looked so alarmingly like the product he manufactured. The Irish tweed suit, in an unfortunate blend of emerald, yellow, and forest green, cast a chartreuse glow on his sallow face. It molded a shape that swelled out at the chest and finally tapered down somewhere around knee level. He was bald. Well, of course, Max thought insanely, who ever saw a pickle with hair on top? There were warts.

The entrepreneur looked them over. His pinched smile faded. "You aren't Percival Kelling."

"Who said I was?" Jem snarled. He pushed past the pickle king and settled his plump haunches in the most comfortable chair. It happened to be the one behind the desk. "Come in, come in. Sit down. We haven't got all day. Mr. Bittersohn is a busy man."

"We won't take much of your time," Max said, watching Jem hoist his feet onto the desk and wondering if this was going a little too far, even for Jeremy Kelling. Maybe not. It seemed to be working. Pilcher sank into one of the hard chairs reserved for visitors, winced, shifted positions, and stared at his visitors.

"What do you want?"

"To get out of this filthy place as soon as I can," said Jem.

Pilcher pulled a handkerchief—green, Max was sorry to see—from his pocket and mopped his forehead. "So do I. I'm flying to Bermuda in a couple of hours. I thought you were Percival. Been thinking of transferring some of my accounts to his firm. But you're not him." He transferred the stare to Max. "You're the one wanted to see me. I know who you are. And that uncle of yours, the lawyer, he's another do-gooder bleeding heart liberal nosey parker. You said something about grand theft and possible prosecution. You can't prove a damn thing."

"I have only one question," Max said. He leaned forward and fixed Pilcher with a stern, accusing gaze. "What did you give your daughter for a wedding present?"

He thought for a minute the man was going to strangle. The pickle king sputtered and stammered and dribbled.

"Just answer the question," Max said.

"What kind of game is this? Oh, well, then, I'll play a few hands. What did I give, uh, Tracy? Enough of my best pickles to supply her and what's-his-name for years, that's what! Fifty cases of assorted delicacies. Bread and butter, kosher dills, spears, slices . . . Are you laughing?"

"I'm not sure," Max admitted. Now that the subject had been raised, he thought he remembered seeing Jed Lomax supervise the removal of multiple cartons from a delivery van. They hadn't been among the wedding gifts. Lomax had probably assumed, as had Max, that the undistinguished brown cardboard boxes had nothing to do with the wedding. "That's all? Nothing else?"

"Why should I have?"

"I can't stand this dribbling cad any longer," Jem announced. He managed to get his feet onto the floor and stood up. "Let's go before I throw up."

Jem insisted he needed another slug of gin, or possibly three, to get the taste of Warty out of his mouth. Max was in complete sympathy. After the medication had been supplied, they headed for home.

Having seen the paternal parent in person, Max was even more astonished at the miracle of his newly acquired niece. Heredity, he mused, was a funny thing. Perhaps Tracy was a throwback to some remote ancestor, or perhaps she'd been switched in her cradle by the fairies. That made better sense. She was a dainty little thing. One could only pity the poor elf that got a true offspring of Pilcher and Jeanne in exchange.

He didn't doubt that the old man had spoken the truth when he'd denied giving his daughter anything more munificent than a lifetime supply of poorly preserved cucumbers. Lying was probably a habit of his, but why should he lie about that? Unless the necklace was hot, and he wanted to get it off his hands. That didn't make sense, though. Tracy was painfully honest (another quality she hadn't inherited), and she'd be as confused and worried about the origin of the necklace as the rest of them were. She'd report it, refuse to accept it, and/or try to figure out where it had come from. Supposing the damned thing had been reported stolen, Daddy would be an obvious suspect. There were easier and safer and more remunerative ways of disposing of stolen property. Even more to the point was Jem's cynical and doubtless accurate appraisal of Warty's character. His daughter was the last person to whom he'd give rubies.

13

Sarah met them at the front door. "Well, did you kiddies have a nice outing? I expected you back hours ago. I suppose Jem talked you into feeding the frogs in the Frog Pond and shucking a bag of peanuts for the squirrels on the Common."

Max gave her a quick but comprehensive kiss. "Sorry we took so long, but we had to go back for Jem's swim fins and Egbert's rubber ducky."

"How far did you get before you missed them?"

"Quite a way. I wanted to keep going, but then Jem started to fuss and Egbert was pouting about his duck, so what could I do? Then there was the corpse to be disposed of."

Sarah gasped. "Another one?"

"No, by a strange coincidence it was the same one. The one I found under the library desk, to be precise. What with one thing and another, it's been quite a day."

"Would you care for some tea or coffee and a sandwich to tide you over for another hour or so? That's how long it will take to get dinner on the table, since I didn't know when to expect you."

"All right," said Max. "Don't rub it in. I know I should have phoned, but things just kept happening. Lieutenant Kilkallen sends you his regards, by the way."

"Do I know him? Oh yes, I remember now. A pleasant-looking man with an old-fashioned air of courtesy that even a crook couldn't help admiring. I trust Louie was properly appreciative? It was Louie you meant, wasn't it?"

"No, he wasn't, and yes, it was. It's too long to tell now," Max said as the thunder of little feet heralded the arrival of his son. How a person that size could make as much noise as a two-hundred-pound man, he would never understand. Davy launched himself at his father's knees, and Max caught him and swung him up onto his shoulder. "Hi there, tiger. What are we having for dinner?"

"How about chocolate-covered pretzels with martinis for a chaser?" Jem suggested.

Davy chortled, and his mother said lightly, "I'm afraid we're out of chocolate-covered pretzels. Unless you brought some home?"

"Unfortunately, no," said Max. "One of the Common squirrels grabbed the bag and ran off with it. You know what rapacious creatures they are; they'll lick anything up to twice their size and brag about it afterward."

Davy didn't always understand all the words his parents

used, but he liked to listen to them talk silly, as he put it, and, as his mother put it, the exercise might stretch his vocabulary. Seeing him grin, Sarah played up nobly. "Really, Max, I don't think that's very nice of them. There they are, right out in front of the State House, wolfing down everything they can get their paws on and not even saying thank you. Uncle Jem, can't you get up a little class on the care and feeding of unprincipled squirrels? You'd have to learn a fair amount of rodent-speak, of course; but think of the difference you could make in their socially stunted lives. And yours as well, I'm sure, Egbert. Maybe you could get those squirrels their own peanut cooker and teach them how to use it."

Davy let out a whoop of laughter. "Peanut cooker!"

"Excellent idea," his father agreed. "Okay, kid, let's get the bags upstairs. Same rooms, Sarah?"

"Unless the gentlemen in question object. You know we always give Egbert the room nearest the stairs because he's an early riser like me. Uncle Jem can snooze all day tomorrow if he wants to, although I'm sure Davy is looking forward to singing all two hundred verses of 'Old Jem Kelling Had a Farm.' And Egbert can do exactly as he pleases."

"Just so you won't keep me out of the kitchen much longer, Mrs. Sarah. You're a better cook than I am, but you know how it is; it's fun to cook in a different place for a change. Sort of like a vacation."

"If that's what you want, that's what you shall have. Everything's set for tonight. There's a little nip in the air, and I thought you might be getting tired of wedding left-overs, so I made a pot roast with carrots and potatoes and so on. I still have to add the potatoes and the so on, so if you really insist on helping, you might fix a tray of cheese and crackers and mix Mr. Jem's martinis. Max, would you like a drink?"

"Please." Max had started up the stairs, suitcases in hand. Davy followed him, clutching Jem's shaving kit. Jem had already retreated to the sitting room in order to snatch a brief snooze before the refreshments arrived.

Davy was allowed to sit up a little later than his usual bedtime so he could have some time with his father and his adored visitors. Sarah and Max were accustomed to squeezing in grown-up talk in between responding to Davy's remarks. By the time supper had been served and eaten, Sarah had reported the news of the day. Most of the wedding presents had been repacked, moved to the carriage house, and tucked into corners where they wouldn't be in the way of the newlyweds. Nothing new had turned up, except, if he could believe it, fifty cases of—

"I know about them," Max said. "I called on the sender this afternoon. If you'd met him, you'd have no trouble believing it."

"Oh?"

"Yes. Keep your comments to yourself, Jem, they wouldn't be fit for juvenile ears. He denied the other thing, and I believed him."

The next exchange was delayed by Davy's request for a

definition of juvenile, and the indignant rebuttal that followed. When Davy had been distracted by a serving of frozen yogurt, his mother went on to the next subject.

"Brooks called. He thinks he may be on to something, but he won't know for certain till Jesse reports in tomorrow. Charles telephoned from Miami; they located the statue at an auction house and are taking the necessary steps to retrieve it. Calpurnia Zickery dropped in—"

Davy's golden head had been drooping over his dessert. It lifted alertly at the name. "The Martian lady," he explained. "She says I can ride in her balloon."

"Great," Max said, thinking that it would be a winter day in the infernal regions before he let his son into any vehicle, much less a balloon, with one of the Zickerys. "What did she want, Sarah?"

"She wanted to apologize for the television crew."

"What television crew?" Max demanded.

"They arrived not long after you left. Some enterprising local journalist heard about the body under the balloon, and passed the word. The story does have its intriguing aspects," Sarah admitted fairly. "Mr. Lomax ran them off before they could lay siege to the house, so they went to interview the Zickerys. That's why Calpurnia popped in, to say she was sorry they had caused such a stir and hope we hadn't been inconvenienced."

"The major inconvenience was their popping in or onto the tent," Max said. "Does this mean we're going to be on the six o'clock news?"

"I hope not. Maybe there'll be an even more intriguing disaster elsewhere and we'll be bumped, or whatever the phrase may be. I couldn't help feeling a little sorry for Calpurnia, Max. She said they were planning to repair the old place; she sounded quite excited about it. I think the poor thing is lonely."

"You feel sorry for everybody," Max said affectionately. "I hope for your sake she doesn't become a nuisance."

"If she does, I'll introduce her to the old yacht club crowd. It would serve all of them right."

Sarah had no fond memories of the yacht club, where, as a young bride, she had spent most of her time sitting in a corner, refusing martinis and fending off the attentions of the drunker male members. That wouldn't have happened if Alexander had stayed at her side like a devoted spouse, but Aunt Caroline's needs always came before Sarah's. After Alexander's death some of the yacht club crew had taken notice of his widow—Bradley Rovedock and his millions, Miffy Tergoyne and her diamonds, Alice Beaxitt and her corrosive tongue, the Larringtons—all of the people whom Sarah had known so long, had liked so little, had been so happy to break away from. They'd tried to keep her on their list not because they liked her, but because they were too hidebound to let go of anybody whom they and their forebears had become used to. There weren't many of the old crowd left, thank goodness, and she wasn't even going to feel guilty about that uncharitable thought.

Observing that Davy was about to fall asleep in his yogurt, she turned her thoughts to happier channels. She graciously allowed Max to do bedtime duty that evening, since he'd been gone most of the day.

Davy revived, as small boys do when bedtime is imminent, but once he'd been bathed and brushed and encased in a manly set of pajamas covered with pictures of jungle animals, he snuggled under the covers and was asleep before Max had finished the first page of *The Little Engine that Could.* Max lingered for a bit, smoothing the blankets and listening to his son's quiet breathing.

He was thinking about the Zickerys. Something about that pair bothered him. Callie and Allie. They seemed harmless enough and no more peculiar than many of Sarah's other acquaintances, but he'd just as soon not have much to do with them. He remembered Alister saying he didn't like children.

They really couldn't be called neighbors, not in the generally accepted meaning of the word. Sarah had inherited thirty-five acres of prime seaside property from her first husband. She'd done the sensible thing, as Alexander Kelling would have wanted her to, and sold off five acres at the farthest end of the property. The money had enabled her and Max to build exactly the house they'd wanted, at a price they couldn't have afforded otherwise; but they had kept the other thirty acres despite the persistent offers of realtors hoping to develop the land.

The Zickery place was about the same size as the Kelling land. Max assumed real estate dealers must have scouted that property, too, but it was on the inland side without a clear view of the ocean and so second-best in the eyes of prospective buyers. Was that why it hadn't sold to developers? Maybe the Zickerys had an exaggerated idea of its value, as people often did, and were holding out for a high price. Maybe they just didn't give a hoot. They certainly had taken no interest in the old place for years. The old house was so obscured now by overgrown shrubs and weeds that it couldn't be seen from the road, but it must be getting rattier and rattier. Max had begun to wonder how soon it would be before some philanthropic soul would pause to light a cigarette and forget to blow out the match before tossing it into the dry grass along the roadside.

And now the Zickerys, two of them, at least, had come back. Nostalgia, fond memories of the good old days when they had ridden rented horses along carefully marked bridle paths, got out the croquet set, and put up the wickets for a real ding-dong battle? There must be money available; getting the ramshackle old house back into livable shape would cost a bundle. And hot-air balloons didn't come cheap, did they? Maybe the estate had been tied up in litigation all these years; maybe the other heirs had died and left Allie and Callie in uncontested ownership of the estate, with a large enough inheritance to restore it.

And why did he, Max Bittersohn, give a damn? He tucked the blankets around Davy's shoulders, patted the tumbled fair curls, and went downstairs.

The others had watched the news and were pleased to

report an absence of the news they didn't want to hear. Jem had given Sarah a pungent description of their visit to the pickle king, which finished that subject to everyone's satisfaction. He and Sarah were sitting side by side on the sofa, looking at old photographs.

Aunt Appie Kelling had salvaged several old photograph albums from the wreckage of the Kelling place when it was being leveled to make way for the Kelling-Bittersohn house. She'd passed them along to Sarah, but only on loan. Various members of the family had voiced their intentions of writing a Kelling family history; nobody had got very far with the project except Sarah's own father. Jem would have been the logical person to take up the job, but he much preferred looking at the photos of himself as a dashing young blade in plus fours or the white ducks and polo shirt worn on Saturday evenings at the yacht club dances. Another favorite occupation was sneering at the photographic images of his friends and close relatives. Somehow Max was not surprised to hear them talking about the Zickerys.

Alone or in couples, even whole septs, members of the Zickery clan had drawn away to revel in pastures new; to opulent suburbs, to in-town apartments that would receive a new cachet as condominiums. With air travel so fast and so convenient, provided the plane didn't fall apart in the air, they could always fly back to Ireson's Landing for a brief visit with those relatives who'd preferred to stay.

"Finally the last of them vamoosed," Jem said. "Once in a blue moon somebody would pull up in a car to walk the boundaries and put up a fresh flock of 'No Trespassing' signs, then drive away and not be seen again until the next blue moon or reasonable facsimile. Didn't you ever see them, Sarah? You and Alexander used to come here a lot."

"We never went that way. There were those 'No Trespassing' signs, after all, and why push through all the brush and brambles when the beach walk was so much nicer? Not that we had much time for walks together."

"Not with Caroline demanding every spare instant of Alex's time and energy," Jeremy Kelling said with a snort.

"There's something about that place that gives me the creeps," Sarah admitted. "When I used to stay at Ireson's Landing as a child, I got so many warnings about staying away from the Zickery place that I developed something pretty close to a phobia about it. I'm sure the grown-ups' warnings were about real hazards like poison ivy and rotted well heads, but I took them all very seriously. To tell you the truth, I'm still scared to death of that house. I wouldn't go there alone if you gave me the whole thirty acres with a clear title. And that's going some for a Kelling."

"Can't say I blame you." Jem closed the album he had been holding and reached for another. "Most of the photos are upside-down or sideways. Just like Appie. She hasn't labeled them, either. Who's this?"

Sarah leaned forward and looked at the photograph. "You'd be more likely to recognize him than I, Uncle Jem. That raccoon coat was surely in fashion during your younger days, and isn't that a Packard he's leaning against?"

"Yes, by Jove, now I've got him! It's the coat. How we used to rag old Alister about that rug."

"That's Alister?" Sarah couldn't believe it. The features under the natty cap were blurry and the photo had faded, but the young Allie was certainly more amiable looking than the present-day version. "Why did you rag him about the coat? They were hot stuff back then, weren't they?"

"Oh, yes. Had one myself. Whatever happened to that raccoon coat, Egbert?"

Egbert stifled a yawn. "Mrs. Emma Kelling borrowed it, Mr. Jem, don't you remember? For one of her theatrical performances, before she began specializing in Gilbert and Sullivan. *Charlie's Aunt* was the play in question, I believe."

"The coat's probably still in her attic," Max said, knowing the Kelling reluctance to dispose of any garment until it had literally fallen to pieces.

"Damn, I had forgotten. Must remember to ask Emma to give it back. Plenty of good wear still in that coat. Not like Alister's. He claimed he'd trapped and skinned the raccoons himself, and the damned coat sure looked like it."

"That's disgusting," Sarah said. "Was he the kind of boy who'd do something like that?"

"No, not really. Alister Zickery was always bragging about what a macho fellow he was—we didn't use that word back then, of course—but he was a wimp at heart. He'd pick a fight with some other boy, but once he'd got the fight all set up, he'd back off and leave it for some other boy to take the pounding. The more I remember that young blister, as Alister was then, the less I'd have to do with him now. I hope my innate tendency toward unbridled geniality didn't come over me at the wrong moment. Was I too cordial?"

"That's not how I'd describe it," Max said. "Are you two looking for something in particular in those albums, or are you just killing time?"

"I thought we might find a photograph that shows the rubies," Sarah said. "It's been so long since I saw them, or even a picture of them, that I'd forgotten exactly what they looked like."

"I haven't," Max said grimly.

"No, darling, I don't suppose you could, after examining the copies and the photographs as closely as you must have done. I suppose I was hoping against hope that it was some other ruby parure, though goodness knows there can't have been many like it. No one would wear such things nowadays, they're too ostentatious."

"You might not, but you have excellent taste," her husband remarked. "Some women would love to flash that ensemble. I haven't had a chance to check the voice mail; maybe Pepe has finally got around to reporting in."

Not only were there telephones of every possible color and type around the house, they were equipped with all the gadgets that might be useful to a man of Max's profession. He turned on the speakerphone so the others could listen.

The first message of interest was from Brooks. Thus far he had had no success in tracing the background of the unlucky Joe Macbeth. "It must be an alias," Brooks said. "We've run the usual name checks, with the usual agencies; you may be surprised to hear that we located a dozen individuals named Joseph Macbeth. All of them are accounted for, however, alive or dead. Sorry to have so little to report, Max, but such inquiries take time, as you know. The police got his fingerprints, and we'll start on that tomorrow."

"Damn," Max muttered.

"Why damn?" Jem asked. "Even if he doesn't have a criminal record, he was old enough to have served in some war or other, so his fingerprints must be on file somewhere."

"Yes, but that sort of search takes a long time. Oh, well, it's probably a long shot. Poor old alias Macbeth may have been killed because he was at the wrong place at the wrong time. Let's see what Pepe has to contribute."

Pepe hadn't much to contribute. The astute lady from Amsterdam had left no direct descendants. Her entire estate had been sold to benefit several lucky charities, including the World Bureau of Art Theft and Forgery, which Max considered a rather nice touch. Her jewels had been handled by a well-known international auction house in Zurich. Pepe had obtained a copy of the catalog, which included a breathtaking range of expensive geegaws. Conspicuous by its absence was the ruby parure.

"It is therefore to be presumed, *mon cher* Max, that the parure was disposed of by some other means, possibly a secret trust. I will endeavor to ascertain more, but you know, my old hat, how these lawyers are. Inform me, if you will, whether bribery or breaking into their offices is to be preferred."

"He thinks he's a comedian," Max muttered, switching off the machine.

"Breaking and entering would be my advice," Jem said. "It costs too much to bribe a lawyer. What a pity my old pal Wouter Tolbathy is singing with the celestial choir. He'd invent some ingenious method of befuddling the legal beagles."

"Such as shooting them with a tranquilizer gun," Max said, remembering some of Wouter Tolbathy's stunts. The tranquilizer gun had been designed for the purpose of shooting at a fuchsia-turquoise-and-chartreuse-colored hippo, also constructed by Wouter, which would begin to snore if it was hit in the proper place. Fearing Jem was about to launch into additional reminiscences about the late lamented prankster, he said quickly, "Isn't it time you and Egbert were in bed?"

Jem tossed aside the album and hoisted himself to his feet. "Time for a final nightcap, you mean. Come along, Egbert, old cabbage. You can brew up some of that tea that's supposed to be good for what ails you, and I'll have a martini straight up."

"Just make sure you're still straight up when you tackle the stairs," said Sarah. "We don't want any more broken legs around here."

Her uncle's response was a hearty, "Bah, humbug," anticipating the season by several months but perfectly in character.

The telephone rang. Max had left the speaker on; Brooks's precise Andover accents came through clear as a bell. "If you're there, Max and/or Sarah, turn on the ten o'clock news. There's just been a teaser, as I believe it is termed, for a story that may interest you. I'll ring off now so you can give it your full attention."

14

"Do you suppose Callie and Allie inflated the balloon for the benefit of the television viewing audience?" Max asked.

"Thanks to Mr. Lomax, they didn't do any filming here," Sarah said. "They had to get footage of something, and you must admit the balloon makes a pretty picture."

"Can't say the same for the Zickery twins."

The swelling, gaily colored shape of the balloon did make an attractive image. Then the camera closed in on the proud owners, standing beside it. Alister was wearing his aeronaut outfit complete with helmet, but Calpurnia had chosen to charm the viewing audience in a purple sweatsuit that did not flatter her lined face. She was all smiles, however, rambling on about how happy she and her brother were to return to their roots and how much they regretted having dropped in uninvited on a family celebration. As for the body under the tent, she had no idea how it had got there or who it was. The police had confirmed that the balloon could not have caused the fatal injuries and that the corpse had been put under the tent at a later time. Alister confined his agreement to vigorous nods and an occasional stretch of the lips.

Callie hadn't hinted by so much as a raised eyebrow that her dear neighbors the Bittersohns must have had a hand in the murder. The commentator was also careful to avoid any statement that might leave the station open to a lawsuit, but innuendos fell hot and heavy. There were references to earlier murders in which various Kellings and Bittersohns had been involved, lurid descriptions of the agency's more unusual cases, and clips from past broadcasts showing, among other victims, an infuriated Jeremy Kelling brandishing a stick at a reporter who had attempted to interview him about the death of his old friend Wouter Tolbathy.

"No wonder they didn't get it on the six o'clock broadcast," Sarah exclaimed. "It must have taken hours to locate those old films and patch them together. Where did they find them? I thought TV studios reused or discarded old . . . Oh, Max!"

There on the screen was the Sarah Max had first seen, white-faced and shivering in front of the family vault, where the skeleton of a former burlesque queen had been discovered.

"I'll give Uncle Jake a call," Max said savagely. "If he can't find a way of suing those sons of bitches—"

"But that's so unromantic, darling. The least you can do

is go to the television station brandishing a horsewhip." After the first gasp of horrified surprise, Sarah had recovered herself. She even managed a laugh. "We do have a colorful past, don't we? Everything the man said was true. I just hate to think—"

The telephone rang. Sarah sighed. "I knew this would happen. What do you bet it's Cousin Mabel?"

There were no takers. It was at least a hundred to one that Mabel Kelling would get her oar in the water before everybody else.

"Sarah, have you gone stark, raving mad? Don't you ever give a moment's thought to your family? Our family, I should have said, just to remind you that you do have one. Staging that ridiculous pageant of a wedding, not that I know much about it since I never got an invitation even though those Bittersky creatures came in droves, I was told, all dressed up to the eyeballs, and now there's Jem Kelling, mad as a hatter, shooting his mouth off about murders and God knows what else. If you ask me, that old fool ought to be in one of those loony bins where they keep them locked up twenty-four hours a day and don't let them have knives and forks."

There was no stopping her; Mabel was off and running again. "It's a wonder Jem hasn't murdered somebody himself. That Egbert of his is about as much good as nothing at all. Percy's the one who ought to be handling Jem's money, but Percy's all for Percy, as you well know. Catch him doing anything for anybody else unless he gets paid in advance. And there's Anne in her own little world, chasing the bugs off her precious roses. I can't stand that woman and never could, even if she is my second cousin once removed."

By this time, Sarah had developed a serious case of the giggles and Max was taping every word because this was Mabel at her most venomous and ought to be preserved for the family archives if anybody ever got around to writing them. Mabel was building up steam and would have gotten around to the rest of the family if Sarah hadn't dropped a gentle hint that this was Mabel's money they were talking on. That did it. Mabel hung up after a final comprehensive "Well!"

Sarah stood up and shook the wrinkles out of her housecoat.

"Thank goodness for Aunt Mabel. A little comic relief is just what I needed. Come on, dear, let's go up. I told Mrs. Blufert to take tomorrow off. She's given us so much time lately that she's gotten behind on her own work, so she won't be here to help out with Davy, and I need to do some grocery shopping, strange as it may seem considering the amount of food that's been in and out of this house during the past few days. Do you have any early appointments?"

"No, my love," said Max. "I don't intend to stir till the rooster crows."

"What rooster?" Sarah had little affinity with poultry in any form.

"Good question. Would you care to go rooster shopping tomorrow? We could send one to your cousin Mabel."

"Nonsense, I wouldn't send Cousin Mabel a pleasant look. At least Jem and Egbert were safely tucked away when she called."

"What did you do with my other bathrobe?"

"What other bathrobe? You only have one here because you took the purple one that Theonia gave you to Tulip Street and forgot to bring it back."

"Then why didn't you remind me?"

"Because I couldn't remember where we'd left it, that's why. You're a big boy now, in case you hadn't noticed. It's high time you started being a role model for Davy, or he for you, whichever gets there first. Weren't we planning to go to bed?"

"That's the best suggestion I've heard all day," Max said.

He didn't sleep well, though. Twice he slid carefully out of bed, so as not to wake Sarah, and prowled the house, checking doors and windows and listening for unusual noises. It seemed to him he had been sleeping only a few hours when he was waked up, not by a rooster crowing, but by a heavy weight pressing down on his diaphragm. When he opened his eyes he saw another pair of eyes inches from his.

"You awake," Davy announced.

"I am now," Max admitted. "What's up, tiger?"

"You." Davy tugged at him. "Up, Daddy."

Max located his sole remaining bathrobe and struggled

into it, then accompanied his son and heir downstairs, where Sarah tenderly assisted him into a chair and waved a cup of coffee under his nose.

"Here you are, you poor old man. Davy, your cereal is all ready; eat it up while I make Daddy his eggs."

Max remembered the first night he'd spent in the Kelling house on Beacon Hill. Someone had tried to burn the house down and had been foiled by Sarah with a pail of boiling water; Max had wrecked a folding chair that was a Kelling family relic and had had a mouse run up his pant leg. Next morning Sarah had fried him two eggs. They'd come out the color and texture of leather. He'd eaten every bite.

"I should have had them framed," Max said.

"What, darling?"

"Those first eggs you ever cooked me, remember? They'd look great on the kitchen wall."

Sarah deposited a kiss on the top of his head. "What a touching thought. Come to think of it, I've seen so-called modern paintings that looked worse than those eggs."

By the time Egbert and Jem made their appearance, Davy had finished his cereal and was demanding action. "What we do today?"

"What would you like to do?" Sarah asked.

"Go see the balloon."

"Not today," Sarah said quickly.

"Why not?" Davy's lower lip went out.

"We haven't been invited."

"The lady said I could bring my alligator to see her."

Max took his mutinous son onto his knee. "The lady doesn't want company yet, Davy. She and Mr. Zickery just got here, and they have a lot of work to do fixing up the house."

"But—"

"Suppose we have a picnic instead," Sarah suggested. "Before we do anything, you have to get dressed. Come on, we'll pick out something to wear. Would you like to be a bluejay, or a pink-and-blue butterfly, or a green turtle with red feet?"

"Like Uncle Jem's turtle," Davy said eagerly. "He had a great big turtle once, its name was Peter, and Uncle Jem used to ride it around and around and win all the prizes at the turtle races."

Sarah laughed. "Did he really?"

"He told me so himself."

"He'd never invent a thing like that," Max said. "Run along, kid, and we'll see if we can find you a turtle race."

Jem's mouth was full, but he nodded agreeably. After Sarah and Davy had gone, he swallowed, stared at Max, and shook his head. "You look like hell. Something worrying you?"

"It's frustration more than worry. None of our leads have panned out, and we don't seem to be getting anywhere. I should be working the case myself, but I don't like to leave Sarah and Davy alone. I can't farm them out to the relatives; I've done that too many times already."

"I think you're being a little hard on yourself, Max. It seems to me that you're doing your full share and quite a bit over. What sort of life do you think Sarah would have had if you hadn't come along when you did? She'd have been trapped by family pressure in the same old net, wearing her mother's hand-me-downs and going to all the family funerals for her entertainment. Alexander was a dear chap, but he'd have been pretty much of a stick even if he hadn't had to be at Caroline's beck and call about twenty-seven hours in the day."

Jem's round, pink face was unusually serious. Max was surprised and pleased. Jem didn't hand out compliments often. Fortunately Jem reverted to type before either of them could get maudlin.

"Anyhow, she's not alone. Damn it, Max, Egbert and I take umbrage at the suggestion that we aren't capable of looking after her. Don't we, Egbert?"

"Decidedly," Egbert said. "Both of us would lay down our lives to protect Mrs. Sarah and Davy. At least I would."

Max grinned at him. "Thanks. I hope you won't take further umbrage, though, if I call in reinforcements. It's time I got in touch with the rest of the crew."

He had meant to call the office, but for some reason he found himself dialing the number of the house on Tulip Street. Theonia picked up on the first ring. Had she expected him to call? Knowing Theonia, Max wouldn't have been surprised. He could hear her rustling something out of a paper bag or perhaps a chocolate box. Theonia liked little snacks that came in small bags.

"Max, is that you? How sweet of you to call. No, of course it's not too early. Brooks has already trotted off to the office. I've been thinking about you."

"Anything in particular?"

"I'm afraid not, Max dear. I'm still getting that strong sense of danger, and it's definitely connected with the necklace." Theonia's soft chuckle sounded like the cooing of a turtledove. "I know, Max, it doesn't take foresight or supernatural powers to suspect that. But it's so strange that the thing has turned up again after all these years."

"You don't have to tell me," said Max. "I was with Sarah the day we walked over to the High Street Bank to see the famous Kelling parure, which was supposed to have been lying in one of the bank's safe-deposit boxes for many years. What we found was a boxful of bricks. That was the day Sarah got her arm broken while I was outside smashing a front windowpane to get at the bastard who intended to kill her and damned near did. I kept tabs on him for a while, but he was moved to another facility for special cases, and I lost track of him. I don't know what I'd do if I ever came face-to-face with him again. I'm not a vindictive person as a rule, but there's one who needs special treatment. Something interesting, with boiling oil in it."

"Not you, Max dear. You just do not have it in you to destroy another human being, however vile that person might be."

Max laughed ruefully. "Sarah said something of the sort while she was supervising the workmen who put up the tent for the wedding. She says I'm not steely eyed enough."

"Of course you're not, and why should you be? Neither is Sarah, as you ought to know by now if you're ever going to. But she's got gumption, Max. She'll cope. You're the one I'm worried about. Do be careful. Watch out for anything that seems out of key, even if it strikes you as stupid or silly. Oh dear, is that our other phone ringing?"

"Answer it," Max said. "If it's Brooks, tell him to cut the billing and cooing short, since I'm about to call him."

Evidently the caller wasn't Brooks, since Max reached him at once. He gave Max a brief and characteristically well-organized summary of the present status of their varied cases.

"Things are getting backed up," Max said with a groan. "I'm sorry to stick you with all this work, Brooks. I know I haven't been pulling my weight the last few days."

"My dear chap, how could you do otherwise? Don't fret yourself, everything is more or less under control. You'll be glad to hear that Charles and Mariposa are on their way home, with the statue."

"Thank God," Max said, and meant it. "Brief them as soon as they get here, will you? I want to get this business of the necklace settled so I can stop worrying about Sarah and Davy. In the meantime, find Jesse and send him out here."

"Has something else happened?" Brooks sounded concerned.

"Hasn't enough happened?"

Brooks agreed that it had. "I'll let you know as soon as I get any information."

Jem had retired to the living room for his early morning, as opposed to his late morning, nap, and Egbert was helping Sarah with the breakfast dishes while Davy towed the alligator around and around the kitchen, making alligator noises.

"He certainly loves that toy," Sarah said, stepping neatly over the string that was about to trip her. "Which reminds me, Max, your father just called to say he's coming over with his tools. Something about the front door of the carriage house. What's wrong with it?"

"Nothing. You know my old man, he wants everything perfect for Mike and Tracy. Maybe he's decided the door might stick some day in the far distant future and he's going to scrape off a few millimeters of wood so it won't."

"I asked him to stay for lunch, but he said he'd bring a thermos and a sandwich, since he didn't want to be in the way. I can't say I blame him for preferring your mother's cooking to mine."

"You make as good a salami sandwich as Mom ever did," Max said loyally.

Davy hadn't seemed to be listening, but he didn't miss much. "Sandwich," he exclaimed. "Picnic! A picnic with Grandpa."

"What a good idea," Sarah said. "What shall we have?"

Sarah made peanut-butter sandwiches and put them in a basket with some oranges and apples and little boxes of chocolate milk, which were a special treat for Davy because his mother didn't think too much chocolate was good for his teeth. Davy suggested cookies, since he was sure his grandpa and the alligator would enjoy them. They were just about to leave the house when the phone rang and the answering machine switched itself on.

"Oh dear," Sarah moaned. "Max, that's Arnold Upthorn's secretary. Do we want to talk to him?"

"We don't want to, but we can't afford not to after all Upthorn did for us on that Artemisia Gentileschi transaction. Grab the phone, will you?"

Upthorn, one of Max's best clients from a prestigious insurance agency in Chicago, was in urgent need of some high-powered expertise, and he needed it now if not sooner. Max started calling airlines, and Sarah suggested to Davy that they turn the picnic into an expedition into the Sahara, sent her son off with Egbert to collect the various items a daring explorer might need, and went upstairs to pack an overnight bag. When Max joined her she was standing by the bed, holding his worn bathrobe.

"I won't need that, süssele, I'm not planning to entertain a glamorous lady spy in my hotel room."

"I'd be embarrassed to have a glamorous lady spy see you in this." Sarah's smile wavered. "Max, do you have to go?"

"We can't afford to lose Upthorn's goodwill, darling, or

the outrageous fee I expect to collect. You never know, Davy may need braces, or a brace of camels. I'll see Upthorn in the morning and be back tomorrow night, come hell or high water." He took her by the shoulders. "Jesse will be here in a couple of hours, and Mariposa and Charles are on their way home."

"Did they get it?" Sarah's face brightened.

"There speaks a true professional." Max kissed her. "Yes, they got it. I have to go, sweetheart. The flight's not till five, but by the time I get to the airport and park the car and pick up my ticket and go through security three or four times because I forget to take all the coins out of all my pockets I'll just about make it."

Max had faced assorted criminals with considerable aplomb, but he wasn't man enough to explain to his son that he couldn't go to the Sahara. He sneaked away while Sarah did her best to propitiate the leader of the expedition. "I'm sorry, Davy, but Daddy has to fly to Chicago and talk to a man about a painting."

"Can we go, too?"

"Not this time, dear. It would be wonderful if we could all go together, but the people in Chicago are going to give Daddy quite a lot of money for bringing back something that somebody else had taken away. Aren't we lucky to have such a clever daddy?"

"But he's going away. Tell him I want him here, Mummy."

"We can't, dear. You see, if you've promised to go somewhere to see somebody who wants very much to see you, it's not polite to stay home."

"Why can't Uncle Jem and Uncle Egbert go instead of him?"

"Because Uncle Jem doesn't know how to drive a car, and Uncle Egbert is going to cook something special for dinner. Let's take our picnic down to the carriage house, shall we? Grandfather Bittersohn will be there, and you can show him how fast his alligator can run."

"But I want Daddy to see, too."

This was awful. Davy wasn't usually so whiny. He had a sunny disposition, and he was used to having Mummy as well as Daddy go away from time to time. At least she had thought he was. Had he reached an age when the absences were beginning to bother him? Perhaps it had been a mistake on her part to have offices both at home and in Boston. Had there been too many paid baby-sitters, too many too willing relatives? But that big, loving family was what she had missed as a child, what she had believed every child should have. Not just Max's father and mother, and sister and brother-in-law, and nephew and brand-new niece, but her own wonderful and weird support group. They all adored Davy, and he adored them. If ever there was a child who did not suffer from neglect, Davy Bittersohn was it. He was just going through a stage, the way children did.

The welcome he got from his grandfather brought the smile back to Davy's face. Isaac had brought his own thermos bottle with coffee in it; he gave Davy a taste, but only a little one, which was all Davy wanted anyway. Grandfather Isaac showed Davy how to pound a nail into a board with both of them holding the hammer at the same time so that nobody's thumb would get banged, and the alligator raced to the satisfaction of all. Then they sat around the boxes of wedding presents that hadn't been put away yet, ate up the picnic, and had a lovely time until Sarah decided that she and Davy ought to go home and let Grandfather Isaac get some work done. Jesse had arrived, brimming with zeal and ready to defend the premises against any invaders that might turn up. Fortunately none did, but Davy refused to take a nap, and Jem spent the afternoon cleaning an antique pistol he had brought back from Pinckney Street, and the phone kept ringing with calls from various clients, and what with one thing and another Sarah was more than a little frazzled by the time her energetic son consented to go to bed.

The last straw was a call from Lieutenant Kilkallen in Boston. The police had finally located Jem's car in one of the lots where abandoned or illegally parked vehicles were taken. An astute traffic cop had noticed the meter hadn't changed for twenty-four hours and had had the car towed. The right front fender was bashed in, and one of the headlights was broken. When he heard that, Jem hit the ceiling and it took an extra pitcher of martinis to calm him down. By the time Sarah got him and Egbert up to their rooms, she was so tired she had barely enough energy to brush her teeth.

She did wonder, though, why Max hadn't called. He usually did when he had to be away from home overnight.

15

Miriam Rivkin was in a swivet.

"Fifty cases of pickles! And such pickles, Sarah! I bought a jar of kosher dills, right after Mike got engaged to Tracy, thought I should keep it in the family, but after I took one bite I threw the jar away. What I'd say is just get rid of the whole lot of them, if you can think of anybody you dislike that much."

"Do you think Tracy would mind? They're hers and Mike's really, I suppose."

Mike's mother snorted loud enough to rattle the phone. "You'd be doing her a favor, Sarah. They aren't going to eat them, you can be sure of that, and it has to be so embarrassing for the poor child to see what her father thinks of her. Her mother's not much better."

"I thought she helped you with the blintzes."

"She tried. I don't think she knows a saucepan from a soup tureen. Oh, she's a nice enough woman in her own way, but the minute she sets eyes on a good-looking man she loses track of everything else. Tracy said she and her mother only see each other a couple of times a year; they meet for lunch if Jeanne happens to be somewhere between downtown Boston, the classier shopping malls, and her latest boyfriend."

"Well, she's got you and Ira now," Sarah said. "That makes her a darned lucky girl, Miriam, and she knows it."

"She asked if she could call me Mum, like Mike does."

"And of course you said yes."

"Of course. As for those awful pickles, get them out of the house before the kids come home, they must be taking up a lot of space. How about donating them to that senior citizens' center your cousin Dolph and his wife started? They aren't actually poisonous, just limp and tasteless."

Sarah thought that was an excellent idea, but she refused Miriam's next suggestion, that she bring Davy over to spend the day with his doting aunt. "To be honest, Miriam, I've got a bad case of the guilts. We've left Davy with other people so much lately, what with the wedding and all the other distractions, and I think he's missing his daddy."

Davy definitely was. He'd waked up that morning demanding Daddy or the balloon, preferably both, and it had taken Jesse's offer of some fast rides up and down the driveway in his wagon to cheer him up. Jesse could run faster than anybody except his daddy, and Jesse didn't keep slowing down for fear a little boy would bounce out of the wagon and land on his head. Jesse shared Davy's conviction that nothing like that was ever going to happen.

Sarah didn't share it, and knowing Jesse's habits, she insisted he put the wooden sides up on the wagon and rig up a temporary but sturdy seat belt. Jem decided he'd time the race with his stopwatch, so Egbert carried out a pair of lawn chairs and a table and they settled down to watch.

After such a strenuous morning, Jesse was ready for a nap even if Davy wasn't. He settled down, though, after Sarah tucked him up under the lions-and-tigers quilt that Aunt Miriam had pieced for his third birthday and gave him fresh water in his small carafe and a few whole-wheat crackers to munch on with his fine new tooth if he felt the need for a snack before it was time for a meal. Sarah went downstairs to do something about the avalanche of mail that had accumulated during the past few hectic weeks. Thank goodness Max would be back tonight. She hoped Upthorn wouldn't want him to go rushing off to Katmandu or Lhasa or some other remote spot. Davy missed him, she missed him, and the paperwork was really piling up.

Then there was the ruby parure. It was still upstairs in the hidden safe in their bedroom. Max had planned to take it to the bank, but there just hadn't been time. She'd feel a lot happier if it were out of the house, but that was silly and superstitious. No outsider knew about the safe, and only a locksmith as talented as the legendary Louie could get into it.

Sarah forced herself to concentrate on her paperwork, so successfully that only a change in the breeze from the open window made her realize how late it was getting. It was coming off the water now and was fairly brisk. She'd better make sure Davy put on his blue sweater; he was probably awake by now and playing on the deck.

He had waked up. His bed was empty except for his usual menagerie of toys. But he wasn't on the deck outside his room. The bathroom?

He was not in the bathroom, or out on the upper deck, or in his parents' bedroom, or in either of the two guest rooms that Jem and Egbert were occupying for their own afternoon naps. She could hear them both snoring: Egbert in a steady, rather pleasant low rhythm; Jem in a raucous crow, proclaiming himself the cock of the walk and perhaps dreaming that he really was.

Then Davy was either on the floor below or on his way back to his room. He knew he wasn't supposed to leave the house and go wandering around outdoors unless he had somebody with him. Davy was a sensible little chap for his age. Nevertheless Sarah went downstairs more quickly than usual.

Jesse was in the living room, watching a soap opera on television. That's what Sarah assumed it was; she caught only a glimpse of two enormous mouths unattractively entwined before Jesse snatched up the remote and the screen went blank. At least the boy could blush, Sarah thought distractedly. The blush was probably on her account, though.

Jesse began, "Oh, hi, Sarah, I was just—"

"Have you see Davy?"

"He's in his room, isn't he?"

"No. He's not in the house."

"Maybe Jed Lomax has seen him," Jesse suggested. "Jed always keeps an eye peeled when Davy's outdoors."

"Jed isn't here. He had to take Mrs. Lomax to the hospital for her therapy session today." Sarah tried not to wring her hands. "Oh, this is silly. Davy wouldn't go outside, he knows better. He must be playing hide-and-seek with me. Under his bed, pretending to be a lion, or on one of the decks talking to a bird, or . . . Help me look for him, Jesse."

She'd never realized how many hiding places there were in the house. It was a modern open structure, not like the rambling old mansion she and Max had had torn down, but a small boy didn't occupy much space. She was beyond caring about disturbing the elders by then. When she burst into Jem's rooms and dropped to her knees to look under his bed, he woke with a snort and a snuffle.

"What? Hey? Who?"

"It's Davy," Jesse said. "Sarah can't find him."

That woke Jem up. "You sure? How long has he been gone, Sarah?"

"Not very long. Twenty minutes, half an hour at the most. But that's a long time to a child as young as he."

"He's got to be around here someplace. Egbert! Egbert, damn it, get your lazy carcass up from that bed."

Sarah couldn't believe Davy wasn't hiding somewhere in the house. She called till her throat hurt, dashing from room to room and looking in places she'd already investigated. Finally she gave up and ran outside, where she met Jem and Egbert coming back from the carriage house.

"Not there," Jem reported. "Jesse's looking in the garage and the shed. Sarah, maybe we should call the police. There's thirty acres out there."

And the cliff and the ocean below. Nobody wanted to say that, or even think it. "Call them," Sarah said. "And Miriam and Ira. Warn them not to say anything to Mother and Father Bittersohn, there's no sense in getting them worked up before . . . until . . . Oh, why isn't Max here? How could he go off this way?"

She left them standing there and ran toward the wooded area behind the house. If she had to search all thirty acres foot by foot, that was what she would do. Time passed; how much she couldn't calculate. Still no Davy, and not much left of Sarah. She was exhausted from all the walking, her voice down to a hoarse whisper from the shouting. She had not yet broken down completely, but she would very soon if her child was not found.

Jem Kelling was doing what he could. He brought his niece a small tot of whiskey and stood over her while she sipped it. He linked his arm in hers and tried to persuade her to go in the house. Miriam and Ira had joined the search; Miriam in her jeans and sturdy walking boots was as tough as any man, especially when her nephew was in danger. Jofferty had come, bringing two of his best men; they were scouring the woods.

Sarah shook her head and handed the glass to him. "I can't sit still, Uncle Jem. It's time Davy's father found out about this. See if you can locate him. Maybe he's on his way home. If he isn't, he'd damned well better be. Call Brooks. Call Theonia. Ask her . . . Never mind, just find Max. I'll come in soon, I promise."

She had been over and over every last inch of the house, outside and in. She'd been down on the beach with field glasses, hating to go, dreading what she might find, and mercifully not finding it. But there was one place she hadn't looked—the Vickery house, the one place that had always been taboo to Sarah Kelling. Why hadn't she thought of it before? Because of the taboo, or the unlikelihood of Davy breaking the strictest rule of all—don't cross the road?

Sarah crossed the road at a dead run and plunged into the narrow opening between the brambly bushes.

The driveway had once been paved, but there wasn't much left of the asphalt now, only broken chunks between the deep ruts trucks had cut through the dirt. Untrimmed trees and shrubs crowded in on either side. Would a three-year-old go this far, into this scary place? He'd been nagging her about visiting the balloon lady, but she found it hard to believe he would wantonly disobey her.

She began calling him again. Between calling and running she was fairly out of breath by the time she came out onto a roughly clipped lawn. The old house was like something out of a horror movie. Shingles and clapboards had been ripped off or let fall, rubbishy remains of furniture had been dragged out on the porch and left to rot, providing a sanctuary for rats, mice, bats, squirrels, voles, and other local fauna. A pile of firewood had been dumped haphazardly next to the rotting steps. As for what might once have been a lawn, it was burdocks everywhere: the misleading kind that looked rather handsome on the stalks but fastened themselves in clumps to people's clothes and animals' fur with myriad tiny hooks, and refused to let go.

Sarah took a deep breath and screamed at the top of her lungs, "Davy! Davy, are you there?"

The form that appeared was definitely not that of her son. Didn't the woman have anything to wear except an aeronaut suit and a tatty purple jogging outfit? Sarah wondered hysterically.

"Why, Mrs. Bittersohn," Calpurnia exclaimed. "How kind of you to call. I'm afraid the place isn't looking at its best, but we hope to get it back in shape before long, so perhaps you could come by another time. After I've purchased a teakettle."

"Is my son here?"

"What on earth would he be doing here?"

Sarah was past caring about good manners. "Miss Zickery, you must have heard us calling, not to mention the sirens when the police arrived. My little boy is missing. He was fascinated by your balloon, and I thought he might have come to see it. We've looked everywhere else—"

Her voice broke, but she cleared her throat and went doggedly on. "He might have crept into the house without your seeing him, and fallen asleep. I hope you don't mind my searching the place, because I mean to do it whether you mind or not, and if you don't help me, there are a dozen people just across the road who will."

"Dear me." Calpurnia looked a trifle alarmed. "I certainly don't want a mob of strangers seeing how run-down the poor old place has become. You just wait there, Mrs. Bittersohn, while I have a look around."

Naturally Sarah did nothing of the kind. The splintery porch steps were a hazard in themselves, but she was right on Callie's heels and she was the first to spot the small bundle curled up on a battered chaise longue in the corner of the room. She snatched him up. He was sleeping so soundly he scarcely stirred, but he was warm and breathing and alive. She turned like a mother tiger on Calpurnia Vickery.

"You've had him with you all this time? And you didn't even let me know?"

"I didn't know he was here, Mrs. Bittersohn. We seldom use this room or the front door." Calpurnia looked uneasily over her shoulder. "You'd better go now."

"Yes, of course." Sarah began backing toward the door. She could hardly wait to get out of the horrible room. It was no wonder the Vickerys didn't use it. It smelled like a moldy cellar, cobwebs swathed the walls, and the chaise longue was the only piece of furniture. "I'm sorry. Thank you. I know I must sound insane, but he's our only child, you see, and we love him so much."

She was out in the daylight at last, trying not to stumble on the splintered boards or the broken steps. Then Calpurnia let out a yelp, and Sarah turned to see a figure out of nightmare burst through the door. He was draped in cobwebs like an animated mummy, and his eyes were bulging.

"A kid! A damned kid! I told you, Callie, I don't want any kids around here!"

"No!" This time Calpurnia did the screaming. "Allie, don't do it! They'll catch you this time, I know they will. You'll be shoved in a padded cell and you'll blame it on me. But I'll fight back this time, I've had enough!"

"You've had enough? I warned you, Callie, I won't take this any longer. Get out of here, Mrs. Bittersohn or Kelling or whatever your name is, and take the brat with you."

Sarah was already on her way. She ventured one quick glance over her shoulder and almost fainted when she saw Alister closing in on her. He was brandishing a big chunk of firewood.

Davy had grown during the summer; Sarah forgot that she was too exhausted to carry a kitten, much less a sturdy three-year-old. From somewhere inside her, she found strength enough to keep ahead of the maniac, but it couldn't last. He was closing in, waving the chunk of wood, yelling at her to go away, get out. In a matter of moments, she and Davy would both be dead. Where was Jesse? Where were the others?

Calpurnia's shrieks rose over the breathless curses of her brother. "Don't worry, Mrs. Bittersohn. I'll save you!"

Sarah fled to her own side of the road, still carrying Davy. And there, finally, thank God, was Jesse, coming full tilt down the driveway, with Jem and Egbert puffing along behind him. Sarah's legs and lungs gave way. She dropped to her knees, clutching Davy, and turned her head. There was Allie, standing still, some distance away, and there, across the road was Callie pointing at her brother. Pointing . . . My God, Sarah thought, she's got a gun! Callie fired one shot and then another. Her brother fell to the ground and lay still.

Sarah held the child closer. He was still too sleepy to know what had happened, she thought, and thank heaven for that. Jesse had stopped and was staring at the motionless form on the ground. "Aunt Sarah! You okay? Is Davy . . ."

"Safe," Sarah panted. "He's safe. Thanks to her."

Calpurnia stood over her brother's body, looking down at him. She tucked the pistol into her pocket and turned to Sarah.

"I do apologize for the mess, Mrs. Bittersohn. Since there is no telephone in my house, would you mind phoning the local police to come and get my brother? Here is fifty-five cents to cover the cost of the telephone call."

Sarah had just enough strength left to carry her son up to his bedroom and get him changed into his pajamas. Jesse tried to take him, but Sarah wouldn't let go, so Jesse went off to tell the searchers that they could call off the hunt. Egbert or Jem would have been more than ready to attend to Davy, but Sarah couldn't bear to let him out of her sight and touch, not even for a moment. The sponge bath she gave him roused him, and Sarah almost wept with relief when he demanded food, a story, and the pajamas with tigers on them.

Egbert rushed off to prepare a tray with a small bowl of milk toast, a tangerine already sectioned, a few grapes on their stem, and a couple of graham crackers to feed Davy's playmate the alligator. While he ate, Sarah sat on the side of his bed, stroking his hair and crooning a silly little song about a mouse and a friendly kitten that her first governess had taught her. Sarah couldn't even remember her name; but the simple ditty had stayed with her all this time, almost entirely forgotten but still here when it was needed. Thank God Davy hadn't had time to become aware of what he and his mother had come within a mouse's whisker of experiencing, what that hideous twin brother of Calpurnia Zickery's had tried to do. He could so easily have killed them both with one heavy blow. Instead he'd wound up with his sister's bullets in his head.

Calpurnia had sacrificed her own flesh and blood for a mother and child she'd barely known. She must have loved her brother, though the hysterical accusations she had hurled at him strongly suggested he had a history of bizarre behavior. Clearly she'd been in a state of shock after shooting him, and who could blame her? And how could Sarah Kelling Bittersohn ever repay that odd-looking woman in her grubby purple jogging suit? Sarah fed Davy milk toast from the tip of his spoon until he turned his head away, coaxed him to eat a segment or two of the tangerine and half a grape, and kissed him good night though he was already asleep. She finished what was left of her son's supper and lay down beside him on the lions-and-tigers quilt. There were voices downstairs, people talking, and somebody singing—Uncle Jem, of course. Something was going on; she didn't know what it was and she didn't care. The only thing that mattered was having Davy back.

She didn't mean to go to sleep, but she was worn out with worry and chasing around. When she woke it was dark outside. Sarah sat up and rubbed her eyes. How long had she slept? Not long, she hoped. There were things she had to do. The police would want to talk to her. They'd come and removed the Zickerys dead and alive, she supposed. Had they put Calpurnia in jail? She must tell the police that Calpurnia had saved her and Davy. Jesse must have told them, but he hadn't realized how dire the danger had been. Calpurnia was a heroine, not a murderess.

Davy was sleeping sweetly, breathing normally. His forehead was cool. He was all right. She switched on the nightlight, made sure the window was locked, and borrowed Davy's comb in order to smooth her hair. Her face was pale and her eyes were heavy, but what did she care? She left his door open and went downstairs.

They were all in the kitchen; she could hear them talking in low voices—Ira and Miriam, Jem and Egbert—and surely that was Brooks? He'd rallied around, bless him. Theonia must be there, too. Sarah hoped she'd brought one of her stupendous coffee cakes or a basket of biscuits. She was starved. No wonder, after all that running around and nothing since breakfast except a peanut-butter sandwich. She was about to push open the swinging door when she heard something that froze her in her tracks.

"Should we tell her?"

"We'll have to," Jem said heavily.

Sarah shoved at the door. "It's Max, isn't it? What's happened to him?"

16

"Nothing." Brooks jumped up. "We just can't find him. Come and sit down, Sarah, before you fall down."

"I'm not going to fall down, and I'm not going to faint." Sarah pushed his arm away and took the chair Ira was holding for her. "I am awfully hungry, though. Is there anything to eat?"

When Miriam Rivkin was around there was always something to eat. She'd snatched up a pot of her made-from-scratch minestrone and brought it along, knowing there's nothing like hot soup on a chilly day when people's stomachs are tied in knots. There were popovers left from breakfast, and applesauce, and Theonie's diet-destroying double fudge pecan rum cake. Sarah ate her way steadily through it all without tasting anything. She'd have devoured pickles if that was all there was, since keeping up her strength was the main consideration.

"That telephone call didn't come from Mr. Upthorn, Sarah. He knew nothing about it."

Sarah nodded. "I didn't recognize his secretary's voice. I assumed he must be new, that Miss Wilson had retired."

"Perfectly reasonable," Brooks said. "Max had no reason to suspect anything, either. He never made it to the airport. He wasn't on the plane and his car isn't in the parking lot. The police are looking for it, but . . ."

"Poor Sergeant Jofferty." Sarah put a bite of something in her mouth, chewed, and swallowed. "He must be sick of us and our troubles."

"He's doing everything he can," Brooks assured her. "And Jesse's searching the byways and side roads. We're assuming Max was waylaid somewhere between here and the highway. It wouldn't be easy to intercept him in the middle of a lot of traffic without being noticed."

"It wouldn't be difficult to run him off the road and cause an accident," Sarah said steadily.

"There wasn't an accident," Ira said. "Well, there were several accidents, there always are, but Max wasn't involved in any of them. That was the first thing the police checked."

Miriam cleared her throat. "He hasn't taken it into his head to go off on some job without telling you, has he? You know Max, here today and off to Kamchatka tomorrow."

"He wouldn't do that, not without telling me." A faint hope stirred. "Have you looked for a note and checked the voice mail?"

"We did," Brooks said. "It seemed unlikely, but there

was always a possibility that he'd come across something that had to be followed up without delay. It's still a possibility, Sarah. We may hear from him yet."

Miriam got up and refilled Sarah's soup bowl from the pot simmering on the stove. Sarah shook her head. "No thanks, Miriam, it's a shame to waste your wonderful soup; my taste buds are paralyzed just now."

"You've got to keep your strength up." Miriam's black eyes snapped. "When I get my hands on that brother of mine . . . !"

She looked so like Max that Sarah's hard-won calm almost cracked. "When you get your hands on him you'll hug him to death. Don't pretend you're not worried, and don't bother inventing comforting theories in order to cheer me up. I'm all right. I may crack right down the middle when this is over, but I have to hold myself together now, for Davy's sake and for Max's. I'd love to believe he saw something suspicious and had to follow it up without taking the time to call me, but I can't. He has a car phone, remember?"

They had remembered. They were all hoping she hadn't. Sarah went on, "Then there's the call that was supposed to be from Upthorn. It was a fake, so it must have been meant to lead Max into some sort of trap. Any number of people could have known that Mr. Upthorn was one of our clients. The Artemesia Gentilischi transaction was even featured on television because it was such a peculiar business, and Mr. Upthorn gushed all over the newspapers about how wonderfully clever Max was. Which he was."

Sarah grabbed her napkin and dabbed at her eyes.

"Now, Sarah, don't you go soppy on us," Jem Kelling muttered. "You know better than I do how many close calls Max has had, but he always comes up smiling. Or swearing, if the occasion calls for it."

Presiding at the head of the table in queenly dignity, Theonia brushed a few crumbs from her magnificent bosom. "He's not dead, Sarah. I'd know."

"Do you know where he is? Can you find out?"

Slowly and regretfully Theonia shook her head. "I've tried, dear, and I'll keep trying. Something's blocking me. All I can see is those rubies. Where are they now?"

"Still in the safe," Sarah answered. "Do you think there's some connection?"

"Has to be," Brooks said. "This whole business began with the reappearance of the rubies. The only way one can explain the presence of Jem's burglarious acquaintance is that he was after the jewels. He failed, and now he's safely tucked away in jail, but that doesn't mean the people who hired him have given up. Breaking into this place would be dangerous and almost certainly futile, so they decided to try another tack. I predict we will receive a ransom note offering to return Max in exchange for the parure."

It was the most hopeful theory anyone had yet proposed. "Makes sense," Ira rumbled. His wife nodded vigorously.

Jem poured another martini from the pitcher at his

elbow. "Try to get some sleep, Sarah," he suggested. "We'll hold the fort."

"No, there's something else." Sarah pressed her hands to her aching head. "Calpurnia. What have they done with her? I want to tell Sergeant Jofferty what happened."

"He said he'd take your statement in the morning," Jem assured her. "We all saw what happened. Jesse was first among the foremost, so he had a better view than Egbert and me. It was obvious that she fired in order to save you and Davy, and that's what we told Jofferty. He had to take her in, of course, but there'll be a hearing tomorrow and I'm sure the judge won't set bail too high when he hears the circumstances."

"I don't care how much it is, I'll post it or sign it, or whatever is necessary. Miriam, can you get Uncle Jake to represent her?"

"Sure, honey. We all feel the same. Don't worry, we'll take care of it. Now you just run along upstairs and get some rest. Everything will look better in the morning."

Egbert, the perfect manservant, had been pottering at the sink. Now he turned to Sarah with a glass filled to the brim with a creamy liquid that smelled finely of freshly grated nutmeg.

"Just drink this down, Mrs. Sarah. There's nothing like fresh eggnog to settle the stomach and soothe the nerves. Mr. Jem always sleeps like a baby after one of my eggnogs."

Sarah didn't want the eggnog, but he seemed so anxious to do something for her, and she wouldn't have hurt his feelings for the world. She still couldn't taste anything, so she choked the liquid down to the last drop while Egbert stood over her like an amiable gnome. Theonia rose in all her majesty, black velvet billowing, and put a plump white arm around Sarah. "Come along, dear," she cooed, "I'll tuck you in."

"Excuse me, folks, I want to make a few phone calls." Brooks followed them out.

"I could use an eggnog myself about now," Jem said complacently.

"What did you put in it, Egbert?" Ira asked with a grin.

"Just a little tot of brandy, sir. Well, perhaps more than a little. I made extra for Mr. Jem, and I can easily make more if you and Mrs. Rivkin would care to indulge."

"No thanks." Miriam spoke for them both. "We may as well get home, since there's nothing more we can do tonight. Tell Sarah I'll call first thing in the morning, and you be sure to call us the minute you hear anything, no matter what time it is."

They took themselves off. Jem found himself with a small problem between his glass and its coaster but solved it easily enough by the simple expedient of drinking the glass dry and dropping the coaster on the floor. "Shame to waste the rest of the eggnog," he remarked. "Finish it off, Egbert, why don't you?"

"Well, Mr. Jem, seeing as how you force it on me. One generally associates eggnog with Christmas, but my mother used to give us eggnog sometimes, for medicinal purposes, you know, when she had an egg to spare and the time to mix it. Sometimes we'd get sick on purpose."

"Getting nostalgic, are you, Egbert?"

"Well, sir, one does tend to count one's blessings at times like this. We've got the little chap back safe, and I won't give up on Mr. Max. He's got out of bad scrapes before, and Mr. Brooks's notion about ransom struck me as eminently logical and on the whole eminently encouraging. As for me—well, Mr. Jem, I don't mind admitting it was a lucky break for me when you happened to see me flipping dough in the window of that crummy pizza parlor and recognized your old army buddy fallen on hard times. Jobs were darned tough to get then with so many being turned loose. Would you care for a small dividend?"

"No, you finish it off, old buddy. I don't want to get too healthy."

It was Sarah who found them, still in their clothes, dozing peacefully in the two easy chairs that they'd staked out as their own for the duration of the visit.

"What on earth are you two Champagne Charlies doing down here at six o'clock in the morning?"

"Good God, is that what time it is? I haven't been awake at this hour since the good old days when I stayed up all night." Jem stretched and groaned. "Egbert, why didn't you put me to bed? Why didn't I put you to bed?"

"I haven't the foggiest, Mr. Jem. Maybe we decided to sit here and listen for the telephone. Could that have been it? I'm sorry, Mrs. Sarah, but there hasn't been any news. Yet."

"I know. Brooks was up half the night, too, in Max's office. Why didn't you tell me he and Theonia were staying? I'd have made the bed and tidied the room."

"That's why nobody told you. You do too damned much for too many people." Jem cautiously turned his head, yelped, and groaned. "I knew I shouldn't have had that eggnog, it's left me with a headache. I never get headaches from gin. Where's Davy?"

"Right behind you. Come on, Davy, let's make breakfast for Uncle Egbert and Uncle Jem and you and me."

"I don't want breakfast. I feel funny."

"How funny, dear? Funny in your tummy?"

"I don't know. I just want to go back to bed, and I want Daddy to come. Mummy, you take me?"

"Of course, dear. Shall I carry you up?"

"Daddy carry me."

Davy was trying not to sniffle and not succeeding very well.

Neither was Sarah. She put her hand on Davy's forehead. He didn't feel warm, but who knew what kind of germ he might have picked up in that horrible house. "I tell you what, you can dress up in Daddy's baseball cap and his Red Sox shirt, and you can be Daddy until Big Daddy comes home. Uncle Jem can be you, and Jesse will drive us to Dr. Colly's office, and he'll give us all something to make our tummies feel better."

"You hold me?"

"If you want me to."

"You hold me?" Davy didn't usually ask the same question twice in a row.

"Yes, I could do that. It's really, really early, though, too early for Dr. Colly to be in his office. Perhaps we ought to try eating something soft and squishy and see how it makes our tummies feel."

"Egbert would be glad to fix you something," said Jem.

"Not eggnog," Sarah said, smiling at Egbert. "How about scrambling a few, or soft boiling them?"

Theonia entered, trailing clouds of mauve chiffon and ecru lace, while Sarah was breaking eggs. Gently but firmly she took the bowl away. "Sit down and drink your juice, I'll do that."

"Not in that gorgeous negligee," Sarah protested.

"There's plenty more where that came from," Theonia said not so enigmatically. She'd been remodeling Caroline Kelling's costly, exquisite lingerie for years, with extravagant success, and hadn't exhausted the supply yet. "Does it bother you to see me wearing her things, Sarah?"

"Quite the contrary." Sarah managed a feeble laugh. "I suppose it could be regarded as a form of revenge, couldn't it? She always had the most wonderful clothes, from the skin out, while I went around in my mother's old hand-me-downs or cobbled-together clothes made out of blankets. Being blind, she couldn't see how awful I looked, but she must have known. How she'd swear if she knew some other woman was wearing her precious silk de chine step-ins."

"Especially a woman she'd never let in her house except

to scrub floors," said Theonia with perfect truth and perfect equanimity. Deftly she spooned the creamy golden eggs onto heated plates and distributed them around the table. "Why, my goodness, Davy, why are you looking so glum?"

"Don't want eggs." Davy drooped.

"You'll hurt my feelings if you don't eat them. I'll cry."

Her face puckered up into a grimace as horrifying as Theonia's perfect features were capable of producing. Davy looked impressed. "I can make a worse face than that."

"As soon as you finish your eggs we'll have a contest."

They had the contest, and Davy won. He and Egbert went upstairs so that Davy could help his old friend pick out clean clothes for the day, and the others put their heads together over a last cup of coffee.

"Thanks, Theonia," Sarah said. "He said his tummy felt odd, but he got those eggs down all right. I think I'll take him to see Dr. Colly, though, just to be on the safe side. You should have seen that filthy place! I hope he didn't eat or drink anything. The well is probably polluted."

"Has he told you why he went there?" Theonia tipped another spoonful of sugar in her coffee. She kept her voluptuous contours from becoming too voluptuous by periods of exercise and diet, but this was no time to worry about calories.

"I haven't dared talk to him about it yet. He was exhausted last night, and he really did look a little out of sorts this morning. It could be he's upset about something that happened over there, and if I press him, I might do more damage. I simply cannot for the life of me understand why he would take it into his head to cross the road, which he's been strictly forbidden to do, and sneak into someone else's house, which is also against the rules, and scare me half to death! I could almost be glad Max wasn't here. He'd have been frantic."

She was lying, and she knew it, and she couldn't keep the smile plastered on her face much longer. She excused herself and fled to the deck. Gripping the rail with both hands, she stared out across the colorful drift of chrysanthemums Anne had created.

"Oh, Max," she whispered. "I miss you so much. Where are you, darling? Where are you?"

17

Max knew where he was. Sitting on a bare rock completely surrounded by water, that was where. What he didn't know was where the damned rock was.

Somewhere in the Atlantic Ocean, at a guess. There was no land visible except for a few other rocks. They were just as barren as his, so there didn't seem to be any point in swimming over to them. The coast must be west of him. He knew which way west was, he'd seen the sun rise once or twice, or maybe it was three times. His memory wasn't working too well. He couldn't remember a damned thing between the time he'd left Ireson's Landing and the unpleasant moment when he had found himself over his head in water and sinking fast. He had grown up not far from the ocean and had learned to swim at Revere Beach and along a fair stretch of the North Shore. That skill and his well-developed survival instinct had helped him fight his way to the surface and stay there, sometimes floating, sometimes paddling, until the sun rose and showed land close by.

Some land, Max thought. He'd been almost at the end of his strength when he'd seen it, and it had been a struggle to climb out of the water, even with the help of a handy ledge. At some point during the night he'd lost his shoes. Maybe he'd managed to take them off, though he couldn't remember doing it. Maybe a kindly mermaid had done it for him.

He was still not thinking very straight. The bump on his head might have something to do with that. Max fingered it gingerly. It was an impressive lump, as lumps went, and he wished it would. He wished he would, too. They must be looking for him by now, but how would they know where to look?

Time to think positively, Max told himself. He could have been worse off, though not much. His head was beginning to clear, and flashes of memory were coming back. Some of them had to be hallucinations, like seeing Louie Maltravers bending over him. Louie was in the clink and unlikely to leave the safety of his cell unless he was forcibly evicted. There'd been something about the Fourth of July, too. Fireworks and rockets going off.

One memory was almost certainly accurate—coming back to consciousness to find himself tied hand and foot, with a gummy gag filling his mouth and a blindfold over his eyes. He'd heard voices but couldn't make out what they were talking about. Then there'd been another stab of pain in his aching head; and blackness.

The marks of the ropes still showed on his wrists, so that part hadn't been a bad dream. He couldn't understand why they had freed him before they'd tossed him overboard. Dying of starvation or exposure was just as final as drowning, or being chewed to meatballs by some monster of the deep, but if they'd meant to kill him, why not do a thorough job of it?

Then there was the plastic bag. He'd run across it during his first feeble attempt at dog paddling, and he'd wrestled with it for a while before he'd realized it wasn't a shark or a whale. He'd hung on to it, for no good reason, and he was glad he had. That bag and its contents might save his life.

That and the seaweed. Too bad Max's old scoutmaster wasn't here to join the party. He'd taught Max all he knew about seaweed, which was more than Max had wanted to know at the time, but thank God he had. Food was all around him, even if it wasn't the sort Max Bittersohn or any member of his family would ever have eaten unless there was nothing else available. Just now there wasn't, but there was plenty of seaweed. Those leaflike forms that Max could see drifting in the water at his feet, too close to his feet, were among the most digestible and easily obtainable edibles in the ocean.

Small silvery fish slid through the weeds, but they weren't so easily attainable. Why hadn't his kindly old mentor taught him how to catch fish with his bare hands? Davy wouldn't like it, though, if Davy's father ate the fish instead of sending them home to their mothers and fathers. He'd better stick to seaweed.

Those fantastically long ribbons of kelp must go all the way down to the ocean floor; Max hoped he himself wouldn't follow them. He saw Irish moss, which was good in desserts and many other foods when treated right in the cooking; Sarah always made blanc-mange when she expected Aunt Boadicea to lunch. He saw the dark purple dulse, so full of iodine that inlanders cursed with goiters would have begged their friends and relatives to send it to them as a remedy for the unsightly and sometimes even deadly ailment, back when no other remedy was available. His old Boy Scout leader would know them all, those that were palatable just as they came, others that would have been the better for warming up if a castaway had had anything to put them in or the means of lighting a fire.

He was thinking negative thoughts again. Time to count his blessings, such as they were. Lots of tasty, juicy seaweed, and a plastic bag, and a worn red bathrobe. His bathrobe. He thought he remembered Sarah tucking it into his overnight bag. They'd joked about glamorous lady spies.

Max rubbed his stinging eyes. If they were a little damp, who would know except him? God, he missed Sarah. She must be worried about him. He was worried about her and Davy, too. An unidentified corpse on their property, the inexplicable return of the Kelling rubies, burglars, car thieves—what would happen next? Damn it, he'd find a way of getting off this rock somehow, never mind how he'd gotten there.

The bathrobe had been in his overnight bag. So someone had taken it out of the bag, enclosed it in plastic, and tossed it overboard with him. His memories of the day he'd made landfall were hazy, but he'd had sense enough to spread the robe out to dry in the sun, along with his drenched clothes. He had spread the plastic bag too, so that it lined a hollow in the rock. The makeshift basin had collected enough dew to give him a drink of brackish but salt-free water that morning. The bathrobe had kept him warm the previous night. It was now spread out again, making a colorful focus for any ship, any plane, any hopeful soul in a rowboat on a trip around the world, anything between a kayak and an ocean liner, on which he could thumb a ride home to his wife and family.

It was too bad that there wasn't so much as a piece of driftwood on these rocks. He could have carved his name for posterity on it with the trusty Boy Scout knife his father had given him on his tenth birthday. They, whoever they were, hadn't bothered to take his knife. It wasn't much of a weapon, and with his hands and feet tied he couldn't have gotten at it anyhow. Another blessing, Max thought sourly. At least it might have been if he could catch a fish, which he couldn't.

Back to seaweed. Max collected a handful of kelp and chewed doggedly. All seaweeds were edible, though some of them were too tough to eat raw. At least one kind could be made into excellent pickles, if a castaway happened to have brought a pickling kettle along. He wondered how long it would take to get thoroughly sick and tired of eating seaweed. He was already sick and tired of sitting there with nothing to do. He took a stroll around his domain, six steps one way and five the other. He tried it with shorter steps to make the walk last longer; but that didn't help much.

He tried reciting poetry he'd remembered from his English classes. Unfortunately, the one that came first to mind was the short piece supposedly written by Alexander Selkirk, a marooned Scottish sailor still known as the progenitor of *Robinson Crusoe:*

I am monarch of all I survey,
My right there is none to dispute;
From the center all round to the sea
I am lord of the fowl and the brute.

Oh, solitude, where are they charms
That sages have seen in thy face?
Better dwell in the midst of alarms
Than reign in this horrible place.

"You can say that again, Alexander," Max muttered.

What the hell had happened to all the shipping? Fishing boats with ship-to-shore radios that could put him in touch with his family, a yacht, the *Queen Elizabeth 2,* one of those huge foreign factory ships that would stay in one place for weeks on end while the smaller boats brought in their fish and went back to get more, if they could find more, a Coast Guard vessel, a submarine? He'd been straining his eyes ever since the sun rose without seeing as much as a periscope.

He had no idea what time it was. A pity he hadn't been able to test the guarantees that came with the outlandishly expensive waterproof, shock-proof, everything-proof watch Sarah had given him for his last birthday. It hadn't been on his wrist when he'd finally got around to taking inventory of his remaining possessions. Nothing else was missing except objects that might have fallen out of his pockets while he was being carried or dragged around. Even his billfold was there, tucked into the zippered inner pocket of his jacket. Somebody had deliberately removed the watch, and Max doubted that the thief's motive had been to deprive him of the ability to tell the time. It was more likely that somebody hadn't been able to resist an expensive watch. Somebody like Louie the Locksmith. But Louie was in jail. Wasn't he?

Sitting around watching his mind wander all over the scenery, such as it was, wasn't getting him anywhere. Max stripped to the buff and let himself down into the water very carefully, not knowing what might be lurking there and not wanting to find out the hard way. He was used to his early morning dip in the sea. He swam slowly at first and was pleased to find the exercise was getting the kinks out of his arms and legs. Everything seemed to be working, including the leg he'd damaged. This past summer, he'd been constrained to spend too much time in the hospital or in outpatient therapy. It was heartening to know that he was by now completely healed, though whether he'd be able to enjoy good health for any great length of time would depend very much on matters beyond his control.

He hauled himself out of the water, feeling a lot better and, unfortunately, a lot hungrier. He dried himself on the salt-stiffened remains of his shirt and stared longingly at a bird skimming across the water. It might have been a seagull, or maybe a fulmar. He didn't really care what it was, he just wished it would have a heart attack or a stroke and drop dead in the water close enough to be retrieved.

If he could catch a couple of fishes, he might use them to lure the bird close enough to be caught. But then if he could catch a couple of fishes, he'd have something to eat that wasn't seaweed. Still no sign of a sail. Would he have to spend another night on this godforsaken rock? Would there be other nights, other days?

Of course there would. Lots of days, years and years of days. Mornings together, noontimes together, evenings together, nights together when Davy was at the lake with the Rivkins and Max and Sarah would have the house all to themselves. Maybe there'd be a nice girl like Tracy by the time Davy was off at college. But first there'd be Davy the king of the sandbox, Davy in kindergarten, Davy in a rowboat with his father, Davy winning a soapbox derby, Davy entering college, Davy magna cum laude in his father's cap and gown. Davy everywhere except here, damn it. Maybe he ought to chew another mouthful of kelp, even though he doubted he could bring himself to swallow it.

18

"Mrs. Flingett, this is Sarah Kelling Bittersohn speaking; I'm sorry that Mr. Bittersohn is not available just now."

Exactly how sorry she was brought a tightness to Sarah's throat that made it hard for her to speak. Fortunately or not, depending on a person's point of view, the woman at the other end was quite ready to do all the talking herself and proceeded to do so for the next twenty minutes nonstop while Davy tugged at his mother's sleeve in the hope of getting her attention and went off pouting to Uncle Jem when Sarah couldn't drop the phone and go with him to watch the seagulls smashing clamshells on the rocks.

Dr. Colly had checked Davy over from his pink toes to the top of his curly blond head and had found nothing wrong. "Keep an eye on him for a couple of days," he had advised. "He's sure not his usual rambunctious self. Could be something's worrying him. I wouldn't badger him about running off, though, at least not yet. I don't hold with this business of interrogating kids about their worries until they get so nervous they start inventing stories they think the other person wants to hear. If he's not back to normal in a day or two, give me a call."

Davy had perked up a bit when his buddy Charles C. Charles carried, complete with trench coat and fedora and a Humphrey Bogart accent. Charles was an actor manqué when he wasn't butling for Theonia or tracking down stolen art objects for Max, and he believed in living his roles. He managed to distract Davy long enough for Sarah to give Sergeant Jofferty her version of the shooting of Alister Zickery. Jofferty assured Sarah that Calpurnia seemed quite comfortable in the local lockup. She had a nice clean cell all to herself, and Miriam Rivkin had already stopped by with chicken sandwiches and salad.

"Bless her," Sarah murmured.

"Well, we're all grateful to the lady for coming to your rescue," Jofferty said. "No question but that she'll be out on bail before long. Jake Bittersohn has already made the arrangements and will represent her when the case comes to trial. She's a queer duck, though, isn't she? Asked me to get her some paper and pens on account of she planned to start writing her memoirs."

Sarah finally managed to get Mrs. Flingett to stop talking, reminding her that they'd been on the case for less than a week and that Max had warned her it would be several days before they could get to work on her missing

Modigliani, what with a family wedding coming up and a large backlog of cases. He had added that he couldn't imagine why anybody would want a Modigliani back, though he hadn't said it to Mrs. Flingett.

Sarah wiped her eyes. The hole Max's absence made in the family circle was growing wider every hour. Jesse was out beating the bounds again, knowing it was probably futile but feeling a desperate need to do something, anything but sit still and wait. Brooks and Theonia had gone back to Boston to pursue other lines of inquiry. Sarah would have been doing the same thing, if she had been able to. Instead she was sacrificing herself to a client, to well-meaning relatives, to her child, to whoever had to be placated or comforted or indulged or paid before she could take the time even to brush her teeth, much less help look for Max.

Although Jem and Egbert wouldn't give up the ship, Sarah knew that Jem was hankering for Beacon Hill and the Comrades of the Convivial Codfish, and Egbert for his own little coterie of lady friends with whom he'd carried on a pleasant, tranquil relationship for many years, mostly playing Scrabble, occasionally making a daring foray into mah-jongg. She couldn't expect them to stay much longer; they'd be stricken with nostalgia for the Hill.

"Mummy, wake up."

Somehow or other, Sarah had managed to drop off for a few seconds. "What's the matter, Davy?"

"You took my alligator."

"No, I didn't. Look under your bed."

"You come with me."

"Davy, I'm very tired."

"No. I want my alligator."

"You didn't say 'please.' "

"I don't have to. I'm the man."

"Who told you that?"

"You did."

Sarah couldn't believe she'd ever been fool enough to say such a thing, but there was no point in starting an argument with a three-year-old. She sighed from the bottoms of her sneakers to the top of her sorely aching head. "All right, Davy. I think you left the alligator in his den under my desk this morning. Why don't you look?"

"You look. You have to get down on your tummick."

"No, I don't. I'm the woman. And it's stomach, not tummick."

Pouting, Davy retrieved his toy. Sarah said with false enthusiasm, "Good boy. Now show me how the alligator wiggles."

"I know how the alligator wiggles. He doesn't like you."

"I don't blame him a bit. Alligators don't like boys who don't like their mothers."

"Yes, they do."

"Never mind." Sarah sighed again. "Let's go see the seagulls."

Sarah made sure the answering machine was working and that there'd be room enough to leave a long message in case the miracle happened. Then she took Davy by the hand and went with him to see the seagulls. It was something to do, at any rate.

But Davy wasn't satisfied. These were different seagulls from the ones he'd wanted to play with, and why couldn't Daddy come home so that they could feed the seagulls together? It was a relief when Miriam came by asking for news, even though she knew there wasn't any, and wondering whether Sarah had enough food in the house. She had brought with her a tossed salad and a casserole just in case.

The day wore on. If it hadn't been for Davy, Sarah could have managed, but he wouldn't leave her alone, not for a single minute. Charles's costume changes failed to interest him; Egbert's noble offer to play camel produced only a scowl and a shake of the head; even Jem's offer to sing all forty verses of "Old Jem Kelling" was rejected.

And the telephone never stopped ringing, and the voice on the other end was never the voice she wanted to hear. Uncle Jem was of some help with the phone, he enjoyed chatting even if he didn't know what he was talking about most of the time.

By late afternoon Sarah was tempted to smack Davy's bottom and make him stand in the corner of his bedroom with his face to the wall, the way Great-Aunt Matilda had chastised Cousin Dolph when he was a boy. She didn't approve of that punishment, even though it didn't seem to have hurt Cousin Dolph, and God willing she wouldn't do such a thing to her dearly beloved child. She knew why

Davy was behaving so abominably. He was just old enough to have learned that parents could be manipulated; he was turning his grief at his father's absence into rancor at his mother's failure to get double duty out of every demand he made on her. She'd tried coaxing, she'd tried pretending that he was the father and dressing him up in Max's beachcombing shorts and jersey. She'd tried to make him understand that parents had to go out and work so that little boys could eat. Nothing worked. He'd never behaved like this before, even when Max had been gone for a much longer time. Was he going through one of those stages more experienced parents had warned her about, or did he know, somehow, some way, that this time was different?

Miriam had seen the way things were going at Ireson's Landing. She turned up again around suppertime with a feeble excuse about being alone because Ira had gone off to some kind of wheel greasers' symposium, plunked herself down in the living room, and suggested gently that while she herself was no great drinker, she just might indulge in a small aperitif if anyone else cared to join her.

Jem was always ready to join in an aperitif or possibly two. Between them they persuaded Sarah to have a glass of white wine, and Davy, who was sagging with exhaustion because he had refused to take a nap, snuggled up to his mother on the sofa and fell asleep. Every time Sarah made a move, though, he roused himself in case she might be having any notions about leaving him alone on the couch.

She rested her head against the pillows and let the others do the talking.

"What is it with that kid?" Miriam asked softly. "Is he coming down with something, do you think?"

"No, it's Max. Davy's become so frantic since his father disappeared that he won't even let me take a bath unless I wear my swimsuit so that he'll have something to hang on to. I can't understand why he's behaving this way, Miriam. Max has been gone for long periods before this."

"But you weren't scared stiff about him," Miriam said shrewdly. "A little worried, maybe, as who wouldn't be, knowing he was chasing criminals, but not plain out of your mind the way you are now. No matter how stiff you keep that upper lip, kids sense your feelings. And the rest of us aren't much better."

"Have you told Mother Bittersohn?"

Miriam always seemed to get stuck with the tidings of no great joy. Sarah had felt guilty about accepting her offer to break the news to Max's parents, but she hadn't wanted to talk about it with Davy listening, and he'd been hanging on to his mother's shirttails all day. At least that was her excuse.

Miriam nodded soberly. "I had to, it's going to be on the news tonight. I wasn't crazy about the publicity, but the cops pointed out we couldn't overlook the possibility that someone might have seen him. Poppa agreed, and Momma gave them that picture of Max Brooks took at his birthday party. They wanted to come over or call you,

Sarah, but I told them to leave you alone, that you had enough on your plate without them asking questions you couldn't answer and dumping their worries on you when you've got enough of your own."

Sarah couldn't throw her arms around Miriam without disturbing Davy, so she had to content herself with a pat and a watery smile. "Miriam, you're wonderful. I don't know how to thank you."

"For what? Acting like a person?" Max's sister didn't go in for emotional displays. "Do you think we can risk turning on the TV if we keep the volume down? I'll keep my finger on the off button and use it if Davy so much as stirs."

Sarah could have predicted what the opening sentence of the story would be. "Foul play is feared. . . ." How they love disasters, she thought, glaring at the announcer's studiously grave face. There was a picture of Max standing beside the car and then a close-up of the photograph that was Sarah's favorite. She gazed hungrily at it until tears blurred the ruggedly handsome features and thick dark hair and familiar smile. The story ended with an appeal to viewers to call the police if they had any information.

Miriam switched off. "Better wake that kid up or he'll never go to bed tonight," she said in a matter-of-fact voice. "I'll see what I can scrape up for supper. How many are we expecting?"

"I don't know where Jesse and Charles have got to," Sarah answered. "I suppose they'll be joining us."

"They're patrolling," Jem said. "And if I know those two, praying they run into an intruder. Jesse is armed with a Malay kris he borrowed from Anora, and Charles has my sword stick. I wanted to join the defense, but Egbert wouldn't let me, so I gave Charles the stick. Did I ever tell you about the time I . . ."

Sarah let her uncle ramble on. She didn't bother asking where he'd obtained a sword stick. It was the sort of thing he would have. Or if he didn't, some other Kelling would. Anora Protheroe's husband, George, had collected Oriental art and antiquities, including a few lethal weapons. She was only surprised Jesse hadn't borrowed a morning star or a few poisoned darts.

The news broadcasts had informed all the family members who hadn't already known. The phone started ringing almost at once and never let up. Jem dealt with some of them while Egbert and Miriam performed their usual miracles in the kitchen. After Charles and Jesse had been summoned by Egbert's energetic performance on the penny whistle, Charles took over the phone. His role of a proper English butler, à la Mr. Hudson, was one of his best. Hearing him intone "I really could not say, moddom" got rid of several importunate callers.

Percy Kelling went so far as to telephone, after the rates had gone down. He was, of course, concerned about how this would reflect on the family, especially the family finances. Between trying to coax a few bites into Davy and taking a few herself, Sarah let him know in the circuitous way Percy favored that this was not a propitious time for family chats. They'd be in touch with Percy and/or Anne as soon as they had any definite information.

"Interfering old ice cube," Jem grumbled.

"No, Uncle Jem, I think he was really concerned. He said if there was anything he and Anne could do, anything, anytime, just let them know. He even asked if I needed money!"

"That's an offer I never expected to hear from Percy," Jem admitted. "He's not so bad, I guess, except for being so damned honest. Did I ever tell you about the quarter?"

"Yes," Sarah said. "Davy, just one more bite of Aunt Mimi's wonderful casserole."

"Miriam hasn't heard it, though," Jem said triumphantly.

Only once in his whole career as a certified public accountant had Percy run into a situation that might have left a black spot on the name of Kelling, Kelling, and Kelling. It was a matter of twenty-five cents. Percy had gone over the books—big old ledgers back then, not computers—over and over and over again. He had forgone the supper that he didn't feel he deserved, he'd racked his brain, he'd gone back in the ledgers as far as he could go. Finally he'd collapsed from overwork and inanition and slept facedown on the ledgers until his father came in punctually at half-past five A.M. Trembling with weakness and the odium of failure, he'd confessed his ineptitude.

His father had taken one look at Percy's careworn face

and stooped over. "Here," he'd said, handing his son the shiny silver twenty-five-cent piece that had rolled under Percy's desk. "Go buy yourself some breakfast. And next time, make damned good and sure that you know what you're looking at."

Jesse's expression showed what he thought of that sterling example of rectitude. "If he was determined to be that honest, why didn't he just contribute a quarter of his own?"

"Your generation doesn't understand these things," Jem retorted.

"Darn right." Jesse always watched his language when Davy was around. "I haven't got time to set you straight, Uncle Jem. What do you say we go back on duty, Charles?"

"You aren't going to stay out there all night, I hope," Sarah exclaimed.

"They're just trying to get out of helping with the dishes." Miriam had begun clearing the table.

"A vile canard, moddom, if I may say so," Charles said. "We will tidy up in our usual efficient fashion before we return to our posts. Would you like me or Jesse to drive you home?"

"No thanks, Charles, I think I can make it, even though it's all of five miles. I'll be on my way, then, Sarah, unless you'll let me put Davy to bed. He's asleep on your lap."

"I'll carry him, he's too heavy for Sarah." Jesse scooped the boy up. Davy roused long enough to demand his mama but accepted Sarah's assurance that she would be up soon and would stay with him all night.

Egbert insisted on escorting Miriam to her car. Leaving Charles to swathe himself in a ruffled print apron before tackling the cleanup, Sarah went to the living room and called the Tulip Street house.

"I tried to telephone earlier, but the house line has been busy all evening," Brooks said. "No, Sarah dear, I'm sorry; there's nothing new about Max, but Theonia wants to speak with you."

Theonia knew what Sarah wanted before she spoke.

"Yes, dear, I've been trying. Have you?"

"What, tea leaves or tarot cards? I don't have your talent, Theonia."

"You have something else going for you, Sarah. It doesn't need props, and it's stronger than any poor talent I might have. Don't worry, it's going to be all right. Go to bed, go to sleep, and dream about Max."

Jem had the same idea. "Come on, Sarah, you need your rest."

"All right, Uncle Jem, I'll be a good little niece and toddle upstairs to my beddy-bye the minute the Sandman shows up with his pail and shovel. What was it you used to say when we children were crammed into cots at the old summer place? Good night, sleep tight, don't let the bedbugs bite."

Jem produced a chuckle. "I'd forgotten about that. It

was just a moronic snatch of doggerel I picked up in the army."

Jem looked a bit moist about the eyes. He kissed her on the forehead and made a quick exit. "You know where to find me if you want me. Just holler."

I wish I could holler for Max, Sarah thought. Where in God's name could he be?

19

Another beautiful morning in a less than beautiful spot. Max greeted the dawn with a growl. He hated to wake up. There was nothing to wake up for, and he'd been having wonderful dreams. Sarah had seemed so real; he'd heard her voice as clearly as if she were standing next to him, seen her so distinctly that he felt as if he could reach up and touch her.

If he hoped to see her again, and he did, he'd better be up and doing. Doing what? For starters, there was breakfast. A scant cupful of brackish water in the plastic cup and a nice cud of seaweed. What should it be this morning, Irish moss or kelp or maybe a tasty morsel of laver?

Bare rock didn't make for a comfortable bed. He'd wrapped the good old red bathrobe around him, over his wrinkled filthy clothes. It provided an extra layer of warmth, but not much padding.

After he'd slurped up the water he shed the bathrobe and

spread it out on the highest point of his estate, anchoring it with a few pieces of rock. A swim would get the kinks out, but why rush it, when it might be his sole means of entertainment for the day? He perched on the ledge and stared out across the water.

So far he hadn't seen any living creature except those daintily streamlined shiners that kept darting in and out among the seaweeds and the big birds overhead, such as the fulmars and the albatrosses. These appeared to be pelagic, however, scorning to rest on his ridiculous apology for an island. For all he knew, there might be seals or walruses or sea lions or hippogriffs or heffalumps on other, larger islands. The briny Atlantic was teeming with aquatic mammals and other wonders of the deep; but so far they hadn't come to call, and who could blame them? He wouldn't be here either if he could help it.

A nice, fat seal or walrus would really hit the spot about now. If he couldn't get a walrus, he'd settle for almost anything edible that wasn't seaweed, even if he had to skin the creature himself.

It was strange how a man who'd always thought of himself, when he did think of himself, as being at least partly civilized could turn into a ravening caveman once the provisions ran low. How long had it been, Max wondered, since he'd carved a roast turkey or barbecued a beefsteak? He'd never been any great meat eater until now, when he wanted it so desperately and saw no way of getting some.

Resignedly he scooped up a handful of seaweed and began chewing.

Perhaps an Eskimo would come along in a kayak full of whale meat and give him some, or a Lorelei would stop long enough to sing him a few lieder before swishing her tail and waving him a cheery "auf Wiedersehen" on her way to the Rhine. He wondered vaguely how much seaweed a person had to eat before it added up to the normal number of calories required by a normal-size adult male, even one whose sole exercise consisted of swimming around and around a rock. A bushel? A pickup truck full? What the hell, it would keep him alive. He wanted to stay alive, for Sarah's sake as well as his own. What was going on at Ireson's Landing? Had there been any responses to the inquiries he and Brooks had set afoot before he was snatched?

That would be one way of passing the time—thinking about the case. He felt hollow and a little light-headed still, but his headache was gone and his brain seemed to be functioning a trifle better than it had the previous day.

The Kelling rubies. That was where it had started. The last time he'd seen or heard of them, they had been in the possession of the lady in Amsterdam. They were Sarah's by rights, nobody denied that except the lady in Amsterdam. She claimed she'd acted in good faith when she paid over a large sum of money to a man who said he was the owner, and who could prove her wrong? Max couldn't prove it, though he had his doubts. Mevrouw Vanderwoude was the only buyer who had managed to hang on to the originals, instead of letting Harry Lackridge substitute a copy. That suggested she'd had her doubts about Harry, or she wouldn't have taken precautions. In any case, she had been informed, by Max himself, that Lackridge had no right to sell the jewels, even if they had been given to him by Caroline Kelling, Sarah's loathed aunt and mother-in-law. Caroline hadn't the right to sell them, either, only to wear them while she lived.

But Sarah refused to go to court over the damned things. She detested them, she didn't want them, they had been bought and paid for. That had been all right with Max. He didn't want the damned things, either. There was no insurance company involved, and the last actual owner, Sarah's husband, Alexander, had left no direct descendants, so the decision was Sarah's.

Mevrouw Vanderwoude had also had no living heirs. Was it possible that she had had a belated attack of conscience and decided that the stolen rubies should be returned to their rightful owner when she was finished with them? That would explain why the parure hadn't been sold with the rest of her jewelry and why it had not been mentioned in her will. She could have made provisions before she died to restore the parure to Sarah, by means of a letter to her lawyers.

Another possibility was that someone had stolen the parure from her. Max doubted that. The lady wouldn't have taken a theft meekly, she'd have reported it to her insurance company and raised hell with the police, maybe even hired

Max Bittersohn to get her property back. Which she hadn't. So, no theft.

Max was beginning to feel a bit pleased with his brilliant reasoning. He reached automatically for another chunk of kelp. All right, let's say it was an agent of Mevrouw Vanderwoude's who returned the jewels. Never mind why she'd chosen a somewhat unorthodox method. People did strange things, as anyone related to the Kellings ought to know. Louie couldn't have been the agent in question. For one thing, nobody with an IQ over thirty would trust Louie to return an object of value. The minute he got his hands on it he'd head for the nearest hock shop or some country that didn't allow extradition.

For another thing, if Louie had been the benevolent Santa, he'd have admitted it when he was cornered instead of risking a charge of assault. And he wouldn't have been hanging around, or under, after the job was done.

So that meant two people or groups of people, one returning the gems, the other trying to steal them back. The unidentified corpse under the tent might have belonged to one of the gangs, or he might have been an innocent bystander who happened to see something he oughtn't have seen.

Max was chewing savagely. He was imagining he was chomping on someone's jugular. Louie. Louie was the key; Louie knew more than he had admitted, and if—no, when—Max got home he was going to get the truth out of the evasive old idiot if he had to borrow Egbert's rubber hose.

That was another thing to look forward to. Looking up, Max realized that the sun was high in the sky. How quickly time passed when a man was enjoying himself, munching seaweed and thinking good thoughts about beating a guy up. The air was pleasantly warm. Time for a swim.

Since there was nobody around but the fulgars, he stripped and spread his clothes out along the rocky spine of the island. He was a fastidious man, when circumstances allowed, and he was beginning to develop a strong loathing for those clothes. If—when!—he got home he'd burn them or bury them. Maybe baking them in the sun would help fumigate them.

Since he didn't know enough about the fickle tides and currents, Max didn't think it prudent to get too far from the rock that had become his by right of discovery. Maybe he could name it after Davy and plant a flag. The faithful old red robe would look fine, if only he had something to use as a flagpole. Swimming around in circles was pretty boring, but the exercise was doing him good.

After a while he noticed something interesting. The fish were swimming faster and more awkwardly, as if they'd lost their way and didn't know how to get back into their normally graceful patterns. Could the unusual behavior of these shoals of fish portend the onset of a storm? He'd really be in trouble if that happened. A supply of fresh water would taste good, but it would soak his clothes and leave him liable to hypothermia if the weather turned cold. He flipped over onto his back and looked uneasily at the sky. Still blue, still cloudless. All the same, it might be advisable to get closer to the rock.

Hanging on to the ledge, he noticed that the turbulence was increasing and the fish were swimming faster. There was a strange noise. Max pulled himself out of the water and scrambled higher up the rocks, straining his neck for a better look at whatever might be there. His hand slipped and he almost fell off the rock.

Could what he was seeing be real, or had he gone irretrievably bats? Was there or was there not a perky little yellow seaplane bobbing gently up and down; and an oddly assembled but demonstrably functional and astonishingly familiar person standing on the wing?

Heedless of the minor circumstance that he hadn't a stitch on his body except for a couple of scars he'd acquired on the football field in his more visibly athletic days, Max yelled and jumped and flailed his arms like a monkey on a stick.

"Tweeters! Hey, Tweeters? It's Max."

"I see you, Max," was the reply. "Of course it's you. Who else would it be?"

"Don't ask me, I'm a stranger here myself. Are you sure I'm not hallucinating again?"

"I don't know what other hallucinations you may have had, but I'm not one of them. How are you?"

"All the better for seeing you, my dear. Was it the Wolf

of Little Red Riding Hood who said that? Stay put, Tweeters; I'll swim over to you."

"Oh dear, no. Stay where you are and put your pants on; you know what a prude I am. I'll taxi right up to your mooring."

Max was mildly amused. "What mooring? I've been over every millimeter of this rock and haven't found one yet."

Suddenly it was Christmas and Easter and Groundhog Day and April Fool's Day and Halloween all together. Tweeters Arbuthnot generally felt more at ease among his feathered friends, but he did make exceptions for a few tried and trusted humans. At boarding school he'd met a chap named Brooks Kelling, who hadn't minded being seen with a fellow student who had a neck like a crane's, a nose like a pelican's beak, and a voice like a booming bittern. They shared a passion for birds, which neither had lost, though in recent years Brooks had been somewhat distracted by a female of a nonavian species.

Recently Tweeters had found another interest, in the person of Sarah's aunt Emma. Thus far Emma had been more amused than impressed by Tweeters's advances, such as they were, but where there was life there was hope, as Tweeters had been heard to say. His seaplane was not for joyriding, but for serious birding. He was built much like a rednecked grebe—the description had come from Brooks—but to Max he looked exactly like an angel. And Max had nothing to offer him but seaweed.

Tweeters hadn't exaggerated his skill as a pilot. He edged

the plane so close to the ledge on which Max was perched that all Max had to do was lower himself onto the wing and crawl along it to the cockpit. He felt like kissing Tweeters but refrained for fear of frightening the timid creature, and also because he hoped to be kissing someone considerably better before much longer.

"How did you find me, Tweeters?"

"Good question, Max. I've been buzzing around these waters like a diving petrel trying to catch up with a wandering albatross. Theonia had one of those flashes of hers, or maybe it was Sarah who had it, something about a quantity of water and a rock shaped like Gibraltar; they've both been pretty worried about you. The rest of us, too, of course. It was a spot of red that finally caught my eye. That's not a color one finds out here, the scenery runs more to blues and greens and browns. Oh, Theonia mentioned that she'd put a lunch basket in the back. She thought you must surely be ready for a change of cuisine by now."

Max's mouth watered. "She didn't happen to include a thermos of black coffee, by any chance?"

"There's one in the hamper behind you. And sandwiches and various other odds and ends, including one of her chocolate tortes. What have you been eating all this time?"

"Seaweed. That's what gets eaten out here. Forgive my bad manners, I ought to have offered you some."

Max was feeling a little light-headed. Tweeters gave him a sidelong look. "I believe Theonia mentioned that the roast beef sandwiches are marked on the wrappings with a big red B. The turkey has a T, and the ham, well, you get the drift. I don't know what else she put in, but it's bound to be good."

"First I have to get in touch with Sarah. She must be as frantic about me as I am about her. You wouldn't happen to have some kind of telephone on board, would you?"

"Certainly. Radio, too, of course, that's standard equipment, but these cordless phones are marvelously handy, aren't they? When they work, that is. What's your home telephone number, Max? Or can't you remember?"

"I'm not at my best right now, but we've got so damned many phones I ought to remember one of the numbers."

Max fiddled with the buttons, got a wrong number, grunted, "Probably a mermaid's," and finally managed to make a connection with the green phone in his office at Ireson's Landing.

Nobody was at home except the answering machine. Max tried the carriage house, then the Boston office, and finally the Tulip Street house. Where the hell could they all have gone?

Looking for him, maybe. Nice of them. Poor Sarah, she must be out of her mind. He wasn't sure he was entirely in his mind.

At last he managed to catch Mariposa, the supremely capable queen of the kitchen of the Boston house, who moonlighted as one of his operatives. When she heard his voice she let out a shriek that half deafened him, then buried him under a spate of Spanish, before she switched over to plain American.

"How come you stayed away so long without tellin' nobody?"

"Because I had no way to get home. How long was I gone?"

"Come on, Max, don't get funny. We ain't in the mood."

"Mariposa, I am not trying to be funny. I'm trying to get home."

"Where are you?"

"With Tweeters Arbuthnot in his seaplane. Don't ask me how he found me, because I'm not too clear on that myself. I don't even know how long I've been away, but it's been too damned long, I can tell you that."

"It sure has. We were pretty scared, Max."

"Me too, Mariposa. Is Sarah all right? I tried to reach her, but nobody's home. When did you and Charles get back?"

"Never mind that now, we'll make our report when we see you, an' it sure better be soon. I'm gonna shut up now so you can keep callin' Sarah. Davy's wound up tight as a torero's pant legs, an' howlin' for his daddy. It's been rough around here, I can tell you. *¡Hasta la vista!*"

"And the same to you, Mariposa." Max took another sandwich and refilled his coffee cup.

"Ah, sweet mystery of life, at least I've found thee! I wish I had a razor so I could get rid of this bush. Mariposa said

Davy's been raising hell because I wasn't around. He wouldn't even recognize me the way I look now."

"Yes, that is a point to consider," Tweeters conceded. "Not knowing much about children, I tend to steer clear of them wherever possible, unless they're seriously interested in the Ciconiiformes. You did mention something during the summer about your son's interest in the herons and bitterns. Three years is hardly a ripe age for a bird lover, but it shows a definite bias toward the proper side, wouldn't you say? Of course you know the young man far better than I."

"I hope you get to know him better, Tweeters. I think you two would get on, and you certainly could teach him a lot." Max scowled at the hand wrapped around the cup. It was scraped and roughened from gripping the unforgiving rocks. He rubbed his knuckles against his cheeks and winced.

"I must look like something that came up out of a swamp. My kid will be wondering what kind of animal his mother's let into the house."

"Oh, if that's what's worrying you, I always carry a fitted shaving kit that one of my cousins gave me. It's a bit la-di-da, but it does come in handy every now and then. Look in that overhead net. There might even be a clean sweatshirt that would fit you. I buy mine a size too large in the vain hope that they won't make me look like the scarecrow from Oz. Not that it ever works. Take the dark blue one with the seahorse on it. Not precisely the style you'd have chosen, perhaps, but needs must, as the old saying goes."

Max didn't care what the shirt looked like. At least it would be clean and dry. For a man who'd been spending more time in the water than out, the warm fabric felt heavenly when he put it on. Sharing a seat with the spider-legged Tweeters was agony for a man as tall as Max, and the way the plane was bouncing around was an added attraction he could easily have done without; but it was a hell of a lot better than the rock.

After he'd finished massaging his jaw with Tweeters's razor, he reached for the phone. "Tweeters, would you mind if I tried again to get through to Sarah? We still have at least an hour's cruising time, haven't we?"

"Yes, we do, and of course I don't mind, go right ahead. I'm sure the wires have been burning with the news, if that is the phrase, but she will no doubt be anxious to hear your voice. While you're talking you just might watch what I do, in case you have to set us down. Not that you will, but I always mention it just so you won't find the trip too dull."

"You're the perfect host, Tweeters. Don't I even get a Mickey Mouse life preserver?"

"Sorry, I'm fresh out of them. But you're a good swimmer, I'm told. Or we could always keep a lookout for a friendly dolphin to give us a piggyback ride. Now look, I'll show you which button to push. This is the one that works, usually."

"That's okay, I know how to operate telephones. Just so I don't have to fly the damned plane or argue with a dolphin. Where the hell could she be? I hope to God nothing has happened. I can't wait to see her."

"I expect you and she will have more time together from now on, won't you?"

Like other shy bachelors, Tweeters had only vague notions about the things that happened in families where the fathers and mothers didn't seem to mind talking with the children. His own childhood memories had been mostly of birdwatching while his tutor exchanged genialities with a young woman who was supposed to be teaching him French. He was extremely well informed about the mating habits of various birds, however, and when Max said, "Sarah? Darling, is that you?" he looked straight ahead and pretended not to listen.

20

Above all other things, Max hoped he'd be able to have a few minutes alone with Sarah before the celebration began. It was unthinkable that there wouldn't be one. Once Sarah calmed down she told him Miriam had started baking a welcome home cake as soon as the word had come via Tweeters and his seagoing telephone that the lost had been found. "She's arranged something for this evening if we're not all too worn out," Sarah had added.

What could Max say except that that would be fine? He was devoted to his family and his loyal cohorts, and a surprising number of Sarah's Kelling relatives had turned out to be more agreeable than they'd first appeared; but at that moment he wished they'd all go away and stay away until he'd had time to show Sarah how glad he was to be back. How many of them would be there? Were Jem and Egbert still at the Landing, or had the call of Beacon Hill been more than the two old men could withstand? Presumably

Jesse and Brooks and Charles and Theonia were around, and Ira, and Lord knew who else. Sarah didn't have the gumption to say no to any of them. Max sighed and fingered his unevenly barbered chin. Maybe he could faint or something, as a gentle hint. No, that wouldn't work. They'd all pounce on him and put him to bed and hang over him, and Miriam would feed him soup.

From then on, Max was too keyed up to do anything except dither and keep his eyes glued to the tiny circular window. Tweeters didn't seem to mind; he was so used to being alone in the cockpit that it was no hardship for him to fall into the silence with Max.

There were still one sandwich and a few ginger cookies in the basket; Tweeters offered them to Max as a good host should, but Max shook his head.

"You have it. I'm too . . . oh, hell. You know."

Being a bachelor, Tweeters probably did not know; but neither did he refuse food at any time, in any quantity or any place. If he didn't eat it himself, which was unlikely, there would surely be a customer among the puffins, the kittiwakes, or some other avian friends. He whiled away the last leg of the ride caroling "Let's all sing like the albatross sings . . ." It was doubtful whether Max heard a single note of the serenade, which was just as well since Tweeters did sound a lot like an albatross.

The welcoming committee was even bigger than Max had anticipated, but they had the decency to stand back while Max extricated himself slowly and painfully from his cramped quarters and limped into Sarah's outstretched arms. Tweeters leaped out on the landing deck and diverted Davy by showing him how to feed the last of the sandwiches to a flock of visiting terns. There was no holding him for long, though, and after a far too short interval the whole crowd converged on the wanderer and bore him in triumph to his chariot. They all piled into various other vehicles and formed a parade all the way to Ireson's Landing, horns tooting and banners flying.

Packed in the backseat of the Thunderbird, with one arm around his wife and the other around his son, Max didn't even bother fending off Davy's hugs. "All right, son, simmer down. Give me a big kiss and I'll tell you about the fish that swam around the rock."

"Why did they swim around the rock, Daddy?"

"Well, mainly because there was no place else for them to go. There wasn't much of a place for me to go, either. I had to just keep swimming around and around and around a big rock that had all kinds of seaweed stuck to it. And that's what I had to eat, all the time I was there. I was out in the middle of the ocean—well, maybe not quite the middle, but pretty far out, and there was nobody there but me, and that's what I did, and I hope I never have to do it again. I don't even want to take a bath in more than three inches of water."

"You mean you were out there all by your only self?" demanded Davy.

He looked so worried, Max tried to think of something

cheerful. "Oh, no. There were a lot of nice little fishes swimming in and out of the seaweed."

"Did you catch any? You could have played with them."

"They didn't want to play," Max said regretfully. By the time Tweeter came he could have eaten one of the nice little fishes raw. "And there were birds. Some of them were seagulls, but the others didn't have the decency to introduce themselves. You'll have to ask our friend Tweeter to tell you about them. He knows everything about birds."

When they reached the house Jed Lomax and Mrs. Blufert were waiting. Finally Max excused himself to wash off some of the encrusted salt and find clothes that had been worn less than three days. He'd hoped Sarah would come and help him, which she appeared more than willing to do. Fortunately or unfortunately, Davy was determined to help, too. So Max cut his shower shorter than he'd have liked and changed into slacks and a shirt and joined the rest of the crowd on the deck, with Davy clinging to his hand.

Egbert mixed the drinks, and Charles served them, and Miriam had made enough hot canapés for an army. Max bit into a delectable concoction involving horseradish and a sliver of roast beef and wondered if the past few days had been only a horrible dream.

"So talk, little brother," Miriam said, putting a platter of cheese puffs on the table. "This is probably the only time in your life you won't be interrupted every five seconds, so make the most of it. What happened?"

"I don't remember. Logic, and the bump on my head,

strongly suggests that persons unknown knocked me out shortly after I left here, tied me up and dumped me into a boat, took me out some distance from shore, and then tossed me out of the boat into the ocean. For reasons that still elude me, they untied me before they dropped me over the side of the boat, so I managed to keep afloat until it dawned on me that I was close to a big rock, which was the only thing I could see except water. I climbed onto it, and then I guess I must have passed out. A few hours or days later I noticed that the stuff clinging to the rocks was seaweed. I happened to remember from my Boy Scout days that seaweed is not only edible, but just about the most vitamin-filled food there is. And that's what I lived on, from the time I opened my eyes and realized what I was seeing until sometime this morning when Tweeters showed up in his seaplane."

Miriam was looking a bit green around the gills. "How ghastly, Max. Now, Mama, don't cry, he's back safe and everything's all right."

"Seaweed!" Mother Bittersohn groaned. "Oh, Max, my poor boy! Is that all you had to eat? You must be starved. Miriam, go make him a sandwich."

Max grinned at her. "It could have been worse, Mama. If I hadn't happened to remember my old scoutmaster, who used to take us down on the beach at Revere and give us lectures on what to eat and what to leave alone, I could have starved to death out of sheer ignorance."

"You wouldn't have starved in three days," said his sister

practically. "What would you like to eat tonight? Not fish, I don't suppose."

"I never managed to catch any, but I have to admit dreams of roast beef danced in my head."

"Then I'd better go and see how soon it will be ready." She gave him a pat on the head as she passed him. So did Theonia.

"I'll help," she cooed. "Max, it sure is good to have you back."

"It's good to be back." Max shaded his eyes with his hand. "Who the hell is that coming up the drive? Not another distant relative with a belated wedding present?"

"Oh, my goodness," Sarah gasped. "They must have let her out. I suppose she's coming to thank us, or—"

"The Zickery woman." Calpurnia was still some distance away, but Max's vision was twenty-twenty. "Let her out of where? The Massachusetts State Home for the Bewildered?"

"No, not exactly. Max, dear, we have something of a situation."

"So what else is new? Care to tell me about it?"

"I'd better, before she gets here." Sarah glanced at Davy and lowered her voice. "What happened was that our friend here took it into his head to go visit the neighbors without mentioning his intentions to anyone. We searched for hours before it occurred to me to look for him there. He'd fallen asleep in the front room, unbeknownst to his hostess. I picked him up and started back, and then . . .

well, then Alister ran after us with a club, shouting curses, and heaven only knows what would have happened if his sister hadn't pulled a cute little pistol out of that baggy jumpsuit she'd been wearing all week and put two bullets into her brother's head, neat as a pin."

"You mean she just walked up to him and bang bang?" Max managed to get his breath back. "And he tried to—"

"Hush, she'll hear you. I'm sorry to spring it on you like this, darling, I was going to break it more gently."

"Jesus," Max muttered. "Gently, she says! Davy, will you do a big favor for your starving dad? Go ask Aunt Mimi for, uh, some cheese and crackers, and maybe a few cookies for the waiter."

That got Davy out of the way. Sarah was not used to having a near neighbor who was a murderess in some degree, if not the first. She did the best she could on such short notice.

"It's nice to see you, Miss Zickery. Lovely evening, isn't it? The sunset over the water is, uh, lovely."

"Which probably augurs a wet day tomorrow." Calpurnia settled herself firmly in the chair Miriam had left. She was wearing a rather smart jumpsuit, dark gray piped in red, and she'd had her hair styled. She turned a curious stare on Max. "So you're back, I see. If you don't mind my saying so, Mr. Bittersohn, it was most inconsiderate of you to leave your wife and child unprotected. If it hadn't been for me, Alister would have done them in. Where is the dear little fellow?"

"With his aunt," Max said. "I'm glad to have a chance to thank you, Miss Zickery. I assure you my absence was, as they say, involuntary."

"You mean somebody kidnapped you? How odd. I wonder if it could have been Allie."

"Is he—was he—in the habit of kidnapping people?"

"No, not really. He was rather in the habit of hitting them over the head, but once he'd done it he usually just let them lie where they fell. He really was a nasty piece of work. Now that he's gone I can start enjoying myself. Perhaps you could suggest the name of a good electrician."

Accustomed as he was to the Kelling clan, Max usually had no difficulty following eccentric conversations, but he wasn't at his best. "Why do you want an electrician?"

"And a plumber and a builder. I'm going to fix the old place up. It will be so nice having you all as neighbors."

"Very nice," Sarah said hollowly.

"I must be running along," Callie announced, reaching for the last of the cheese puffs. "So much to do, and finally the money to do it with. I expect I'll see you in court, Mrs. Bittersohn, if not before."

"How can she stay there?" Sarah demanded as the convivial murderess jogged briskly away. "The place is a wreck. It would probably cost less to tear the house down and start all over again."

"Sounds as if she's expecting to come into an inheritance," Jem said. "Hmmm. Have you ever heard of Plato Zickery?"

"No, I can't say I have. Enlighten me."

"Happy to." Jem refilled his glass. "Plato was a miner who struck it big in the Gold Rush of 1849 and spent the rest of his life dinning it into his sons that they'd better hang on to their money because there wouldn't be any more where that came from. Needless to say, that was not the case. My great-aunt Cerissa either married Plato or didn't, I forget which."

"You never mentioned that," Sarah said.

"No, it slipped my mind. Things do. What the hell, I can't keep track of everything. But as I recall, the Zickerys each owned his or her personal bank, and every one of them was too mean to spend a nickel that they didn't have to. It wasn't until the great-grandchildren began flocking around with hope in their hearts and greed in their eyes that some of the older generation figured it was time to loosen the purse strings a little. Once they got in the habit they couldn't stop. Old Plato's legacy was gone when they used to come here for the summer, or so people said, but maybe one branch of the family managed to hang on to part of it. I can find out if you want me to."

If it was anything about money, Jem got it right, but Sarah shook her head. "It's nothing to do with us, Uncle Jem. I hope the poor thing has enough to enjoy herself with, that's all. She must have led a horrible life with Alister, never knowing when he was going to attack someone."

Brooks had been fidgeting, in his controlled way. Max

was beginning to sag, but he knew his right-hand man well. "What's up, Brooks? Something on your mind?"

Brooks hesitated. "It can wait till later. I think I hear Miriam calling us to dinner."

The food was superb, as it had to be with Miriam and Theonia cooking and Egbert helping. Davy behaved like a dream. All he'd wanted was his father back, and now he had him. He didn't even object to going to bed so long as it was Max who put him there, so Max tucked him in and told him a story about the little fishes swimming in the kelp and stroked his curly head until he fell asleep. Max would have given his eyeteeth to follow his son's example, but duty called. He dragged himself back down the stairs to join the party.

They were still gathered around the big table in the kitchen, and it looked as if the celebration was in full swing. Max fixed his smile back in place, straightened his shoulders, and prepared to be a jolly good fellow for God alone knew how many more hours.

Sarah came to meet him and took his arm. "Excuse me, everyone. May I just say a few words?"

The tumult and the shouting died. Smiling faces looked expectantly at her.

"I love you all," Sarah said. "And so far as I'm concerned you can sit here and celebrate till the dawn comes up like thunder, or however it comes. If any of you want to stay the night, you know where to find sheets and towels and anything else you may need. We will see you in the morning. Late morning. Good night."

A hearty cheer, led by the unmistakable voice of Jem Kelling, followed them as they left the room.

21

Max could be almost preternaturally clever when it came to making coffee, sectioning grapefruit, and finding the bag of muffins that Sarah had brought home from the new bakery down near the Landing; but he had never yet been able to grasp the method by which a person of reasonable faculties and attainments could go about extracting the inside of a raw egg from the outside without making an ungodly mess.

Such a foray into farmyard matters must surely require iron nerve and careful treatment, which it was not going to get from Max Bittersohn. Not this morning.

He had waked up at dawn and found himself snuggled into bed with a beautiful women who happened by a felicitous coincidence to be his wife. It seemed a pity not to take advantage of the coincidence, and he was pleased to find that Sarah was of the same opinion. The next time he woke she looked so tired and so beautiful, he decided to surprise her by getting breakfast. He felt wonderful. He felt capable of anything. Except breaking eggs.

They were in the refrigerator, neatly arrayed in their individual cardboard coops. Max brooded over the eggs for a while, put them back in the refrigerator, made coffee, found the muffins, ate one, and was about to make it two when Sarah appeared in a ravishing garment of blue-and-white gingham with approximately twenty yards of ruffles around the edges.

"Goodness, Max, how can you make such a mess just standing in the middle of the floor?"

"It isn't easy, but I'm a man of many talents, in case you haven't noticed."

"What are you grinning about?" Sarah asked suspiciously.

"If you don't know, you weren't paying attention last night."

The mating call of the ruffled grouse echoed along the hall. It was answered by the seductive response of the female grouse. Brooks and Tweeters had met on the stairs. When the birders came in Sarah was breaking eggs and Max was busy with the coffeemaker, since he'd drunk the first batch.

"Ah," Brooks said. "You're alone."

"We were," Max said.

Brooks tactfully pretended not to notice Sarah's pink cheeks. "Well, once this business is settled we'll all leave you in peace."

Sarah turned, the egg whisk in her hand. "Oh, Brooks, dear, Max didn't mean—"

"Yes, he did." Brooks and Max exchanged man-to-man smiles.

"Mean what?" Tweeters asked.

"Never mind, Tweeters." Sarah patted him on the head.

"I believe"—Brooks took up his narrative—"that we are one step nearer to a solution. I didn't receive the news until yesterday afternoon, and what with all the excitement I decided it could wait until this morning."

"What could wait?" Max poured coffee all around.

"Well, you see, I had a hunch," Brooks said in a pleased voice. "After we realized Max had been snatched, as we say in the PI business, I got to thinking about Theonia's warning. They were after him this time, she said. That sounded like something personal. So I went back through the files, endeavoring to ascertain whether any of the individuals he had put away might hold a grudge."

"I should think all of them would."

"No, no, you'd be surprised what nice chaps the majority of art thieves are. Quite the gentlemen, some of them. The real professionals dislike violence. I concentrated on the ones who had committed violent crimes or who had expressed antagonism toward Max. One name stood out like the proverbial sore thumb. The man who deliberately and cold-bloodedly broke Sarah's arm, whom Max beat to a pulp immediately thereafter, and who was intimately connected with the Kelling jewels."

"Good heavens," Sarah exclaimed. "Aunt Caroline's little lover? But he's in jail, Brooks."

"Where Max's evidence put him," Brooks pointed out. "However, Harry Lackridge is not in prison. He'd been a model prisoner, it seems, and he had developed a serious heart condition. The doctor gave him less than a year to live. Taking those factors into consideration, the parole board let him out three months ago. Sarah, do you remember what he looked like?"

"Physically, he was a watered-down version of Alexander. Alexander was the handsomest man I ever saw. Harry wasn't; but he had Alexander's height and thin build, and aquiline features, and of course he'd gone to the same schools, so their accents were similar. I suppose," Sarah said slowly, "he'd have been a fine-looking man if he'd been a better man. Character does have an effect on a person's looks, you know. Harry always looked as if he were sneering. There was no kindness in him, and it showed. I suppose some women find that arrogant manner attractive, though I can't imagine why. Aunt Caroline certainly did. She bilked Alexander and me of everything we owned in order to please her little lover."

"Who proceeded to bilk her of everything she gave him." Max still looked a little dazed. "Damn! Why didn't I think of Lackridge?"

"You wouldn't have recognized him," Brooks said. "His hair had turned snow white in prison, and there wasn't much left of his face."

"You mean Lackridge was—is—the corpse?" Sarah gasped.

"The identification has been confirmed," Brooks said precisely. "Once we had a name it didn't take long to get a fingerprint comparison. I haven't been able to trace his movements between the time he was released and the day he signed up as a member of the tent crew, but we're working on it."

"Macbeth," Max muttered. "It makes sense, doesn't it? 'Infirm of purpose! Give me the daggers!' Caroline Kelling was the one who committed the murders, not Harry. That's why he got off with a relatively light sentence. I suppose he blamed her for instigating the whole ugly business."

"That's the way a mind like his would work," said Theonia, sweeping into the kitchen in a flutter of silk and lace. "Many people think in those terms, I'm afraid, always trying to shift the responsibility onto someone else. Sit down, Sarah, I'll wait on myself."

Brooks wouldn't allow that, of course. He seated his lady and brought her juice and coffee.

Max had been thinking. "That still leaves a lot of questions unanswered, Brooks. If Lackridge was trying to get the rubies back, who brought them here, and who killed Lackridge?"

The discussion had to be postponed. Davy came in, towing Jesse and demanding watercress sandwiches so they could go feed the gulls. He graciously agreed to eat his cereal and drink his juice first. Before long the whole group was assembled, except for Charles, who had gone back to Tulip Street. Sarah was cooking eggs as fast as she could. When the eggs ran out, there was one of Theonia's almond coffee cakes to be devoured and a few more pots of coffee to be drunk. Before they finished, Mrs. Blufert arrived. She had brought her grandchildren, who were great pals of Davy's, and the three were soon happily having alligator races on the upper deck.

Mrs. Blufert cast an appraising eye around the kitchen and reached for an apron. "Now you all just get on out of here," she ordered. "No, Mrs. Sarah, don't you dare touch a single dish, just go and set a while in the sun and rest. I don't want any help from anybody. Leave me to get on with things."

There was no arguing with Mrs. Blufert when she was in that mood. They retreated to the seaward deck, from which Sarah could keep an eye on Davy, and Max said, "We need to settle our plans for the day. Jem, I can't thank you and Egbert enough for keeping the home fires burning and the martinis mixed, but you must be yearning for Beacon Hill."

"We have no intention of deserting the ship, Mr. Max," Egbert said stoutly.

"I think we're almost out of the woods now, Egbert, if you'll excuse me for mixing my metaphors." Max had been thinking. "It must have been Alister who killed Lackridge. Didn't Calpurnia say he had a habit of hitting people on the head, more or less at random? He was loony enough to go in for smoke bombs and stupid enough to think hiding the body under the tent would get the police off the track."

"You were hit on the head, too." Sarah shivered. She was remembering the maniacal look on Alister's face and the club he had brandished.

"That could have been Alister," Max agreed. He rubbed his head. "Damn, I wish I could remember more. He must have done something to get me to stop the car and get out. Ran out in the road waving his arms and yelling for help, maybe. After he knocked me out he could have dumped me in the backseat and driven to the shore, kept me tied up and unconscious till after dark, then transferred me to a boat. Do the Zickerys own a boat?"

"Easy enough to rent or steal one," Brooks said thoughtfully. "There are a lot of boats and a lot of docks in this neck of the woods. Could he have done all that by himself, Max?"

"No. He had to have had help with some of it. Calpurnia might have lent a hand with moving the corpse. Once the deed was done she might have gone along with Alister to keep him from walloping her. She wouldn't admit it because that would make her an accessory after the fact. I can't see any sane person conniving in premeditated first-degree murder, though, which is what it would have been if they'd dumped me into the ocean with my hands and feet tied. Somebody did untie me. Maybe that was Calpurnia. Then there's that balloonist or handyman, or whatever he is; is he still there?"

"Why don't I just wander over to the Zickery place and look for him?" Jesse suggested hopefully.

Max grinned at him. "Aching to punch someone, are you? You probably couldn't find him, Jesse, he seems to be good at being inconspicuous. There's somebody else who knows some of the answers, and this time I'm going to get them out of him one way or another. Maybe with Egbert's rubber hose."

"Louie," Jem said. "Good thinking, Max. I'll be happy to lend a hand with the rubber hose. That's probably the only satisfaction I can get out of him for wrecking my car."

"Charles is going to get your vehicle out of the police lot and take it to a body shop he knows," Brooks said. "It's still driveable, but I'm afraid that the fines and the repairs will amount to a tidy sum."

Jem looked as if he had been struck in the face. "Never mind the rubber hose, Max. Where can we borrow a rack?"

He cheered up, though, at the prospect of returning to the beloved apartment on Beacon Hill. He and Egbert went off to pack. Brooks and Theonia followed them upstairs; they had brought clothes enough for only one night, and the office work was piling up.

"Do you have to go, Max?" Sarah asked.

Jesse was looking tactfully out to sea, so Max gave his wife a quick kiss. "I have a feeling we're on the verge of ending this thing, süssele. It would be good if we could clear it up before the kids come back from their honeymoon; you don't want it hanging over them, do you? Don't worry about me, I'll have Jem and Egbert with me, fully armed with penny whistles and rubber hoses. Jesse will stay here with you till I get back, which won't be long. Stick close to the house, and don't fall for any phony telephone calls, okay?"

"You'd better tell Davy you're going," Sarah said. "I hope he won't be upset."

Davy took the news far better than she had expected. Max promised to be back by suppertime and assured his son he wouldn't go out in the ocean anymore without Davy to look after him, and that did the job.

"He's a changed child," Sarah said wonderingly. "He knew, Max. I swear he knew you were in real danger."

"So did you." He hadn't told her he had dreamed of her, heard her voice calling him. " 'There are more things in heaven and earth . . .' as Mortlake the tent man might have remarked." Max put his arm around Sarah's shoulders. "There's nothing to worry about this time, love. I'll have those two stalwarts Jem and Egbert with me."

By the time everyone got packed and collected it was almost time for lunch, so they finished the rest of Miriam's salad and the last of the bread and cheese and ham, and finally Max got his elderly passengers into Sarah's little compact. The police had found no trace of his car. He'd better talk to Ira about a replacement, Max thought. If the Mercedes hadn't been found by now, it was probably gone for good, driven over a cliff or sold to a dealer in stolen cars.

Jem was still brooding over the damage to his cherished

vehicle. He sang songs about bodies and hangings all the way to Boston.

As Max had expected, Louie was still incarcerated. The new Charles Street jail, as it was still called, wasn't as easy to get out of as the old one had been, but Louie didn't want to get out anyhow, as he was the first to admit.

"Good of you to drop in," he said, rising politely to meet them. "I trust that's all you have in mind. If you've any intention of offering to make bail, forget it. I'm quite comfortable here. The food is rather boring, of course. If you can believe it, they refused my request for Gorgonzola. I haven't tasted the ambrosial stuff since I was locked up. And unfortunately I lack the facilities for entertaining visitors properly. You didn't happen to bring an electric teakettle and a supply of Lapsang Souchong, did you?"

"Cut it out, Louie," Max said. "Since we last spoke I've been kidnapped and cast out to sea, where I spent three days sitting on a rock eating seaweed. I'm not in the mood for fun and games."

"Oh, dear." Louie remained standing, since Egbert and Jem were occupying the bunk. "I'm sorry to hear that. You don't think I had a hand in it, do you? I have the perfect alibi, best one I've ever had."

"No, but I think you know who did. Your brother Dewey."

"Why on earth should you suspect Dewey?" Louie's close-set eyes shifted. "There isn't any such person. I made him up."

"Like hell you did. One of the few things I remember from my lost weekend, or weekday, is seeing a face resembling yours bending over me. There can't be more than two people in the world who look like that, and one of them was here in Charles Street Jail at the time. What does Dewey do for a living? I know, I know, he's an actor and you're his stand-in and if you think I'm dumb enough to believe that, you can think again. Does he pick locks, too, or has he other equally unacceptable skills?"

Louie sighed. "I suppose I had better come clean. Dewey's a basket weaver. He's quite good at it, too." Seeing Max's expression, he added hastily, "That's the plain truth, Mr. Max. How do you think Dewey broke out?"

"Of prison? Now we're getting somewhere. So Dewey's on the lam, eh? What was he in for?"

"Oh, Dewey isn't violent. He's a very gentle soul. They got him for bank robbery, but he never hurt anyone, and he always wrote 'I apologize for the inconvenience' on the notes he handed the tellers."

"Very considerate," Jem said.

"Oh, Mother brought us up right, at least until she went into detox. So you see, there was poor Dewey in one of those tedious prisons where there's nothing to do but listen to psychologists explaining about your childhood neuroses and ministers insisting that you find Jesus and earnest people trying to teach you various crafts. You know, turning pots and weaving mats and, in Dewey's case, learning how to make baskets. After five years he got to be very good at it, and then it occurred to him to turn his newly acquired talent to practical ends. He began weaving a particularly large basket. The guards were very amused. One of them said it reminded him of his aunt Matilda; she liked to knit socks, but they got out of hand, or foot, as the case may be, and kept getting longer and longer. She used to give them to a bird sanctuary, for the flamingos."

"Louie," Max said.

"Yes, of course. So there was Dewey with a very large basket and a yearning for freedom. It was full moon that night," Louie said dreamily. "Can't you picture it—the accordion wire lacy black against the sky, the balloon rising gracefully over the wall, silhouetted against the big silver globe of the moon, and Dewey leaning over the basket, waving his hankie at the guards down below?"

"No," Max said. "I can't."

"Really? I thought I expressed it quite poetically. Well, you're right, of course. Dewey toyed with the idea, he'd always been fond of balloons, but he decided that even the guards might get suspicious if he asked for several hundred yards of nylon and a propane burner. What he actually did was climb in the basket under his used sheets and unmentionables, and wait for the laundry people to pick him up. It really was a most inefficiently run establishment," Louie added critically.

"Fond of balloons, was he?"

"Very. Dewey's a free spirit, he never could stick to one job for long. One of his jobs was as assistant to a balloon man at a carnival. The old fellow was really a wizard with balloons, he taught Dewey everything he knew. Said Dewey had a real aptitude. One can't actually steer the things, you know, but one can direct their course to some extent. It requires study of upper air currents, and knowing just when to let the air get cold and when to heat it up again. I never understood those things myself, but Dewey took to them like a duck to water, so to speak."

"How did Dewey get involved with the Zickerys?"

"The balloon, of course. They were looking for someone to handle theirs, and there was Dewey—"

"Oh, for God's sake," Jem shouted. "I've had enough of this. Not even a profound knowledge of English music hall songs can excuse your dithering, Louie. Hit him, Max. Or let me hit him."

"That won't be necessary, Jem." Max reached into his briefcase, took out a package, and began unpeeling layers of plastic wrap. Louie stiffened.

"The carrot and the stick, Louie." Max smiled fiendishly. "The Gorgonzola sandwich is the carrot."

Louie's greedy eyes were fixed on the sandwich. "What's the stick?"

"We drop all charges and throw you out on the street."

22

Tweeters didn't want to go home. Considering what they owed him, Sarah hadn't the heart to come right out and tell him to leave. She tried an indirect approach.

"You haven't mentioned your puffin, Tweeters. How is his damaged beak coming along?"

"Oh, Sarah, I am so sorry. I was supposed to give him his beak builder two hours ago, but I've been having such a wonderful time that I completely forgot about Cuthbird. Can you forgive me if I rush off in a swivet?"

"Of course I can, Tweeters. I understand perfectly. I'd feel just the same if it were my puffin."

Tweeters still wasn't quite ready to fly. "I may have to fashion him a prosthetic beak."

"Oh, is it that bad? Do keep us informed, won't you?" This was a hint that even Tweeters Arbuthnot couldn't miss. He looked around for a hole to fly out of. "Where did I leave my plane? Do you happen to remember?"

"No problem," said Sarah. "Brooks and Theonia will drive you down to the landing and your plane will be right there with its pontoons on. It shouldn't be more than a fifteen- or twenty-minute hop from here to Jamaica Pond. Isn't that where you park?"

"Sometimes. There's a lot of sky out there, you know, and quite a bit of water under it. Well, I suppose I'd better get back to Cuthbird. Thank you for a lovely time."

"The thanks are all on our side, Tweeters." Sarah gave him an impulsive hug. "I don't know what we'd have done without you. Perhaps you'd like to come for dinner one night next week, after things get sorted out here. Give our regards to Cuthbird."

"I did mention to you, I hope, that the blue-faced booby with the sore claw is coming along well, and we hope to have some good news for you very soon."

She and Theonia followed Tweeters and Brooks to the latter's car. "I always have the feeling that Tweeters is looking around for a good place to roost," Theonia said. "Do you think it's because he's lonesome?"

"I suppose he must be. I've only been there once, but Tweeters has this big old Victorian house with nothing in most of the rooms but birds in big cages. They go in and out just as they please."

"Who does the cleaning up?"

"He has a man and wife—I guess they're man and wife—who take care of the place. Between them they do most of the daily chores like the cooking and housekeeping and keeping up with the bird counts and all that stuff. They're both pretty old, they get somebody in a few times a week to scrub out the cages and sweep up the birdseed that gets kicked around. Most of the birds seemed to be damaged in one way or another, broken wings or blindness, things like that. Some of those birds are real bastards. There's one called a skua that will hatch an egg, then take that one and feed it to the next in line if the supplies run low."

"Oh, dear. Brooks never mentioned the skuas."

"He was trying to spare you, I expect."

Theonia laughed, and then grew sober. "Take care, Sarah. Are you sure you don't want me to stay?"

"Absolutely. Jesse will be here, and Mrs. Blufert, and Mr. Lomax is somewhere around, and Miriam and Ira are ten minutes away if I need them. The most important thing is to find out what Harry Lackridge was up to. It's a terrible thing to say, but I have to admit I'm relieved he's dead. He was a dreadful man. Now if we can just dispose of those rubies! You know, Theonia, I'd like to throw the case over the cliff and be done with it."

"We'll figure it out, Sarah." Theonia enveloped her in a soft, sweet-smelling embrace. "You take it easy today, you've had a bad time. We'll let you know as soon as we learn anything."

Sarah was glad to take Theonia's advice. Davy told her ominously he was getting too old to take naps, and Sarah was afraid he was right. He finally consented to make camp beside a pyramid with his trusty crew, so Sarah bedded them down in Davy's room with ample supplies of molasses cookies in case the camels deserted them. Then she sent Jesse in the office to field business calls and stretched out in a deck chair on the lawn. She was too old to take naps, too, but the strain of the past few days wasn't something that passed in a night.

She was still worried about Max. That was something that wouldn't pass, either. She would always worry about him. But she'd have to get used to it; danger was part of his life and part of Max. Maybe that was one of the reasons why she loved him so much. He wasn't afraid of life.

Alexander had been afraid. Afraid of hurting people, of being hurt, of living. And because of his fear she and her husband and her son were still in danger. Talk about the Hope diamond! The rubies were beginning to look like the Curse of the Kellings. I'll get rid of them, Sarah thought drowsily. They aren't mine anyhow. Percy's daughter, Belinda, should be next in line because she's a triple Kelling, though she did have sense enough to pick a fourth cousin twice removed for a husband. I was afraid for a while that Belinda had her eyes on Kenneth's brother James, and he's only twice removed. No wonder the Kellings are so peculiar. . . . Thank goodness I had sense enough to marry a man who wasn't even distantly related to me. I hate to think what a child of mine and Alexander's might have been like. . . .

She hadn't meant to fall asleep, but when she opened her

eyes the sun was halfway down the sky and Davy was sitting on her lap.

"Is it suppertime yet?" he demanded.

Sarah rubbed her eyes. "No, not for a long time. Where is everybody?"

"I'm here. Josie and Jim are helping Mrs. Blufert make cookies."

Sarah gave him a hug. "Why don't you go and help, too? I'll come as soon as I wake up."

She had seen something that made her want to get Davy out of the way as quickly as possible. He ran off, and Sarah braced herself for another visit from her homicidal neighbor. Calpurnia was tastefully attired in a navy sweatsuit, and she was showing all her teeth in a smile.

"I thought you might condescend to join me for tea this afternoon," she called as soon as she was within earshot. "You've entertained me so nicely, the least I can do is return the compliment."

Sarah wasn't in the mood for Callie, here or at the Zickery house, but good manners prevailed. "I thought you didn't have a teakettle."

"I'm afraid I was teasing you. The fact is, Alister and I have had quite a lot of work done on the old place. I didn't want to encourage you to come while he was there, but now that he's out of the way I mean to begin entertaining again. I'd like you to be my first guest. You and your dear little boy."

Sarah thought quickly. It might be cruel and unfair, but

she didn't want Calpurnia having anything to do with Davy. "I'd love to come, Callie, but Davy has friends visiting. May I bring my cousin Jesse?"

Calpurnia considered the suggestion. Finally she nodded. "Certainly. What's one more?"

"Damned car phones!" Max tossed it into the backseat. "Keep trying, Egbert."

"It's all the traffic, I expect." Egbert redialed.

"Can't you go any faster?" Jem demanded.

"Oh, I don't think that's possible, Mr. Jem." Egbert pushed his employer off his lap and propped him against the seat. Max didn't believe in collecting unnecessary traffic tickets, but on this occasion he was driving with panache, cutting in and out of traffic and exceeding the speed limit whenever the chance presented itself. He wished a cop would pull him over so he could demand an escort. Naturally there were no police cars to be seen.

"I'm sure there's nothing to worry about," Egbert said. "Mrs. Sarah is too intelligent to take chances. She wouldn't go over there by herself. Anyhow, what could the woman do?"

"I don't want to think about it," Max said. "She's killed one man and tried to kill me. Alister or Dewey must have untied me while she wasn't looking. Try again, Egbert."

It wasn't until after they had turned off the freeway and were tearing along the road to the Landing that Egbert got through. Max heard him say, "Oh, dear."

"What?" he demanded.

"It's Mrs. Blufert," Egbert reported. "Davy is fine, he's with her and the grandkids, they're making chocolate-chip cookies."

"Where's Sarah? Tell Mrs. Blufert to put her on the phone."

"I'm afraid she's not there, Mr. Max. It seems Miss Vickery came by and invited her to tea. But don't worry, Jesse has gone with her."

"How long ago?" Max put his foot down.

"Just a few minutes."

"Faster," Jem urged.

A tree branch lashed the windshield. Egbert moaned and covered his eyes.

At least the phone call had saved a few minutes. Max turned straight into the rutted path that led to the Zickery place. They bounced along the road and came to a crashing halt in front of the house. Max was out and running before the engine died. Rising over the roofline was a big round thing striped in bright colors.

He crashed through the overgrown bushes next to the house. Behind it was a pasture-size open space, knee deep in nettles and weeds, and in the space was the balloon. No wonder he had had hallucinations about the Fourth of July. What he had heard as he'd floundered around in the cold water was the *whoosh* of the engine that heated the air for the balloon. The flare of flame had suggested rockets and fireworks to his dazed brain. How they'd got the damned thing back here he didn't know, but Dewey was a wizard with balloons, according to his brother.

Dewey wasn't visible. Calpurnia was in the basket of the balloon, which was anchored only by two ropes. It rocked wildly as Calpurnia pulled at Sarah, trying to drag her into the basket. Sarah dug in her heels and resisted, but she was losing the struggle.

"Hit her!" Max yelled. He jumped a recumbent body, saw that it was Jesse's, and ran faster. "Slug her!"

Sarah heard. She'd never hit anybody in her life, but this seemed to be the time to forget her Back Bay training. Calpurnia's grip loosened when Sarah's fist smacked into her nose. Sarah fell back, rolled, and scrambled away on hands and knees. Calpurnia leaned over the side of the basket. Two quick slashes, and the balloon was free. It rose ponderously into the air.

A tatterdemalion figure reeled out of the house, holding its head. "Stop her," Dewey gasped. "She doesn't know how it works!"

Max couldn't have cared less. He was holding Sarah, and she was holding him just as tight. But Sarah wouldn't have been Sarah if she had thought only of herself. She raised her head from his shoulder. "Jesse. She hit him with the gun and tried to make me get in the balloon. Is he all right?"

Jesse sat up. "What the hell happened? Ouch. My head!"

The balloon had cleared the treetops. It rose higher, drifting south across the Kelling acres, heading seaward, sailing beyond the sunset and the baths of all the western stars, until . . .

"Oh, my God," Max said.

A flight of birds—terns, seagulls, they were too far away to identify—swooped gracefully down, greeting a fellow flier or, more likely, curious about what the peculiar thing might be. The basket rocked wildly, spilling out an object that flapped and flailed its limbs as it fell, passing out of sight below the trees.

Dewey shook his head sadly. "I told her she didn't know how to work it."

23

"Caroline Kelling wasn't the only woman who fell for Harry Lackridge," Max said. "Calpurnia had carried a torch since the good old days, when the Zickerys and the Kellings and their guests used to spend summers here. Their paths diverged after that; Harry married Leila and became involved with Caroline, and Calpurnia went off and did whatever the hell she did all those years. When the law finally caught up with good old Harry, Calpurnia heard about it; it made headlines in every newspaper in the country, as you recall. Caroline was dead and Leila promptly sued for divorce, so there was Harry, womanless for the first time in years, and locked up in a maximum security prison, where he couldn't get away from Calpurnia. She visited him almost every week, and I expect he played up to her; why shouldn't he? There was nobody else."

The police had come and gone, Davy was tucked into bed with his alligator, and the members of the Bittersohn

Detective Agency had assembled in the living room with tea and coffee and, in Jem's case, a large pitcher of martinis.

"I've read about women like that," Theonia said with a delicate moue of distaste. "It is not at all unusual for prisoners to receive proposals of marriage from women who've not even met them. Sometimes the poor fools actually marry convicted murderers."

"There are a lot of weird people in the world," Max agreed, trying not to look at certain members of the group. "In this case Calpurnia had known Harry before and, God knows why, taken a girlish fancy to him. It was a nice, bloodless affair, consisting solely of whispered endearments. That's about all you can pass through a sheet of Plexiglas with a guard watching you. It might have ended as harmlessly if one of Harry's other old flames hadn't died."

"The lady from Amsterdam," Brooks contributed.

"Mevrouw Vanderwoude. I wish I'd known her better, she was obviously quite a gal. She was smart enough to hang on to the original jewels instead of letting Harry pull one of his little switches, but they apparently had a closer relationship than I had thought. She left instructions that the parure should go to Harry after her death. It was meant as her last malicious joke; the letter she left with her lawyer stipulated that Harry had to collect the gems in person. If he was unable to do so within six months, they were to be returned to the original owner—Sarah Kelling Kelling Bittersohn, by name. She assumed Harry wouldn't be able to comply with the conditions, since he was safely locked up. In case Harry missed the joke, she wrote to him and told him what she'd done. I'll bet she was hugging herself with girlish glee as she pictured him in a frenzy of frustration.

"In the meantime, however, Harry had got religion. There are no atheists in foxholes, as the saying goes, and Harry wasn't getting any younger. He had a bad heart, and I'll do him the credit of believing he honestly did want to make peace with the people he'd swindled before he had to make peace with his Maker. He was due for another parole hearing, and figured he had a good chance of getting out, thanks to his reformed character and poor health. His intention was to collect the parure and return it to Sarah. Where he made his mistake was to tell Calpurnia what he meant to do.

"Calpurnia wasn't what I would call normal to begin with, and that news tipped her over the edge. All those years of visits and cake baking, and what was she going to get out of it? She'd assumed that if he ever did get out, he'd marry her. Instead he blandly informed her that he meant to spend the rest of his life, what there was of it, in prayer and good works, beginning with the restoration of the Kelling jewels to their rightful owner. Calpurnia knew about the jewels, of course. The thought of those rubies made her mouth water. She lost her temper and told Harry what she thought of him and his plan. He told her what he thought of her, and she went wild. The guard remembered that last visit of hers; she started screaming at Harry and had to be dragged out of the room.

"Harry had got the message. He took pains to elude her after he was released, since she'd made it clear she intended to stop him from returning the parure, whatever it took. Alister felt he had to go along with her plans. He was terrified of her, and he had enough family feeling left to hope he could prevent her from doing anything drastic. Apparently Callie had also been a habitué of Danny Rate's; she remembered Louie from the old days, and figured a locksmith with few moral scruples might come in handy."

"How did she get in touch with him?" Sarah asked.

"Through the want ads, if you can believe it," Jem said disgustedly. "That's how *we* found the verminous little wretch. He recommended his brother, Dewey, who'd run out of raffia and was planning his prison break, to Calpurnia. It was a pretty damned ineffectual bunch, in fact."

"Very amateurish," Brooks agreed. "One must make allowances, however. Calpurnia hadn't had enough experience with organized crime to find better material."

Max grinned at his second in command. "A pity she didn't ask our advice, isn't it? They didn't do that badly for a bunch of amateurs. Harry wasn't as careful as he might have been, either. Before the blowup he had told Calpurnia about his pretty fancy of returning the rubies in person. Isn't there something in the Bible about doing good without proclaiming your deeds aloud? You get extra points for anonymity, I think. When he heard about the wedding he decided his best chance of sneaking into the house was during the confusion of an event like that. He applied to Omar Inc. for a job, which they were happy to give him since they were having trouble finding suckers who'd work for pennies and no benefits."

"He could have sent it by mail," Brooks said. "Registered, of course."

"Maybe he didn't trust the U.S. Post Office, or maybe he was afraid we could trace him that way, or maybe he'd got it into his head that he had to deliver the damned thing in person. Don't ask me to account for the actions of a religious fanatic. Harry was wearing a plain white shirt and black pants and bow tie under those coveralls; in that outfit he could pass as one of the waiters. After he'd managed to sneak the jewels into the library among the wedding presents, he changed back into his coveralls and hung around, in case Calpurnia had figured out what he meant to do. Which she had. Then the balloon descended, and there, to his horror, was dear old Calpurnia.

"According to Louie, who is not, I admit, the most reliable witness you could find, Harry then followed the Zickerys home and started delivering a sermon. Louie said it was quite a performance. The more Harry talked about righteousness, the madder Calpurnia got and the more nervous poor old Alister got. He knew his sister had gone off the deep end and was capable of almost anything. He finally broke in and suggested Harry had better leave. The minute Harry turned his back she grabbed a two-by-four and let him have it."

"Do you believe Louie?" Brooks asked skeptically.

"Oh, yes. He's no killer. Neither is Dewey. But she had them over a barrel; there was Harry, dead as a mackerel, and there was Dewey, an escaped convict on the lam, and there was Calpurnia, a respectable elderly female from a good family. Whom would the cops have believed? They had to do as she directed."

"I suppose it was her idea to put Harry's body under the tent," Sarah said.

"So Louie maintains. It took her till morning to think that one up, though, by which time the tent people were on their way here. The smoke bomb was Calpurnia's idea, too. Not a very bright idea, but it worked. They trundled poor old Harry up the back road on a wheelbarrow, with Louie carrying a lantern to guide them. He said it was one of the most horrible times of his life, feeling his way through that black fog, hearing the puffing and panting and the squeaking of the wheelbarrow following him. He decided he'd had enough. While the rest of them were dealing with the corpse, he went looking for transportation, recognized Jem's car, and took off. He was too unnerved by his experiences to think straight, but after we'd had our little talk he came to the conclusion that he'd be safer in jail than with a madwoman on his trail. She scared the bejesus out of him."

"So it was the rubies she wanted all along," Sarah said.

"She wanted the money she expected they would bring," Theonia said soberly. "And revenge on Max. She'd heard Harry cursing him before he saw the light, and in her twisted way she blamed Max for having Harry put in prison."

"But she hated Harry, too," Sarah protested.

"She hated both of them. She wasn't exactly reasonable toward the end," Theonia said. "She'd come to believe the rubies were hers by rights, that she ought to have been Harry's sole heir. When Louie failed to get them back for her she thought of another scheme. She persuaded the others to help her kidnap Max, telling them she meant to exchange him for the rubies. But once she had him in her hands she went completely berserk. She ordered Dewey and Alister to take him out in the balloon and drop him overboard to drown. They were afraid to disobey, but neither of them wanted to commit murder, so they untied him before they threw him into the water."

"Nice of them," Max grunted. "Dewey claims he was the one who thought of putting my old bathrobe into that plastic bag. He hasn't admitted it yet, but I'm pretty sure he was also the one who stole my wristwatch. That's what Louie would have done. Petty larceny runs in the family."

"Alister wouldn't have swiped your watch," Jem said. "But he hadn't changed from the old days, when he'd pick a fight and then back off."

"Same old Alister," Max agreed. "He was afraid to defy Calpurnia and afraid to cooperate fully with her. Having, as she thought, disposed of me, she needed another hostage to be exchanged for the rubies, so she lured Davy over there with promises of balloon rides and God knows what else. A trip to Mars, maybe. I don't think she'd have hurt him, but Alister was afraid she might."

"He was chasing us to get us to run away," Sarah said with a shiver. "To run away from Calpurnia. He knew she had a gun."

"And that she was crazier than a loon. It was the first time he had had guts enough to defy her. I have to give the guy credit, he acted to save you and Davy. Calpurnia had to shoot him. He knew too much, and after that she couldn't count on him to keep his mouth shut."

"What are you going to do with the rubies?" Theonia asked.

"According to Uncle Jake, the question of legal ownership still presents a problem," Max answered. "It may take years to work it out. In the meantime—"

"In the meantime they're going to the police," Sarah said firmly. "They're evidence, aren't they? I don't ever want to see them or have them in the house again. If they do come to me, and I don't see why they should, I'll sell them and give the money to Dolph and Mary for the senior citizens' center."

"Sounds good to me," Jem said. "What do you say, Egbert? Shall we head for home? Brooks and Theonia can drop us off."

"We can retreat with honor," Egbert agreed. "Having done our duty like gentlemen."

Sarah and Max exchanged glances. "If you're sure," Sarah began.

"They're sure," Max said firmly.

"Quite," said Brooks, rising. "We'll have a real celebration after we've caught up on sleep and office work and a few other things."

"Miriam will certainly want to throw a party," Sarah said with a smile. "I must call her."

"Tomorrow," Max said.

The hints were falling as thick as autumn leaves, not that anybody needed them. Jesse had been put to bed with an ice pack on his head and a hefty dose of painkillers. He'd sleep till morning. Max helped Brooks transfer Jem's and Egbert's suitcases from Sarah's car to the company vehicle Brooks was driving and stood waving till the taillights disappeared.

"Nice night," Max said. "Are you cold?"

"No, I have my nice woolly sweater."

He put his arm around her anyway.

"Do you think Davy's old enough now to have a puppy?" Sarah asked.

"What brought that on?"

"I was just thinking. They say, whoever they may be, that a properly trained and cared-for dog can be worth a whole kennelful of police. If you're having spasms about villains and vampires peeking in the windows, a watchdog might not be a bad companion to have around."

"Who's going to train it?" Max wasn't ready to commit himself, and for cogent reasons.

"Why, you, my love." Sarah was quite willing to take a chance. "Growing up in the city, I never had a dog of my own."

"I always wondered why your mother-in-law didn't have a Seeing Eye dog. They can be trained to help the deaf as well as the blind, and she was both."

"She wouldn't have wanted a smelly, messy dog around, fastidious as she was. Anyhow, why would she need a dog when she had Alexander?"

Max was sorry he'd brought the subject up. The moonlight was silvery bright and the air was cool, and Sarah was a warm weight against his shoulder. He was sick and tired of hearing his beloved talk about poor Alexander, but he'd never say so, not to Sarah.

"He didn't have much of a chance, did he?" Max tried his damnedest to sound sympathetic.

"I don't know about that, Max. I think you take your chances as they come and do what you can with what you get. Some people get more, some get less because they're afraid to hold out their plates for what they really want. I sometimes wonder what I'd have done with my life if Alexander and his mother hadn't been killed in the old electric car. Alexander would have been kind to me as he always was, he'd have puttered around with his odd jobs and visits to the relatives and waiting on his mother hand and foot. Eventually I'd have become an old woman and died without ever having had the chance to be young.

"Can't you just see me, sitting in a rocking chair that had been my great-grandmother's, working a piece of needlepoint one tiny stitch at a time, wondering whether anybody was going to drop by unheralded by teatime and whether Alexander had remembered about the acidophilus milk for Aunt Appie, which of course he would have had on hand in a carefully stoppered pitcher. He was always thoughtful about small matters. Where he failed was in the big things."

"I've never heard you talk about him that way," Max said in surprise.

"You won't hear me talk about him a lot from now on. He was a dear, sweet man, and now he's gone. I've said good-bye to him." Sarah turned to face him and put her hands on his shoulders. "I knew I loved you, Max, but I didn't know how much until I was afraid I'd lost you."

He took her in his arms. "I don't even know what the hell acidophilus milk is, but if you want some, I'll track it down."

"I think there's some in the fridge. Would you like a glass?"

"No thanks. What I'd really like—"

"So would I," Sarah said. "Let's go in."